DANCING IN CIRCLES

DANCING IN CIRCLES

Julia Hawkes-Moore

HONNO MODERN FICTION

Published by Honno
'Ailsa Craig', Heol y Cawl, Dinas Powys,
South Glamorgan, CF6 4AH

First impression 1995
© Julia Hawkes-Moore, 1995

British Library Cataloguing in Publication Data
A catalogue record for this book is available from the British Library

ISBN 1 870206 15 0

*Published with the financial support of
the Arts Council of Wales*

Cover illustration by Penni Bestic
Cover design by Penni Bestic
Typeset and printed in Wales by Dinefwr Press, Llandybïe

With thanks for all the support and encouragement from Honno, my family and friends and the Company of Eight – but with special love to Bob and the little angel Gabriel

1

At noon every Midsummer's Eve, the Glasmaen Methodists take their harmonium up Bryngaran Hill on the border of Wales and Herefordshire and hold a service in the middle of the ancient stone circle. This year the heat was intense and the sky was veiled with the threat of thunder. When the harmonium was set up it went so badly out of tune that the singing had to be unaccompanied. The voices of the singers were thin and querulous in the hazy air. A party of hikers sat on the fence and dangled their lumpy brown knees as they watched the Methodists. They joined in with the words they recognised in some of the hymns, but their baritones and basses buzzed like gnats in the spongy heat.

'Bizarre,' muttered one in a flat Brummy accent.

'Religious weirdos,' observed another. 'Watch them glare when I pass you this can of lager.'

'Oh, 'Rock of ages, cleft for me'. I like this one. Very suitable for Christians in a pagan stone circle.' The short fat one sang along with the chorus, and then sneezed violently. 'Ugh, hay-fever. It's like breathing in treacle.' He mopped his nose. 'Perhaps it's better in the valley. There's a Norman chapel, a ruined castle, and a pub with five stars in *The Good Beer Guide*.'

'I'll be glad to get back to Birmingham, where they only sell lager,' groaned the first. 'One more pint of real ale and I'll keel over.' He fumbled in his knapsack. 'Let's take a few photographs to show the lads in the office.'

The hikers were not to know that the magnetic powers humming in the stones had in fact caused all their films to go blank.

An artist had propped up his home-made easel in the shade of the solitary oak tree to the south-east of the circle. He was busy splashing paint onto his canvas, and could not hear the singing. He listened to the faint trills of an invisible skyborne lark instead. His stomach felt queasy. He wondered fleetingly whether this might be the fault of the rather elderly goat's milk yogurt which he had eaten for breakfast. He glared at the view.

The valley dipped before him, patchworked fields scattered with sheep and sturdy red-and-white cattle. It was hedged about with high, rambling barriers of hawthorn, oak, elderflower and dogrose. There were all the shades of sun-bleached green, and where the turf had been scarred by tractor wheels the earth was a livid red. The thatched roofs of Glasmaen gleamed like lumps of amber among the slate roofs. Westwards, the mountains of Wales hung dark as thunder-clouds. To the artist the view was his palette of ochre, umber and emerald, and not the fluorescent yellow of the one field of rapeseed which sickened him with its alien ugliness.

Half an hour or so later the disgruntled Methodists packed up their useless harmonium and departed. The service had been singularly unsuccessful. They all proudly remembered Midsummer Eves when their powers of righteousness had left Arthur's Circle silenced and defeated. This year, they felt that the circle had somehow defeated them. They did not discuss, or even mention, the low vibration which had emanated from the stones. They twisted their feet on the floors of their cars to get rid of the sensation of pins and needles which had crept up from the earth. They swallowed hard and rubbed their ears as they drove back down Bryngaran Hill, assuring themselves that the buzzing and popping was the result of altitude. Next year, they vowed secretly, they would build up the power of prayer, before they returned, to an irresistible strength. The stones would be quelled.

Once the Methodists had gone the power in the stones surged. The air took up the humming of their energy and quivered. The hikers from Birmingham felt unsteady on the fence, and climbed down. They packed their empty lager cans into their knapsacks, sensing the otherworldly atmosphere growing around the circle. Striding away down the hill, their spirits lifted and they began their usual banter again.

The heat intensified.

Isaac Talboys, the artist, only became aware of his solitude gradually. Tourists and religious ceremonies had been regular events at Arthur's Circle for as long as he had lived in the valley. He had never taken much notice of such oddities of human behaviour.

He gazed at the unfinished canvas on his easel and moaned. He threw his smeared palette to the ground and tore at his streaming black hair and beard with his hands. He left paint stains flecking the darkness, alongside the strands of grey. His hair was thick and long, and matted into his untrimmed beard and moustache; it grew out bushily from just above his shaggy eyebrows. His nose and cheek-bones were sculptured and tanned by sun and wind. His clothes rambled around him, stained into earth colours by sweat and dirt. His nails were torn and blackened on his strong, long hands. Only his eyes had a clean blue glitter.

The heart of his picture was empty where the lurid yellow of the rapeseed lay on the bed of the valley. Isaac could not imagine any way to smooth over this hideous eyesore. He turned away and concentrated on rolling up a cigarette. As he licked the paper, he glanced up and noticed that the stone circle was empty of visitors. Glancing higher, he saw that storm-clouds were piling up in the sky above the hill.

His first thought was not for the canvas, but for the safety of his violin. Had he wrapped it securely before he set out? He couldn't remember. If there was to be rain, then he had better check that his old waterproofed jacket was tight around the instrument.

Or better, he decided, he could fulfil a lifelong wish and fiddle up a storm. Folding up the easel and packing away his paints took a few minutes, during which the sky darkened to purple. As he passed the stones Isaac finally became aware of their tingling powers. His long hair crackled with static, and he shuddered as the fine dark hairs rose across his neck and shoulders. Isaac's eyes flashed a brilliant electric blue as he felt the energy welling up from the circle.

His long stride carried him quickly to the place where he had hidden his ancient black Ariel motorbike amongst the bracken. With spider clips he fastened his easel and haversack to the rack. Then, with a flick of his bright eyes to the glowering sky, he changed his plan and unfastened them again. Pulling out a springy coil of thick copper wire from his sack, he twisted it

3

along the length of the folded easel. Now he had his own personal lightning conductor. He unclipped the bundled jacket which contained his precious old fiddle in its battered leatherbound case. Then he returned to the edge of the circle.

Here the energy from the nine stones had increased so much that Isaac felt dizzy. The dancing waves and spirals of magnetic power seemed to crackle and shimmer around the entire circle.

Isaac hesitated. Would it be better to sit under the oak tree, and be sheltered from the rain but threatened by lightning-strike? Or should he brave the spinning potency of the ancient stones, which must have resisted thunderbolts for five thousand years? He realised that he wanted to join the stones, to become part of their vitality. He decided to sit below the tallest stone, from where he had a clear view down the valley, now shadowed by the dark clouds. He entered the ring of stones, and immediately felt the energy gush around him. Within the circle the crackling magnetism died away, and a smooth, timeless peace descended: the eye of the storm.

He drove the steel tip of his copper-bound easel into the hard earth beside the stone, and then knelt down to unwrap and tune his violin.

He began to play melodies of exquisite sweetness and sadness, and the circle of ancient stones seemed to draw in closer to listen. Isaac was the best fiddle player for miles around, and perhaps the best to have played within hearing of Arthur's Circle since the stones were raised. He played folk music, ancient and vibrant, and the stones began to vibrate to Isaac's rhythms instead of their own. The air inside the circle rang with music. Outside the circle the thunder-clouds piled ever higher.

Isaac played on, losing himself in the enchanted sounds. As he reached the crescendo of his tune the air about the circle was ripped apart by an ear-splitting explosion, and a dagger of lightning half a mile long hurtled down to earth. It hit the huge stone at its tip, and for an instant the ancient quartzite slab glowed like an electric light bulb. Then a branch forked off and leapt over his head, hitting the primitive conductor which sizzled with a green-and-blue flame.

Isaac dropped the bow and clutched the fiddle. He shook his head to clear his ears, and his long hair floated and crackled

4

with static. As his stunned vision began to focus, he looked out across the valley.

The combined effect of the vibrating magnetic powers of the stone circle and the massive voltage of the lightning-strike which had momentarily enclosed him had wrought an extraordinary change in Isaac's vision. He could see the countryside about him with perfect clarity, but superimposed over it he could see something else: a glistening cobweb of shimmering silvery lines, centred on Arthur's Circle. His memory instantly convulsed, and responded to his puzzlement with an explanation. These gleaming snail trails must be the legendary ley lines. They marked a system of primeval pathways running as straight as rulers between points of importance, such as the circle in which he now crouched like a dark spider.

Heedless of the danger of lightning-strike, Isaac stood up and looked about him. The glistening lines fanned away from Bryngaran Hill in all directions, up and down hills, regardless of contours. They crossed lines from elsewhere, and wherever they met Isaac could see some ancient feature appear. He recognised the squat belfry of St Briavel's chapel and the turret of Hay Castle aligning with the mound of Glyn Tump at the mouth of his own valley. The sculptured hook of Hay Bluff showed clearly as the nexus of many lines running through Wales. At several crossing places, moats or pools of open water shone like mirrors to catch the eye. Across into the rich plains of England the spires and towers of churches and cathedrals soared, each aligned so as to partially obscure the next. Circular copses and spinneys of oak trees formed dots on this extraordinary map, new to Isaac and as ancient as time.

He turned around towards the south-east and gazed down the length of the valley, catching his breath in excitement as he did so. A broad and brilliant line shone all the way to the estuary of the river Severn, over thirty miles away. At the limit of the horizon Isaac could see the shimmer of the Severn, and the gleam of rocks at Lydney Sands. Instantly he knew that something very special indeed awaited him at Lydney. He had to go there.

He plucked his bow up from the scorched grass and packed it away with the fiddle. Then he ran across to his motorbike and strapped the bundle on to the rack. He fastened on his small black helmet and pulled the greasy Belstaff jacket over his shoulders before hoisting the bike upright. Oddly enough, the bike started first time. Isaac crouched over the machine and set off down the hill.

The narrow lane, with hedges at either side higher than a tractor-load, took him past The Knapp, where Bryn Jones lurked, and past the organic orchards of the Mortimers' nurseries. At one point he squeezed past two car-loads of excited witches following a van laden with firewood, all going up Bryngaran Hill to prepare the bonfire for their solstice ceremony. He shot out of the lane and into the valley road without looking, confident that no traffic would trouble his route, and only just missed colliding with a sleek black BMW saloon which was coasting towards Hay. Isaac took no notice of the angry blast of the horn, which he barely heard over the pounding of his heart and the motorbike's engine.

As he passed the first cottages of Glasmaen on his left Isaac glanced across. A tiny boy tumbled on the lawn of the first house, playing with a bouncing mongrel dog.

From the top of the thatched roof of the second cottage, Don Craven the thatcher waved as Isaac hurtled past on the noisy bike. As he swung around the corner below the church and the castle, an old woman glared at him from the rose-covered porch of the Post Office. Passing the tiny school, Isaac glanced appreciatively up at the crêpe-paper tropical rainforest festooning the windows of the end classroom. He tore past the group of people shoving the harmonium about outside the Methodist chapel, and shot by the elegant new craft workshops at the edge of the village without noticing them. Soon he had reached the stretch of Roman road aligned with the ley line, and tucked his head down and concentrated on the journey.

The rain began at Grosmont Castle, and he had to peer through his goggles to see his way between the sheets of falling water. Before long, he was passing beneath the fortified arch on the ancient stone bridge over the Monnow at Monmouth, glancing up at the castle to check his position. Threading his way through the lanes towards Lydney Sands took more calculation, but eventually he found a railway crossing he could use and reached the bank of the River Severn.

Isaac concealed his motorbike among the brambled undergrowth in the pine wood which ran along the bank, and unpacked the bundle from the rack. He discarded the helmet but drew the Belstaff around him more closely. The noon heat had dropped since the rain began, and the earlier pressure of the air had lessened noticeably. The downpour dissolved away to a gentle dripping and the earth gave off a clean, fresh fragrance. The scent of pine trees and wild flowers tingled in his nostrils.

Isaac stood still for several minutes to get his bearings and then moved off downstream until he sensed the place where the ley line met the river.

Here an outcrop of mica-studded rocks tumbled down to the beach below. The wide river wound its lazy way through the broad flat sands, late-afternoon shafts of sunlight gliding over its surface. The sands were still firm and damp from the rainstorm, and glistened as the clouds faded away and blue skies reappeared.

There was no trace of human activity anywhere. Isaac sighed and understood that he had to wait for his promised event, probably until dark fell after high tide.

Locating a dry cleft amongst the rocks from which he could easily see the expanse of sand, he coiled himself up on his outspread jacket, lit up a cigarette to lull his hungry stomach, and prepared to wait.

2

Dr Edward Keynes was angry. Everything about this trip had been infuriating, and was likely to continue to be so. He had not wanted to come to this wretched corner of Wales, but he strongly suspected that his job was on the line. Deeply-rooted spite must be the only explanation for the fact that the Department had sent him out here. The journey, through a thunderstorm, had been long and unpleasant, and reaching the dilapidated hotel was no comfort. He had driven round and round tortuous lanes, narrow and winding, for an hour and forty-three minutes, completely lost. His embarrassment was completed by having to negotiate with the bad-tempered old woman in Glasmaen Post Office to locate the whereabouts of St Briavel's Hotel. On his way to the hotel a maniac on an old-fashioned motorbike had shot out right in front of his car, causing him to brake sharply and apply the horn, two actions which he particularly hated having to perform. The maniac had not even acknowledged his emergency manoeuvre.

When he finally arrived at the battered-looking Victorian hotel he had to find a parking space for his muddied BMW amongst tractors and Land Rovers. He had been waiting and ringing the reception bell for seven minutes before a slovenly and overweight woman turned up. Her brown hair was unkempt, and her cheeks flamed with large red patches of colour – certainly not flushes of embarrassment.

'About time too!' he snapped. 'My office has registered by telephone. My name is Dr E. Keynes.'

The woman stared at him with sleepy grey eyes. 'Totterikins?' she asked. 'Niver heard that 'un before.'

Her accent was so thick that he had to waste nine minutes making himself understood. Worse, when he eventually signed the register he had been disgusted to discover that his survey team had been booked in at the same hotel. Were there no bed-and-breakfast establishments for them to use? Would the Department expect him to dine in the company of such juniors? Surely not.

The room to which he had been shown with a proud flourish by the maid was evidently the best which the hotel could offer. The air and the mattresses were distinctly damp. Inexplicably, there were three beds of various sizes. The grimy little shower room appeared to be the main feature of the room according to the verbal ramblings of the maid. There were no shampoos or soaps, or even towels. Doubtless the locals all had standards of hygiene similar to hers. If so, they were unlikely to object to their neighbourhood being used as a deposit for intermediate nuclear waste, which could only be a plus factor for choosing this site.

The view offered some compensation. After studying the outlook over woods and unruly hedges westwards into Wales, Keynes turned away from the rather grimy window.

Pulling the crisp new map out of his briefcase, Dr Keynes checked his position. St Briavel's Hotel was, surprisingly enough, extremely conveniently situated for his research. The valley of impermeable igneous rock which the geological team had identified as the optimum site was very close. The small-scale map even gave the valley's outlandish name: The Glyn. Only one building was marked in the valley, an empty rectangle which indicated a ruined cottage. The accompanying report stated that the valley was uninhabited. The certificate of ownership stated that the land was owned by a farmer, one Bryn Jones. This was the man with whom Keynes was empowered to negotiate. Correspondence with him so far suggested that he was amenable to the possibility of selling all this inaccessible and unfarmed land.

Keynes pulled his father's gold hunter watch out of his pocket. Six o'clock. Tomorrow was June the twenty-first, the longest day, so there would be plenty of daylight for him to take a walk before dinner, distasteful as the idea was. The thunderstorm had come to nothing despite a short burst of rain, and the clouds had cleared.

Removing his grey pin-stripe suit, Keynes hung it carefully in the spacious wardrobe since there was no trouser press. He dressed in the tweed jacket, corduroys and sturdy walking boots which the gentleman's outfitters back in Cambridge had assured him were suitable for country wear. Combing back his hair in the mirror, he glared at the reflection of a tall, straight-backed, dignified man in the prime of life. His hair was dark brown, flecked with grey, and waved softly over his high smooth forehead. He should have remembered to get his hair trimmed before he set out, he realised. It was almost over his ears. It gave a sloppy impression. He sighed. There was not likely to be anyone his intellectual or social equal out in this wild place, so perhaps it did not matter.

As he passed the empty reception desk a roar of drunken noise from the depths of the building suggested that some popular sporting event was in progress on the bar television. This was undoubtedly the reason for 'the multiplicity of farm vehicles parked outside. Keynes shuddered at the thought of such vulgar carousing in the middle of a Saturday afternoon. He marched through the vast entrance door, which stood wide open.

At the mouth of the valley rose Glyn Tump, a Norman castle mound according to the report. This stretch of Wales was infested with early earthworks, Keynes knew, so if this one were included in the development it would hardly be missed. On an impulse he climbed carefully to the top, observing the buttercups gleaming among the grasses, and looked out from the summit. No buildings were visible; Glasmaen village, half a mile away, was screened by trees. At the top of what must be Bryngaran Hill, Keynes noticed something odd. He unpacked the binoculars from the case over his shoulder and focused them.

There, as he had expected, he could see the ring of Neolithic stones which the map identified as 'Arthur's Circle', lit by the mellow afternoon sun. To his surprise, a number of people were moving around up there. Adjusting the focus again, he saw that they were holding hands and revolving in a ring within the stones, around a heap of wood. They all seemed to be wearing long white dresses.

This was something quite beyond his experience. Some peculiar little voice in the back of his head whispered 'Witches,' but he quickly dismissed the thought as nonsense. There would be a sensible explanation. He repacked the binoculars and descended the hill rather too fast, giving his trousers a green stain.

His interest in the walk had faded. He returned to the hotel, changed, and descended to the bar to drink several sherries before dinner. The curly-haired barmaid at least seemed to be articulate, if rather prying. By responding to her chatty questions with cool politeness, Keynes managed to maintain his privacy. He noticed that the two young men from the survey team looked in briefly, then wisely went back upstairs to change from their scruffy jeans and jumpers. When they reappeared in decent casual wear, he nodded to them courteously, and returned to studying the report.

This subtle warning was enough to persuade them to eat the unattractive meal at a table on the opposite side of the restaurant from Keynes. To have to put up with their foolish chatter would have irritated him even further.

As he was finishing his coffee Dr Keynes glanced up to see one of the young men standing in front of him.

'Excuse me, Doctor, but we were wondering … Well, that is, Graham and I thought that …'

Keynes glared at him. 'Yes?' he rapped, offended by the intrusion.

The young man shuffled his feet and took a deep breath. 'Well, sir. *The Good Beer Guide* recommends the Golden Oak pub in the village, and we wondered whether you might like to come with us.' He adjusted his heavy steel glasses, then shoved his hands into his jacket pockets. 'It's not far,' he added, lamely.

Keynes considered. The other young man had come up behind the first. 'Richard Beavis, isn't it?' Beavis nodded. 'And Graham Ferris?'

Ferris grinned. His front teeth had a gap between them, yet he didn't seem to mind. 'Yes, Doctor Keynes. Since we've got to work together for the next few weeks, it might be a good idea to get to know each other better. And they do Owd Roger at the pub. We thought it would be a good opportunity.'

'Did you, indeed,' commented Keynes. 'I do hope you realise that you are here to work, and not just to tour public houses on expenses.'

Ferris grinned again. He really should get that unsightly gap seen to, thought Keynes – and both youths could do with haircuts. 'That's what expenses are for, after all, Doctor. Getting to know the locals, etcetera.'

Keynes frowned, but decided that it might be politic to go along with their suggestion. If he could show them the right standard of dignified behaviour now, then it should eliminate future problems. The survey team was notorious for sending in ridiculous expenses claims. Under his supervision this would not occur. He nodded graciously. 'Very well. And since this is the first evening, I shall drive you there in my car and pay for the drinks.' Their eyes lit up, doubtless at the opportunity of riding in such a superior vehicle.

'That's very kind of you, Doctor Keynes,' said Beavis.

Keynes led them silently out to the car park, and unlocked the doors of the BMW with his automatic device. He could see that they were impressed from the way they immediately got into the back, lounging over the pristine grey leather seats. He pulled carefully out of the hotel drive and drove smoothly into Glasmaen. Graham Ferris seemed to know the turning to the pub already, and directed him into the narrow car park below the castle ramparts.

As they entered the low thatched porch of the attractive pub, Beavis seemed inclined to enter the bar. Keynes deftly prevented this error by pushing the lounge door open. The low-beamed room was almost empty. Beavis nodded and smiled at the smartly-dressed elderly lady and gentleman sitting by the window, and walked over to reserve a table by the fireplace.

Ferris followed Dr Keynes to the bar, which was draped with dusty dried hops. Keynes shuddered at the unhygienic nature of this practice.

There seemed to be a lot of people in the bar-room, judging by the noise of voices. It took several minutes for the barmaid to appear. When she did, Ferris leapt to attention.

'Oh, hello again!' she cried. 'Graham, isn't it? And Richard?' Ferris grinned and Beavis actually waved from his chair. She turned to Keynes. 'And who's your handsome friend then, boys?'

Keynes was taken aback at her familiarity. She was surprisingly young for such a job, he thought. He felt that her extremely long yellow hair, worn loose like that, must be a hygiene risk, too.

'This is our boss, Lucy. Allow me to introduce Dr Edward Keynes,' smirked Ferris.

'Welcome to the Golden Oak, Doctor! I'm Lucy Goldhanger. You can call me Lucy, if I can call you Edward. And what's another Doctor doing out here in Glasmaen, then, when we've already got Doctor Llewelyn over at the Surgery?'

Her smile was so disarming that it was several moments before Keynes realised that he was staring at her, and that she was waiting for him to reply.

'I'm not a medical doctor, if that's what you mean, Miss Goldhanger. I have a Doctorate in Applied Physics, a PhD.'

'Physics is it, indeed. Well, I'm sure I don't know anything about physics.' She stretched, and lifted her hair back from her face in a rather appealing gesture. 'But you're a visitor, and welcome for all your 'Missing' me! What can I get you to drink, then?'

Her smile was charming. Keynes generously ordered three pints of the mysterious Owd Roger. She vanished into the barroom to pour it, bringing back a tray laden with three chunky glasses frothing with dark brown beer.

'The best of health to you, then,' she said as she changed Keynes's twenty pound note. 'You've come in at a good time; we've got the folk band in tonight, in the bar. Lovely music, except the fiddler's not here. He's an artist, so you can't rely on him.' She glanced over at Beavis, who was still gazing at her. 'Is the fire still alright, Richard? I know it's midsummer, but it makes such a difference. Do keep an eye on it for me, won't you, sweetheart?'

Keynes observed that his companions drank their pints quickly, as though planning to rush back to the bar and accost Lucy Goldhanger. He purposely drank his rather more slowly, and then returned for refills. Lucy was brisk and efficient in replenishing the glasses, and the hubbub from the other bar was increasing.

As he sat down again, loud jangly music began in the other room. By the second pint he found that his foot was tapping to the rhythm. They were drinking more slowly by now, and his companions had asked for a different type of beer. Keynes, however, had developed a taste for Owd Roger, which reminded him of some of the beers which he had tried in his University days. Beavis and Ferris were very interested in this subject, he discovered.

During the third pint, Ferris and Beavis both excused themselves in turn to visit the Gents, which was through the bar. They each took a long time, and returned praising the music from the band. Keynes found himself to be unexpectedly relaxed, and persuaded Lucy, Graham and Richard to call him Edward. They even discussed Lucy's spectacular fall of golden hair in a friendly way. At the end of the fourth pint, Keynes began to feel much more energetic than he could remember feeling for years. His fingers were tapping on the table top in time with his toes. The fire was so bright and warm that he actually removed his jacket and loosened his tie. Keynes was surprised to discover what personable and interesting young men Graham and Richard were, and told them so. He also told them that he had forgotten what a pleasant place a pub could be. When Lucy came to clear their glasses, he told her how charming she and her pub really were, and admired her swirling printed dress. She told him that the dress had come from India, which impressed Keynes very much.

Lucy brought them more beer and persuaded them to come into the bar to listen to the music. Richard and Graham sprang up at once, but Keynes found the stone-flagged floor treacherous underfoot, and fell against furniture several times. The bar proved to be very full of people, smoke and bright lights, and Keynes only paused to finish his pint before slumping against a wall. He asked several of the locals about the witches dancing in the stone circle, but no one seemed to know anything about it. The music was excellent, and he joined in, singing as loudly as possible. He had forgotten what a splendid voice he had. The crowd seemed to appreciate this, by falling silent when he was singing. Someone put another pint into his hand. He tried to persuade Lucy to dance, but she insisted that she was too busy. Instead, he taught the band several rugby songs which he suddenly recalled.

The band put away their instruments and went home. Lucy and Graham cleared away the remaining glasses. Keynes felt happier than he could remember feeling since he was a student. He even let Richard borrow his car keys and drive them all back to the hotel. It had been a splendid night, he thought, as he tumbled into bed after removing most of his clothes. Perhaps this was not going to be such a bad project after all.

3

Isaac had waited since long before nightfall, half asleep, but when he saw the first movement in the river only his fingers tensed. A dark shape bobbed in the moonlight, then warily approached the shore. Another and another appeared, until a dozen sleek round heads turned toward the sands. Seeing no threat of danger, the gleaming shapes moved closer. As they reached the shallows they gradually lost their fluid, graceful movements, and the land-bound seals lumbered ashore.

The broad and shining path of moonlight ran over the flat silver sands on either side of the Severn. Isaac lay hidden and alert amongst the twisted rocks, as spangled with mica as the sky with stars. He watched in easy, relaxed silence, and yet there was a hint of tautness, of waiting, in his long, fine-boned hands. One gripped the springy arch of a bow; the other caressed the outer curves of the object which lay by his side.

The seals rolled and stretched out on the beach, working away the weariness of their long swim. The full moon shone dully on their wet fur and on dark but luminous eyes.

Lifting up their sloping necks and pointed faces, they began to sing.

The song of the seals was a slow one, sibilant with the sounds of the sea, deep and rolling as the ocean. Then a thin, clear keening rose above their chant and the first seal stood upright. Flippers grown long and slender lifted off the cap of sleek grey sealskin. A wave of fine pale hair tumbled slowly down over the naked shoulders of the small, slim woman who sang. One by one, the other seals raised up their voices and bodies and concealing caps, until all twelve stood swaying and singing in a circle on the sand. Then they slowly began to dance, touching their thin wet fingers together as they moved in a ring.

Amongst the rocks Isaac tensed himself and lifted up his bow. He listened for a long while to the rhythm of the women's song, then began to hum the tune to himself, very quietly. As the dance continued he reached smoothly down to his side, poised in a crouch, and levelled his bow. His eyes did not leave the circle of shining dancers. In one fluid movement he drew the bow.

The note he drew from his fiddle was as pure and clear as the voice of any of the singers, and fell into place with their tune as smoothly as a single hair in a well-brushed lock. He followed it with further sounds, higher and deeper, sweeter and sadder. Their song did not waver, so smoothly did he play, but took on a richer quality. The notes of their song, inhuman and eerie in their sadness, were strengthened and structured by the violin. So gently as to be imperceptible to the circling dancers, the musician took control of the music, until they danced enraptured by his tune. He bowed and twisted the instrument whilst he quickened the pace from a gliding to a sliding step, a waltz that became a polka and spiralled into the bright, crisp steps of a jig.

The dancers loosed hands as they broke their stately circle and revelled in the reeling tune. Their singing faded as they needed all their breath for dancing. Faster and faster he took them, their long pale hair floating out like seaweed as they stepped and span. They threw back their heads in abandoned joy, and closed their eyes the better to hear the rippling tune.

Isaac wove every tune he had ever heard into that dance. He danced those creatures faster and harder than ever human beings danced. Long into the night he danced them, and gradually they began to tire. The older and larger of the dancers tumbled onto the sands, gasping for breath, until the beach was littered with their naked bodies, sweat gleaming on their pale skin. Still he played, until only one dancer still spun and twirled; the youngest and sleekest of them all. Isaac grinned and tossed his long hair. His eyes flashed and glittered in the moonlight. Then he quickly laid down his bow and fiddle, and leapt as swiftly as a young stag down from the rocks and towards the girl.

It was as though he stepped into a pool of minnows, so quickly did the women seize their grey caps and clap them to their heads. They fled towards the shallows as they began to transform. Sleek seals slid into the water in an eyeblink. But he had tired them by his playing, so that they were much slower than they should have been. Even so, the last girl had her cap in her hand as she reached the river's edge. Thin waves seemed to rush out to meet her, trying to suck her back into the safety of her element. But Isaac gave one last great jump, and threw his full weight onto her slender body in a rugby tackle remembered from his schooldays. Together they crashed into the water and he caught up her wrists as she tried to cram the sealskin cap over her hair. He pushed her hands, cap and all, behind her head, then pressed her face down into the water and sand until she ceased to struggle, and fell limp beneath him.

Isaac crouched beside the girl. He laid his head between her small pointed breasts and listened. After a moment he became aware of her heart beating slowly, and of the sound of shallow breathing. Looking up at her narrow pale face, turned slightly away from him amidst the tangle of her dim hair, he thrust his long forefinger into her mouth, between her small sharp teeth. Hooking out a crust of wet sand, he pushed her over onto her side. Giving her back a sharp blow with the side of his hand, he watched as she moaned and spat out sand and water. The shadow of a bruise blushed over her pale thin skin, between her shoulder-blades.

Now he could hear her breathing clearly, and he pushed her over onto her back again. Brushing her face clear of hair and sand, he looked at her for a long while. Then he hoisted her over his shoulder, turned and strode away from the sea.

Out in the moonlight, the seals bobbed and dived, frantic with panic for their sister. Their great dark eyes blinked and rolled in fear, but they dared not swim closer to help her. They watched as Isaac picked up her limp, cool body in his arms, her dripping hair trailing like seaweed. They saw him bend again to catch up her sealskin cap with one hand and stuff it into the pocket of his worn trousers.

He clambered slowly up the rocks and moved away, out of sight of the river. The seals bobbed in a close huddle for a long time. Large slow tears like pearls rolled from their staring eyes. As the dawn began to filter over the land they turned and dived away, all eleven moving as one.

Once he was deep into the pine wood, Isaac lowered the body of the girl and examined his trophy. She lay on her back upon a quilt of pine-needles. The narrow sandy path which he had followed faded into the pungent blackness of the resin-scented pine wood. It was still too dark for bird-song, and the soft rust-lings of invisible small animals were silenced by their passing.

He stood up and, recovering his violin and bow, walked away into the wood. Once he was certain that he was out of sight he drew out the sealskin cap from his pocket. Folding it up into a narrow parcel, he tied it with a strand of horsehair plucked from his bow. Then he carefully pushed the small roll through the sound-hole into the cavity of the fiddle. He tested the result by drawing out the notes of an old tune, listening intently. Rather than being muted or muffled by the roll of skin, the fiddle played with a sweetness and clarity it had never held before. It was as though the ancient magic in the enchanted sealskin infused and thrilled the battered old instrument. Isaac nodded, satisfied, then swung around and returned to the side of the motionless girl.

He knelt down beside her, laying down the bow and fiddle nearby. Gripping her slender shoulders, he shook her gently until she moaned again. A smile lifted one side of his dark mouth and his eyes gleamed blackly in the dim light reflected from her skin. She blinked, and looked up into his shadowy face for a moment with wide, liquid brown eyes. Her pupils were dark holes of unfathomed depths, the soulless eyes of the Faery people. Then she shut her eyelids tightly, like translucent scallop shells closing.

With that one glance Isaac's body relaxed. He still held her close, but with a new gentleness. He became aware of the chilly dampness of her downy skin, and bit his lip. Laying her down again, but tenderly, he removed his old Belstaff jacket from his own broad shoulders and placed it around her body. Then he slowly ran his warm hands over her cool thighs and down her smooth pale legs. He wiped the sand from her feet, and from the filament of skin which webbed her small toes. Holding her feet between his palms until her skin darkened with a faint flush of warmth, he lifted them to his lips. He kissed her soles and toes softly, then turned his gaze back up her slight body towards her face. His eyes glittered, but he spoke quietly, with firmness and decision.

'Tell me your name.'

She sighed, with a shudder that ran the length of her body, and opened her wide brown eyes full upon Isaac's face. Her look was without emotion, clear and cool as the disc of the full moon above them. Then she spoke, slowly, as though tasting his language and finding it bitter to her tongue. 'My name is Ainee Sealfin. Return me to my sisters, and we will give you silver, stolen from wrecked ships, as much as you can carry.'

Isaac considered the image of the girl surrounded by the sheen of silver, threading its light through the fronds of her pale hair. He shook his head and gazed hungrily at her pearly beauty. Ainee raised herself up onto her elbows, the jacket falling back to the ground. He laughed sharply and moved quickly into a crouch across her faint white body, pinning her down. The girl's dark gaze did not waver, but she spoke again: 'Release me, and you will be given barrels full of ancient Spanish gold.'

In Isaac's mind she curled deliciously, Danaë in a shower of golden coins, but he shook his head again.

'Pearls, then,' she sighed. 'Precious, deep-sea pearls as large and white as eyes and teeth. My sisters will hurry them to you, if you will let me call to them.'

Isaac shuddered, a long tensing and resettling of desire and fear and hope. He tangled his long fingers in her silky hair, forcing her face closer to his. 'No, you are here now, and in my arms, Ainee Sealfin! I am the artist, Isaac Talboys. I have searched for you throughout my life. I don't want your treasures, but I do want you. Be my muse, my model, my subject. Be my lover, Ainee. Come and live with me.'

Ainee stared up into his glittering eyes, and considered for a long while. No fear showed on her smooth face, but a tremble of excitement ran across her lips as she began to smile softly. Then she laughed, a small, quiet laugh like a silver bell sounding in the tower of a sunken village. 'To live on the earth with all its mysteries; to escape this dull, wide, dirty ocean? Yes! I may do that … for a time. So long as you enchant me with your music, and your strong warm hands, then I will stay with you, Isaac Talboys.' She pursed her lips in a tiny wicked smile, and lowered her eyelids over her dark and liquid eyes.

Isaac pulled her mouth to his and kissed her hard and long, biting at her lips and tongue until she writhed beneath him. She tasted of the salt sea.

Then he lowered her back down to the ground and gazed at her, enraptured by her smiling nakedness. His head span as he realised that she had captured him, not he her. His heart turned to Ainee Sealfin in that instant, and he knew that he could never love anyone else.

As for Ainee, she pressed her cold body up against his warm one. Here was novelty, she thought, as her blood tingled with his closeness. This was certainly a great deal more interesting than dreaming in her dark cave for decades more. She had heard old stories and fables of Selkies and Mermaids who had been seduced onto the land, and of the wonderful things which they had experienced there. Some had returned to tell their tales, but others had found human life so fascinating that they had left the ocean for ever. Well, now she too, Ainee Sealfin, could taste that forbidden life and devour its fruits. Especially as the seas had become filthy during the last century. Here she could breathe sharp sweet air, and move about freely, untrammelled by the tattered banners of fishing nets, unstained by gouts of oil. Ainee stretched her body luxuriously, pushing her toes into clean, dry sand.

She smiled her slow wide smile into Isaac's glittering eyes as she considered. She could begin by exploring human love. The few humans she had seen were corpses which hungry mermaids had tugged down to the grottoes of the Selkies, and they had remained beautiful for only a few short hours. Not like this warm and living man, adoring her as though he wished to devour her. Ainee twisted her hands up into her victim's hair, and pulled him down into a kiss so deep that Isaac felt her draining the blood from his soul. He struggled to tear aside his shirt and unfasten the buckle of his belt, sensing her skin warming as it came into contact with his.

Ainee and Isaac discovered their hunger for love by the light of the full moon that Midsummer's Eve, and although the night itself was short it was many hours before they fell asleep in each other's arms.

Isaac was woken by the song of a blackbird applauding the first glimmer of dawn. As he opened his eyes he saw the sheen of naked skin beside him, and fine pale hair tumbling over that skin like waves over sand. Recalling the extraordinary events of the previous night made him smile and press the slender body of Ainee Sealfin close to his own. Ainee stirred in his arms and turned to look into his dazzled eyes.

'Good morning, Ainee,' he whispered.

For a moment she gazed at him impassively, then a smile of welcome dawned over her face. 'Greetings to you, Isaac. So here is daylight breaking on your world. Now you will show me your home?'

Isaac began to nod, but then the difficulties of transporting a naked seal-maiden on the back of his motorbike across thirty miles of Britain began to occur to him. She could be wrapped in the jacket on which they presently lay, but a helmetless passenger on a small bike with battered L-plates might attract unwelcome attention. For the first time, he wished that he had bothered to take his test. Ainee's lilting voice interrupted his reverie.

'Do you live close to water?' she asked.

'Yes, I do, on the bank of a stream,' he replied. 'But quite a distance away.'

'Well, then,' Ainee said decisively, 'give me back my sealskin cap, and I will swim to you.'

Isaac sat up. 'Oh, no. If I do, you'll swim back out to sea and leave me alone again. No, I'll take your cap back to my house. You can make your own way there upriver. You might not be bothered about where I am, but I'll bet you'll know whereabouts that cap is. Speaking of which, is it true that a human can – how does it go? – lay a taboo or *geis* on a … a fairy?'

Ainee's pout became more marked. 'Fairy, indeed! I'm a princess among the Selkie people, the cousins of the noble seal. You'll be calling me a mermaid next, and you know what they're like – ugly great flapping fish.' She clicked her tongue angrily. 'But yes, I suppose it is.'

'Good. Right then, listen carefully. You must never, ever touch my violin. Understand?'

Ainee glared. 'So that's where you've hidden it.' She sighed crossly. 'Very well. And I'll have to swim all the way then, I suppose. Still,' she announced, brightening, 'it will give me the chance to look at this land of yours, and to get used to the brightness of sunlight. Swimming is easy enough. I'll find you.'

Isaac nodded, and leaned forward to kiss her once more. Her lips were soft and inviting. He hesitated as he felt the warmth of her body, then stood up quickly. 'That's what we'll do, then. Take care going through Monmouth – that's the town where our river meets the Wye, and a lot of people live there.'

He caught Ainee's wrist, and pulled her to her feet. He dressed quickly, then picked up the Belstaff and slung it over his shoulders. They stood looking at one another for several minutes. Then he pushed her gently. 'So off you go, then. The river's that way. Good luck.'

He watched as she turned and walked delicately over the pine-needles, until she disappeared between the trees. A sigh caught in his throat, and he frowned, wondering whether he would ever see her again. Then he turned, recovered his violin, and made his way to his motorbike.

Ainee heard the engine start after several tries, and then waded into the river. She stretched out her arms and luxuriated in the fresh water. Turning downstream, she slid into the current as smoothly as an eel.

4

'Oh no, he's crying again.'

Gareth Hopkins-Jones didn't bother to reply to the obvious, and pretended to continue sleeping. Then Sue jabbed her finger in his ribs. 'It's your turn. Go and give him a bottle.'

Gareth groaned inwardly at the unfairness of it all. Sue might well have fed him before bedtime, but she didn't have to go downstairs to a cold kitchen and mess around for half an hour with pans and kettles. She was definitely getting the better end of this deal.

'You feed him, Sue. It's your tits he wants, not me.' Immediately Gareth realised his mistake.

'Okay, so you go around with a couple of milk bottles strapped to your chest for six months.' Sue's voice was icy. 'See how you like it.'

Gareth thought about this for some time. How wonderful it must be to have such soft cushions for Berian to nestle against. What a joy it must be to have an ever-running fountain of warm, sweet milk with which to content your baby.

This bottle business was all a part of Sue's new hardline feminist manners. She insisted that Berian would soon learn that the night feed was no fun any more, and start sleeping right through. Gareth knew better. If Berian was hungry, then he should be fed. To curl up against Sue, all warm and milky, must be so pleasant ... No wonder he yelled for Sue. Berian's cry took on a new note of desperation.

'That's a circular saw we've given birth to, not a baby,' Gareth announced, then realised that he had just made another mistake. Sue's warm, soft body beside him had gone rigid. She heaved about and switched the light on, flooding the room with painful brilliance.

'We've given birth to! Oh, yeah, so just how much did you really suffer in the process? At exactly which point did you think that your body was going to split apart? Don't give me that crap. You don't know anything about it.'

Gareth sat up. How could she say that? He had been there every minute. He had done everything he possibly could. 'Christ, Sue, you really do want blood from a stone, don't you? There's not many men would have been as involved as I was! I do my share, and more than my share too.'

Sue remained lying motionless, her back turned towards him. Berian screamed. Gareth sighed. He was going to have to go, after all.

Clambering out of bed, he walked round and switched Sue's light off. On the broad landing, where the boys slept, the dawn light filtered through the thin curtains, a rainbow design which Gareth had woven when Emrys was born. Berian's howls quietened as he saw someone coming to his rescue. Emrys, mercifully, slept the unconscious sleep of a four year old. Gareth scooped Berian out of his cot and carried him downstairs.

Berian was grizzling with hunger. Gareth bounced him in his arms, wishing yet again that he had the facility of shelf-like female hips to rest babies on. His arms ached from a vigorous night's drumming. He pushed aside one of the blue-and-yellow curtains with his shoulder, and looked out of the window. Early roses draped the window-frame, and fronds of deep blue iris curled around the sill.

'Look, Berian, pretty flowers. Pretty long grass, too,' Gareth sighed. 'Lawn-mowing today, I think ... Oh, no, looks like we've got company.'

A rackety motorbike pulled on to the gravelled driveway and shuddered to a halt. Isaac climbed off it and removed his scuffed helmet and ancient Belstaff jacket. Gareth glanced at the milk bottle in its steaming pan, and struggled to unlock the door before Isaac could hammer it down.

'Morning, Isaac. Early morning call? Here, hold the baby while I get his milk.'

Isaac caught Berian in his arms and stumbled over the dog basket. Skip snarled, suddenly alert, then recognised the artist, and went back to sleep. 'Useless animal,' growled Isaac. 'Why don't you get a decent guard dog?'

'Because then it'd bark the house down whenever some idiot came visiting at an unholy hour. Honestly, Isaac, you look rough. Where've you been? You missed a good session in the pub last night.'

Isaac grabbed the bottle and rammed the teat into Berian's mouth. 'Oh, you noticed I wasn't there, then?'

'You're never all there. Here, come and sit down. That baby's dangling like a string of sausages.' Gareth collapsed into the old rocking chair and stretched his arms out for Berian. Isaac passed him over then lay down on the sofa, which was draped with old Indian bedspreads. 'Boots!' yelled Gareth.

'You're turning into a real nag with all this child-minding you do,' grumbled Isaac, pushing off each boot with the other foot. A shower of sand and pine-needles fell with the boots onto the rag rug. He pulled out his tobacco tin and began to roll a cigarette.

'Oh, not when Berian's feeding ...'

Isaac took no notice, and lit up.

'Okay, so I am turning into a nag. I'm too knackered to care just now. Sue can give you hell – if she catches you. Hopefully, she's fast asleep by now. Give us a roll-up.'

'Out dancing round Arthur's Circle until the small hours, was she, the old witch? Was Bryn Jones there?' Isaac grinned as he rolled another cigarette for Gareth.

'Yeah. Her dad, and the rest of his mob. Crazy family I married into. They've all been working like lunatics to get the tickets out for the Folk Festival this week, plus Sue doing everything for the concert at school. They deserve a wild night out. Hey, there was a good laugh this evening. There was this bloke, suit-and-tie type, completely pissed in the Oak tonight. He was well into the Owd Roger.'

Isaac groaned. 'Stranger, was he? Strong stuff, that. I remember the first time I tried it. Or rather, I can't remember.'

Gareth nodded. 'Singing rugby songs, would you believe. Asking everyone questions about witches dancing in the Circle. He even tried to dance with Lucy. Total idiot.'

'Her dad on duty, then?'

'No – Vin was up dancing round the Stones. Lucky for that bloke, that was! Anyway, why weren't you there? We could have done with your fiddle, to drown out this bloke's singing. Out ladykilling, were you, you lucky bugger?'

Isaac tapped off a column of ash into the saucer on his lap. 'Sort of.'

There was a long silence, broken only by Berian's contented sucking noises and Skip's snores.

'I'm in love,' announced Isaac. Gareth looked up in genuine surprise. 'She's really ... marvellous.'

'Hey, that's terrific! When do we meet her, then?'

'She's coming over today. That's why I'm here. Saw the light on. Lend us some things, will you?'

'What sort of things?' Gareth grinned. 'Don't say she's going over to your place. Get tidying, will you! Any ordinary woman would run a mile!'

Isaac considered this. 'She's not exactly ordinary. I don't think she'll run, somehow. Anyway, I need some food ... some clothes ... and some flowers.'

Gareth gaped. Berian had fallen asleep. 'Clothes? Some of Sue's old stuff, d'you mean? Food? Flowers?'

'Yeah. Get a move on. I reckon you're right about the tidying, for once.'

Gareth carried Berian upstairs, then went to rummage in the cupboard while Isaac emptied the contents of the fridge into a carrier bag.

* * *

Isaac left his motorbike on the side of the narrow roadway and plunged past dock leaves the size of rhubarb to reach the gap in the hedgerow. Once through, the hillside fell away and the wood sprang up to claim the valley. Slender, smooth trees competed for roothold and light. Insects buzzed invisibly, and pigeons chanted in the high vault of interlaced branches. Wild flowers pierced banks of ivy with splashes of colour like paint drops: campion, violets, and late bluebells. The smell descended; the heavy fresh green smell, damp and clammy in the nostrils, laden with the base notes of wild garlic.

The trackway descended like a stairway over roots and boulders. All around, the woodland grew fiercer and greener. The air was wet with the breath of trees. Small animals crackled behind ferns, and a row of sheep droppings added their sharp sweet scent.

At last Isaac glimpsed a patch of wet grey, far below; the low slate roof of his long stone cottage. Studded with carved red gables, it rambled alongside the brink of a clear and noisy stream. Early sunlight splashed onto the tiny bridge, a single slab of local slate. The terrace was formed of coloured stones, set with the upturned bases of green glass bottles. He stooped to study one of these, and saw that a fragile moss had grown like coral within this miniature greenhouse.

Around the terrace set into the rising hillside of the sunny side of the valley, a lifetime's collection of obscure machine parts lay rusting. Wind chimes rang softly as he passed the walls of flaking grey stone which he had cemented with mud from the bed of the stream. Enamelled advertising signs for Pear's soap rested against great baulks of seasoning timber. A zinc bath flooded gently with icy spring water from a hose; the dark clothes bumping against its sides were being washed by the flow of water. A week's washing took a whole month here.

Isaac never locked the blue and red striped door. Lifting the latch, he entered a room as cool and dark as a cave. Oil lamps, lutes and cobwebbed mandolins hung from the walls among stencilled cabinets and unfinished canvasses. Huge heavy wooden furniture slanted across the stone-flagged floor. An unleaded Aga slumbered in the corner. The smell of the place was the smell of the man; musky, woodsmoked, paraffined animal.

A small marmalade tomcat yawned and sauntered toward him as he lay down the fiddle, the carrier bags, and the great fragile parcel made from all the flowers from Sue and Gareth's garden. It sniffed his outstretched fingertips, then deigned to accept his stroking hands. It survived by devouring voles and mice. When he began to pick it up, its long warm body slipped through his fingers, and it stalked away, offended.

Isaac crossed to the Aga, but it was as cold as iron; out for several days. Sighing, he knelt to riddle the ash and load the furnace with sticks and crumpled newspapers dated from the previous year. As the small yellow flame struggled into life, he went to the stone sink to fill the heavy iron kettle with spring water from the hosepipe. He left the stream filtering over the pile of washing-up in the bowl. The sticks were alight by now, and he fetched wood from the neat waist-high pile outside the door and lowered the kettle over the heat.

He looked around at the paintings pinned to the wall; wild, dark, windswept paintings. Gnarled hawthorns and brooding yews were outlined amongst ochre skies. Rusting harrows showed like ribcages and claws against tangled briars. A young girl played the viola; a study of springy, concentrated curves. A group of friends from the village shared tawny wine at dusk. Berian gurgled in his big brother's arms. The marmalade cat slept. Not one was finished.

During the last five years Isaac had rebuilt this derelict cottage hidden in the valley above Glasmaen. Before settling here, Isaac had explored Europe and Asia, sketching but failing to recapture the raw energy of his days at art college and in the student riots of Paris.

Eventually he had decided that the peace and solitude of one home were preferable to the turmoil of vagrancy. Serendipity had introduced him to this hollow of Britain, where wild Wales marched alongside rural England. The tangled beauty of the countryside had wound itself around his heart, and marvellous paintings had floated from his brushtip. Now his cottage had been finished for several months and he had lost his inspiration. He was lonely, and weary of the few local women who had once appealed to his seductive artist's eye.

Isaac stood before the small mirror, contemplating his own dark beauty. His eyes glittered electric blue as he thought of Ainee Sealfin in his arms.

Turning away, he climbed the narrow pine stairs, crossed the landing, laden with shelves of dusty books and unplayable records, and went into his bedroom. The high small window caught the first shafts of dawn light piercing the dark valley. The rafters were lined with ancient sewing-machines.

Plunging his hands into his rail of clothes, he pulled out a hand-woven Indian shirt, a dark embroidered waistcoat from Bulgaria, and wide Kurdish trousers. He quickly dressed, rubbing off the remaining sand and pine-needles from his body with a ragged yellow towel.

Turning back the heavy blankets, he yanked the faded flannel sheets from his wide bed, replacing them with cleaner ones from the shelf. He had brought upstairs a spray of Gareth's best damask roses, and now he stripped the petals off, sprinkling them between the sheets. As he did so, Isaac listened to the stream outside. It sounded like falling rain. Here he would hold her, stroke her, kiss her. Here they would sleep dreamless sleeps, and awake to love. The valley, the ocean and the world would cease to exist as they lay tangled in each other's arms. He smiled at the prospect. Only the hiss of the kettle boiling disturbed his reverie.

After he had eaten and had swept the dust, fluff and mouse bones out of the door, Isaac made his way downstream to bathe in the deep green pool beneath the waterfall. The water was stinging, cold and sharp as knives, and sparkling with tiny rainbows. The rainbows slithered down his dark wet hair, across his broad muscled shoulders, over his clean amber skin. Fronds of fern caressed his arms, spread wide to receive the brightening sun and the shimmering water. He watched an otter playing with her cubs, and heard the rattle of a heron flying past. Then he dressed, and returned to doze in the patch of sun on the terrace, waiting for Ainee Sealfin to appear.

5

When Dr Keynes woke up the following morning he discovered that he was in intense pain. His skull throbbed to the pounding of the blood in his brain, like tom-toms. Every bone in his body had been disconnected and then badly replaced. The lining of his mouth had been stripped away by powerful chemicals. His intestines and stomach were as swollen as sausages. Even his finger-nails felt bruised. He began to moan, and quickly cut the noise short as its booming reached his trembling ear-drums.

By forcing open his uppermost eyelid Keynes eventually managed to focus on the digits of his portable alarm clock, despite the awful glare of light in the room. He felt a slow wave of disbelief as he identified the time as nine o'clock. He always breakfasted at seven-thirty, but today the thought of breakfast brought a violent lurch to his stomach. To be kind to himself, he lowered the eyelid slowly and returned to sleep.

At noon Dr Keynes, awash with black coffee and wearing sunglasses, walked unsteadily out into the sunshine. The maid had informed him that the survey team had set out shortly after an early breakfast, apparently keen to do some work. The absence of the two main witnesses to his beery indiscretion had given him a little relief. He had become sufficiently aware of the heat of the day to have left his tweed jacket in his room, together with the tie which had seemed to be far too complicated to bother knotting. The act of shaving had been exhausting enough already. There were several bloody nicks in his chin.

He automatically walked towards the Glyn, clambering painfully over the boundary fence. Glyn Tump appeared far higher today than it had done yesterday, when he had so blithely scrambled to the top of the mound. Today it seemed as unscalable as the Matterhorn.

Keynes glanced warily up towards the summit of Bryngaran Hill, which blazed like a furnace in the midday sun. No flicker of movement was apparent from the stone circle, and he let out a sigh. The white-robed dancers must have been a trick of the light, after all. This made him feel slightly better, and he stepped out boldly towards the woodland filling the valley of the Glyn.

The shade of the leafy green trees was welcoming in its coolness, and the dappling of sunlight over the undergrowth and slender tree trunks was merciful to Keynes' tender eyes. He even removed his sunglasses once he was well inside the wood.

There was no trace of a path, but Keynes found that he could pick his way alongside the rippling stream which wound along the floor of the valley. The banks were dry, not muddy, and little beaches of gravel stretched out for a few yards here and there. He could jump across the stream if necessary. He came across a lawn of emerald green grasses, around which the stream looped in a wide meander. He sat down carefully to enjoy the cool shade, listening to the chatter of the water and the humming of bees in the wild flowers. It was all rather pleasant, he thought with some surprise. He eased off his walking boots from his overheated feet and waggled his toes inside his socks.

Then a naked girl stepped out from behind a tree and smiled at him.

In her arms she held a large shining salmon. Its head lay between her small pointed breasts, and its broad tail lay along-side her thigh. Long fair hair draped her shoulders, but did nothing to conceal her pale flesh. She continued to walk towards him, smiling, as Keynes was suddenly released from his initial shock and scrambled to his feet, stumbling over one of his loose boots as he did so. He momentarily wondered whether this was the smiling barmaid from the pub last night, with all that long fair hair; but realised that this girl was smaller and paler, and – well – of a more delicate build. She was very close to him now, and looked up at his face with eyes so large and brown and deep that he was reminded of photographs of seal pups about to be clubbed to death for their skins. He shuddered at the curious sensation of cruel power over her which this thought gave him.

She adjusted the heavy salmon in her arms and stretched up one slender hand to touch his chin, seeming to marvel at its hairless state. She ran her fingers over the shaven skin, pausing to touch the scars of his clumsy razor. She continued to smile and her teeth were as trim and gleaming as a string of pearls.

Keynes's throat convulsed as he attempted to speak to her, but no sound came out. He glanced down at the salmon. Its eye swivelled to glare back at him, and it opened its jaws to reveal teeth like those on a new steel saw. He leaped back in horror, tumbled over his other boot, and fell heavily into the stream. The girl threw back her head and laughed with thin, tinkling notes which mingled with the notes of the stream. Then she paused and began to listen to a distant sound. Keynes dragged himself out of the stream and started to move towards her, his hands outstretched hungrily, dizzy with desire for her slim body.

She spun around, clutching her salmon, and leapt away from him, bounded into the woodland like a deer, and vanished from sight. As he gazed after her he became aware of the faint sound of a violin being played, deep in the wood.

Keynes sank slowly down onto his knees, and then collapsed on the grass, shuddering in disbelief. A sob shook his wet and sweating body and for the first time since the death of his mother fifteen years ago, Keynes laid his head on his arms and wept.

It was several hours later when he woke and made his way back to the hotel, feeling curiously refreshed. When he glanced into the speckled mirror in his bathroom, he noticed that his shaving scars had all vanished.

*   *   *

Sue Hopkins-Jones finally came downstairs at midday. She felt rested and restored after the stately circle dancing and the soothing rituals at the Sabbat the previous night. This morning, after a good night's sleep – interrupted only by Gareth's outburst at dawn – she had listened to the 'Archers Omnibus' in bed, and then taken a leisurely bath. Her pale skin was flushed with warmth from the hot water, and her short hair was freshly washed and hennaed; it was pink and bouncy on her head. She wore a bright yellow T-shirt and turquoise shorts. Her grey eyes were luminous and shining as she smiled at Gareth and wished him good morning. He was greatly relieved to see that she was in a cheerful mood. Whilst she stooped to check the sleeping baby in his cot, Gareth rinsed his rubber-clad hands free of blue dye and peeled off the gloves. The kitchen was fragrant with the warm wet wool in his steel buckets, whilst the tangy herbs of the dye itself mingled with the savoury scent of roasting chicken and potatoes. Sue stood upright and stretched deliciously, her fingertips just touching the low ceiling. Her milk-heavy breasts rose under the yellow cotton. Stepping up close behind her, Gareth caught her around the waist and kissed her neck. She smelled of cream and peaches, and he nuzzled into her ear as she wriggled against him. She revolved in his arms, turning her wide slate-grey eyes up to meet his soft hazel ones. She wrapped her hands around the back of his neck and returned his kiss.

'You've been busy this morning, my love,' she murmured to Gareth. 'Dyeing your next batch of wool, dinner cooking, and a sleeping baby. What more could a woman ask of a man? Where is Emrys?'

'Playing with the dog in the garden. That gives us a good hour before your father turns up to eat us out of house and home. What would you like to do best?' He nibbled at Sue's earlobe, and she giggled and pushed him away.

'I'll go and play with my little boy while you finish your wool. Don't pull such a face! After all, you get him all day and I only see him at evenings and weekends. Never mind, sweetheart, term ends on Wednesday, and we can all be together all day long, for six weeks. Lovely!' She writhed with pleasure, then prised Gareth's arms from about her and almost danced with joy over to the open window. She leaned out, calling and waving to four-year-old Emrys as he chased Skip the dog across the lawn. Then she froze as she saw that all the flowers were missing.

'What's happened to the garden?' she asked in a cold voice.

Gareth had his explanation ready. 'I went out and did the dead-heading earlier. Been meaning to do it all week. Think I went a bit wild with it, though, don't you? Still, the flowers will all be back in a week.'

'A bit wild!' Sue groaned. 'All my irises ...'

'And I mowed the lawn while you had the radio on, see. Didn't I do well?'

Sue struggled with her temper for a moment, and then heaved a deep sigh. 'Yes, love, you did. I did agree to leave the house

33

and garden to you until the school holidays. You're quite right. Well done.'

Gareth grinned, and she turned to run her hand through his thick brown curls. 'Tell you what,' said Sue, 'I'll stick a bottle of Frascati in the fridge and we'll have drinks on your newly-mown lawn before lunch. If we're quick, we can down most of the bottle before Dad has it all! Howzat?'

She had swung across the room, grabbed a bottle from the wine rack and pulled open the fridge door before Gareth remembered.

'Where's all the food I bought on Friday? This fridge is practically empty!' She glowered at Gareth, her good mood forgotten. 'What have you been doing?'

The baby began to cry. Skip began to bark as Bryn Jones drove his elderly Rover 2000 onto the gravel drive, arriving early for his Sunday lunch. Gareth groaned.

* * *

Isaac, alone, was racked with love for Ainee Sealfin.

The impossibility of his passion did not occur to him. He had captured a vision; she had been chilly in his arms and yet warmed by the furnace of his desire. To the artist, Ainee was the ultimate, the immaculate concept. Yet he had not imagined her; she had responded to his kisses in wild, unwary ways. He had played out his need in fraught notes of his finest music; his leap of capture had resulted in her opening melting dark eyes to his. She had promised him an eternity of rapture; all he needed was long enough to paint her. She was as salt and moist as oysters; she was as soft and liquid as his dreams.

He sat in the shade and moaned as he played the fiddle, eloquent with its new timbre of magic. A haunting Irish melody floated up over the slates of his cottage, tangling in the trees of his valley.

He paused, glancing up to wipe his eyes, and saw Ainee Sealfin naked in the sunshine. She had stepped out of the stream, and glistening rivulets of water coiled down her ankles like chains of silk. Her hair shone like ripening corn in sheaves, trickling over her shoulders, and her smile sparkled at him. But

34

what made him moan aloud was her skin; she was covered in the sheerest down of tiny golden hairs, from the shallow dome of her forehead to her shell-like toenails. This faint fur captured the sunlight and gleamed as she moved. She shone like a candle against the dark woodland, a spirit of light.

Isaac set the fiddle aside in a daze, then reached down to his sketch book and charcoal. 'Stand still,' he commanded, his eyes photographing her incandescent splendour. He drew her image rapidly, in sure and confident strokes, hardly glancing at the paper. Then he compared the two and a smile crinkled across his face, spreading into a grin of complete pleasure. His muse had arrived. He cast aside the sketchbook, and rose to greet Ainee with his arms spread wide.

'Welcome to our home, Ainee Sealfin,' he whispered as he reached for her waist, but she raised a finger to hush him.

'I have brought you a gift, Isaac Talboys. Wait!' As he obeyed her command, startled, she leapt down into the stream again, and thrust her hands into the shimmering water. She span around and stepped up again, lifting up to him an enormous flapping salmon, flashing in the sunlight. She laughed with the sound of bells ringing as he stepped back before its grinning teeth, then she looked around. She carried the salmon over to the zinc tub beside the house, and slid the great fish carefully into the flooding water. It revolved slowly, spinning the sodden clothes around the tub.

Then she returned to Isaac and reached up to tangle her pale hands in his long hair, her fingers like streaks of white ageing his blackness. She opened her eyes wide and gazed into the blue depths of his.

'Here I am, Isaac,' she whispered in tones which made his mouth water. 'Love me.'

Isaac swung her into his arms, then carried her into his house and upstairs into his rose-petalled bed.

*   *   *

35

MONDAY 22 JUNE

Over an early dinner at St Briavel's Hotel Dr Keynes considered his position. Because of a series of peculiar distractions, he had not yet begun his mission to Glasmaen, but it would be healthier not to think about them, he decided. As he stirred his coffee his mind wandered, wondering if he dared to ask the chatty barmaid why an obscure Welsh saint should have had need of an hotel. Then he dismissed the thought rapidly. Why, he was verging on joke-telling, which he had always left to more frivolous mortals. He gave a brisk sigh. He was wasting time.

The barmaid had told him that the young men with whom he had dined on Saturday night were now taking bed and break-fast at the Golden Oak. She had gone on to describe their appearances around the village with 'some sort of funny tele-scope and stripey poles all day long,' and then asked him flat out whether he knew what they were up to. He had evaded her question with a shrug, but he realised now that he had felt a curious compulsion to respond to her inquisitive smile and bright eyes, to tell her everything. Why did he find the local women so tempting?

Keynes suppressed this unsavoury thought and concentrated on his mission. If the survey team was busy, then so should he be.

Keynes pushed back his chair, nodded curtly to the smiling barmaid as he passed her, and strode out directly to his car. He would go and see this farmer Bryn Jones at once, and open negotiations with him. Then he remembered that his car keys, briefcase, and suit jacket were all still in his room, and rather angrily returned to fetch them.

6

Bryn Jones was a man who preferred to live an easy life. He had systematically arranged things so that living cost him the least amount of effort and cash. Consequently everything about him was elderly, frayed, grey and dusty. Tall but stooping, overweight and slow-moving, Jones shambled along like a much older man. His hair was uncombed and overgrown, as was the tea-stained moustache and beard (which hid a weak chin), all in shades of tough grey pepper-and-salt. His dark eyes glittered slyly in a craggy, crinkled face, and his clothes had all been bought long before his wife died fifteen years ago. Since it was summer, he wore a pale blue cotton suit with wide lapels and a hint of flares. The blue had turned almost to beige with dust and grease.

Bryn Jones had emerged from the slums of Manchester into comparative affluence and exoticism. At the age of twenty-one he had written a highly controversial and scandalous novel about demonic possession, the result of several months of carefully-researched and calculated effort. This was salacious to the point of obscenity and had become an international best-seller, as he had designed it to do.

Within a year Bryn Jones had married a quiet, intelligent middle-class young woman, bought 'The Knapp', a vast and crumbling Victorian country house and estate in the hills above Glasmaen, and settled down to complete happiness. From then on he took life easy. He spent his time reading, being fed, and sleeping. His wife quietly bore him a daughter and brought her up largely without interference in his leisurely life, sent her off to teacher training college, and then quietly hanged herself from the banister rail. He only missed the women because he now had to do his own cooking. He saw his daughter Susan, who had now presented him with a pleasant son-in-law and two fine grandsons, at Sabbats, Folk Club meetings, and at her house for Sunday dinner.

Occasionally he had summoned up the energy to write another book to his established formula, under a pen-name to preserve his privacy, and used the proceeds to have a part of his mansion restored. He would then sell off that part at a comfortable profit, which he invested in safe shares. The buyers took over the responsibility for the upkeep of the structure and the rambling gardens. He had moved within the house several times during his married life, each time to a smaller apartment, which he considered cheaper to run. Now he lived in the ballroom.

His main expenditure was on books, almost all second-hand from nearby Hay-on-Wye. They lined the corridors, loaded onto sagging shelves and built up in tottering piles on the furniture and in the corners of every room.

Otherwise he lived surrounded by souvenirs of the Thirties in Manchester; airing frames, string vests, cinema projection lamps, pianolas, bakelite, feather bolsters, newspapers. He had few heating or washing facilities, or none. Nothing was antique; everything was junk.

Jones had never raised a duster since he moved into this mausoleum, and every surface was insulated with a layer of thick and woolly fluff. One Easter holiday, his newly married daughter Sue had spent the fortnight cleansing and scouring. She began with the disgusting kitchen, in which he stored tinned food of more use to the props-buyer of a BBC classic serial than to living mortals. She persuaded Gareth to spend seven days building and stacking bookshelves. After this Herculaean effort, she realised that her father had no intention of protecting all the newly naked surfaces from the invading dirt, and gave up. Jones could easily have afforded to pay a troop of daily cleaners, but he preferred his home filthy, or what he called 'homely'.

His ballroom was a separate wing stretched above the stables and coach-houses, entered by a flight of marble steps rising from the conservatory. The ballroom was a lavish and impractical addition to the house; it was immensely long and far too narrow to accommodate even a small orchestra. Had they played at one end, the other would have been plunged into silence. Had they squeezed into the middle there would have been no space left for the dancers to pass. Dances there must have been dismal occasions.

Jones spent most of his time in an echoing space at the north end of the ballroom. The centrepiece of this room was a sumptuous fireplace; a huge kaleidoscope of brilliantly-coloured marble. Bryn Jones bothered only to light a fire in it when temperatures dropped below freezing on his conservatory thermometer. Even so, it had no effect whatsoever in warming the room further than a yard from the hearth. The windows, too, were unreasonable. Nine feet of vertical glass facing north-east provided views and light, but no heat; especially since there were seven of these absurd stained-glass refrigerators. Jones wouldn't afford curtains, and the original builder had only bothered to provide shutters over the lower halves of these windows, so the overall result was to provide the ambient temperature of a morgue all year round.

In winter, the cold controlled his life. Every movement had to be made after due consideration to the prevailing draughts; trips to the toilet had to be planned well in advance, and usually after visiting the kitchen to boil up a kettle of water with which to defrost the lavatory. Moth-eaten fur coats hung behind the door, as protection for the march to the Siberian bedrooms. Jones had installed night-storage radiators, but despite his comfortable investment income was too mean to pay for their electricity, therefore they crouched in dank corners. The only way Jones could survive an evening spent in that room in February was by being fully dressed and in thermal underwear, huddled like a caterpillar in a sleeping-bag, creeping within the tiled hearth to lie shuddering inches from the flames of the log fire slumbering within its iridescent marble.

The place certainly had capabilities for improvement. From where he lay in the grate, Jones would study the cavernous room and imagine what it would be like if he could be bothered to decorate it. The cracked grey ceiling would shimmer with golden stars in a vault of midnight blue, hung with gleaming bronze chandeliers. The drab, unpainted walls would be defined with rose-coloured dados and cornices, and would glow with all the subtle shades of tapestried wallpaper, hung about with icons and sensuous Pre-Raphaelite oils. Great folding screens of hand-painted silk would close off the dark corners and hide the hideous – but active – radiators. The windows would be swathed in luminous velvet curtains, all swagged and looped. A lush meadow of ruby carpet would be scattered about with jewel-like oriental rugs and Knole sofas, and the flickering firelight from the logs blazing in the magnificent marble fireplace would sparkle over this glorious chamber, a temple to Poetry and Love. He would hug himself with pleasure at the thought that all this was possible, despite the effort and expense, and go back to reading his book.

The views from Bryn Jones's ballroom were exhilarating; wooded green hillsides tumbling down towards the silvery gleam of the river. Hang-gliders swung past the Knapp's topmost turret, waving through the bathroom windows as they passed. The surroundings were gothic to an almost nightmare degree. Sheep drowned in the bog alongside the driveway, and a hurricane once barricaded the inhabitants in with felled beeches for three days. Snow often shut the lane for weeks. All that could be heard up there was the hissing of the wind amongst the yew trees, and the cries of foxes and owls long into the night.

As he parked his BMW at the top of the long and sinuous drive to the Knapp, Dr Keynes was impressed. The views over the unspoilt countryside were charming, and the peace and quiet were like a warm blanket in the cool of the summer evening. The turreted Gothic Revival house was magnificent in its setting of cedars and yew trees. It was all rather different from the small farmhouse which he had expected. For several minutes, he rather envied the owner.

After he had knocked at three separate front doors, to be re-directed each time after a lengthy wait, he was not so sure. Bryn Jones could not be as affluent as he had at first appeared, if he had had to subdivide his house in this way. Once he had finally located the correct door, its paint peeling away, at the top of a flight of slippery marble steps in an otherwise splendid conservatory, Keynes wondered how far he could drop the price of the land he had to purchase from the farmer. The man must be in sore need of money, living in a scruffy corner of this vast house.

The large door swung slowly open with a painful groan from its hinges, and a hunched figure peered out. Keynes looked him up and down and shivered faintly in disgust, then recalled his duty.

'Good evening,' said Keynes crisply. 'We haven't met, but my Department has been in correspondence with you for some time concerning the purchase of an area of land known as 'The Glyn.' My name is Dr Edward Keynes. I am here to conduct the final negotiations with you. Is now convenient, or shall I arrange for a later appointment with you?'

Bryn Jones considered this. He enjoyed forthrightness in money matters. He nodded his head slowly, and opened the door wider to permit Keynes to enter his house.

He led the way through dark and narrow passageways, carpeted with inadequate scraps of scuffed rugs over bare boards, and lined with mouldering old books. Then he opened a wide door into a vast and echoing room which smelled strongly of stale woodsmoke and damp. He directed Keynes to a greying and overstuffed armchair and lowered himself into another.

Keynes sat down carefully on the greasy needlecord surface and glanced around. He failed to repress a shudder at the dank and dusty room, which made Jones smirk.

When Jones spoke, it was slowly, and with a nasty quiet sibilance which he had practised on his family for years as he strove to get rid of the Manchester accent. 'So how much are you offering me for the Glyn?' he enquired.

Keynes frowned. 'We are currently surveying the area. It has no potential for arable or pastoral use, as you know, being extremely steep and covered in uncoppiced shrubby growth. There is no access by road or footpath, and the valley has been uninhabited for seventy-three years. You could not expect a high price, and we will offer what the market can bear.'

Jones coolly repeated his question. Keynes sighed. Well, at least this forthrightness would speed up negotiations, he thought. Then he could get back to civilisation. 'Ninety three thousand pounds,' he replied.

Bryn Jones gasped and lurched forward, clutching at the arms of his chair. 'That seems very … reasonable,' he murmured as he tried to recover his balance. 'But what do you want the land for?'

'The land is an investment purchase by the Department. It is highly probable that it will not, in fact, be used in your lifetime or in mine. After a full survey, the task of preserving the land as a nature reserve will be handed over to a local nature conservancy council, with a small annual grant for running costs. Nothing will change, except that the area will become even more of a public amenity than it is at present.' Keynes offered one of his thin smiles as he spoke. This was an extremely generous arrangement, he felt, and one calculated to receive public acclaim.

Bryn Jones nodded, and returned the small smile with one which revealed his broken yellow teeth. 'And what might you use the land for?'

This was the tricky bit. Keynes drew a sharp breath. 'Oh, there will be scientific exploration of the underlying geology of the area.' He paused for a moment, and then added firmly: 'But that is an expensive option, and may well not be taken up.'

Jones frowned, and considered for a moment. 'I take it this has to do with the fact that there's a major fault line in the old red sandstone running right along the Glyn?'

Keynes was surprised at the old man's perspicacity, and reviewed his opinion of him. 'Well, yes, it is a particularly interesting area, geologically speaking. That is our main reason for wanting the site, yes.'

'And the other reasons?'

Keynes glanced out of the window. 'Remoteness from large centres of population, really. This would be the main benefit to the nature reserve, of course.'

Jones nodded, and heaved himself up to his feet. 'Well, Dr Keynes, I'll consider your offer. Thank you for your visit.'

Keynes escaped from the chair with relief. 'I'm staying at St Briavel's Hotel for several days, if you wish to discuss the matter further. Let's see; today is Monday; I will visit you again on Friday, if that is convenient.'

'No, not Friday. I won't be here. Busy all weekend with the Festival. Next Tuesday will do, afternoon I think.'

After noting this neatly in his diary, Keynes followed Jones back to the conservatory door, and shook hands in a stiff farewell. Then he hurried back to the leather-lined cleanliness and comfort of his BMW.

Jones watched him negotiate the tree-lined drive far into the distance, before grinning and rubbing his hands. 'Now I have to go and see that Isaac Talboys,' he hissed to himself. 'I'll buy back the Glyn from him. Perhaps I better even do it formally this time, with documents and things. Otherwise, we may well be in a sticky situation.'

Bryn Jones sloped back down the corridor, whispering 'Ninety-three thousand' to himself, like a mantra.

7

Ainee Sealfin was fascinated by her new life and, enthralled by Ainee Sealfin, Isaac constantly drew her and painted her, capturing every new curve and shadow which she revealed. His greatest difficulty was in persuading her to hold still for long enough. He had solved this problem when making portraits of children by drawing them while they were frozen into immobility by watching 'Neighbours' on television. But Ainee was different in so many ways.

She was enchanted by music, and insisted on listening to his entire cassette collection, which would exhaust his batteries in a matter of days, he grumbled. But whenever she discovered a sound which interested her, she would crouch or stretch wherever he posed her for long enough to complete a pastel image. She listened most closely to women's voices, mouthing the choruses as she memorised the words; she enjoyed all the old sad folk ballads just as much as the passionate songs of unrest and pain of the sixties and seventies – Isaac had nothing more recent. She was particularly impressed by the anthems and polyphonies of nuns in French and Greek abbeys, and by the crystal choirs of Bulgarian women.

'My sisters could learn this,' she would sigh, and gaze silently into space whilst Isaac feverishly scribbled, trying to describe her lostness.

Dance music excited her, and it was hard to prevent her pacing the measure of a sixteenth-century pavane along the length of the sunlit terrace, or curling around the pillar dividing the main room in a lifting Irish jig. She traced out the spiralling sidesteps of branles, her fingers entwined with the invisible hands of her invisible sisters, and she adored the soft swayings of fandangoes and waltzes. Best of all was when Isaac laid aside his charcoal and brushes, and took up the forbidden violin, and she danced with her eyes half-closed to his eerie Balkan melodies or worked out complex stepping-patterns to his Celtic rhythms. Her dark eyes flashed as she twirled, spinning and laughing.

Constantly, she asked questions. She followed Isaac about the cottage, pointing and enquiring, querying and investigating everything he did, or had, or said. He showed her bookfuls of pictures by all his favourite artists, and photographs and paintings of the loveliest places which he had visited; she collected music and images as though they were all created just for her.

Isaac had lived alone for fifteen years, and in silence, and struggled to reply, and explain, or describe. But he would weary of finding encompassing answers, and grow short-tempered with her. When he felt the helpless impatience of a bad teacher surging within him, he would lay aside his mug of cider, or his fiddle, or his palette, and step over to Ainee Sealfin and seize her in his arms. He would pull up her face to meet the force of his rough kisses, his fingertips beneath her chin, twisting his long fingers into the loose silk of her shimmering hair.

Silencing her tongue with his, he would lower her onto the broad cushioned sofa, or lift her light weight against his hard body and carry her upstairs to his bed. And there he would prove his love for her again.

*   *   *

TUESDAY 23 JUNE

Bryn Jones arrived in the Glyn as Isaac was killing the salmon. For several days it had swum in circles in the tub, grinning at Ainee or snapping at Isaac as he snatched pieces of washing out of the water. He had finally found the time and energy to yank it out and hit it on the skull with a mallet. Bryn sauntered across the sunny stone-flagged terrace to watch Isaac dragging out the salmon's entrails.

'What a beauty,' Bryn Jones remarked. 'I'd be happy to take a few steaks off you. That's too much food for a man alone, without the benefit of a deep freeze.'

Isaac stood up, his hands filled with slippery innards. 'Afternoon, Bryn. I've got company, and anyway most of this fish is going to Sue and Gareth, so I expect you'll have some ready-cooked from them next Sunday.' He turned and walked over to the mound of decaying rubbish at the far end of the garden, which he loosely termed his 'compost heap'. Throwing the entrails onto the pile, he shouted for the cat.

'Quite a midden you're building there, Isaac,' commented Jones when the younger man returned to rinse his hands in the brook before beginning to slice the fish apart. 'You'll be able to make a splendid vegetable garden out of it some day, if you ever decide to tidy up and sell.'

Isaac looked up at Jones warily, suspicious of his smiling countenance. 'Why should I sell?' he asked. 'I'd never be able to get all that heavy furniture I've built up the bank again, and who'd want to buy? A three-room cottage with no access except by a winding path, and no mains services? You'd have to be as mad or as anti-social as I am to want to live out here. No, I've made my bed and now I'll lie in it, so to speak. And I like it here.'

Jones watched him work for several minutes in silence before he spoke again. 'You've done a damned good job here, you know. No one would believe that this cottage was just two tumbledown walls with the stream flowing between them when you bought the Glyn from me, five years ago. I certainly never believed that you'd do such a lovely job on it, or I might have charged you more for it all!' Isaac glared up at Jones for a moment and then returned to his work. 'You know, Isaac, I'm thinking of moving. That ballroom is too big for an old man like me. It should have a family living in it. I might let Sue have it, instead of that poky little cottage of theirs, and find somewhere smaller for myself. Like this, for instance. Yes, this would suit me very well. I like the peace and quiet, and you've made the cottage very comfortable. A lot warmer than my place in winter, I'm sure! I could offer you quite a bit to buy it back, Isaac. You'd have made an excellent return for all your hard work. I could offer you enough to buy any interesting old ruin you fancied having a go at, within reason. You could end up somewhere pretty amazing in ten years or so, if you keep doing up places as well as this and selling them for such a tidy profit.'

Isaac laid aside the large knife he was using, leaned over into the stream to wash his hands, shaking them dry, and then slowly stood up. He looked steadily at Jones for a while, and then laughed. 'How tidy a profit, Bryn? How much are you offering me for the Glyn?'

Jones could not entirely restrain a grimace from appearing briefly on his face as he offered to give money away, but eventually muttered 'Forty thousand pounds'.

Isaac sat down on the block of wood which he used for chopping kindling and rolled up a cigarette while he considered this. 'That does seem to be a tidy profit, I agree. I bought the whole valley off you for only four thousand. But I must have spent, oh, let me think, about fifteen, say twenty thousand, on all the building materials. And I paid for that by selling my paintings, a lot of paintings, for not very much money each. I put a lot of time and care into those paintings, which I won't ever get back. And then there's all the work I've done on the cottage, rebuilding the walls, laying a new roof, never mind building up these stone walls for the stream to run between. Carpentry; making new stairs; lugging the stove down here. Decorating. Cutting a path in the bank. Laying this terrace. Re-laying the slates hurt – it was like hundreds of knives slashing the palms of my hands. So you could really say that I built the place with my own blood and sweat. You see, you can't expect me to suddenly give it all away, for a mere wad of money. It has cost my time, and my effort. And anyway, I'm not sure whether I want to move.' He thought about Ainee for a few moments. 'And I've got a woman living with me, now. I'd have to see whether she likes the Glyn. It may be just the right place for her, we'll have to see. No, I don't think I'll sell.'

Jones glanced about, but could see no sign of any woman. 'Have a think about it, Isaac. I'll see you again soon, perhaps at the Folk Club? Last meeting before the Festival, and we'll need your help. Damn good posters and programme covers, by the way. Send in your receipts for expenses. Enjoy your salmon with your lady friend.' He nodded at Isaac and shambled slowly away up the winding path.

As he reached the top of the bank he paused to open the small gate and looked back down at the cottage. His eyesight was poorer lately, but he could have sworn that a naked girl was crouching over the corpse of the salmon, tearing at the raw flesh with her teeth. He almost made his way back down the path to investigate, but it might just have been a trick of his eyes, after all.

*　*　*

WEDNESDAY 24 JUNE

Isaac and Gareth sat in the late-morning sun and watched Emrys wander down the path towards the wood, hand in hand with Ainee Sealfin, who now seemed to be decently clad in an old black dress of floating cotton. Her hair was twisted up onto her head, wisps falling among the tails of red satin ribbon. The sun shone through the dress as she led the way into the trees, outlining her body and making the men shiver.

'Wow, Isaac, she's something else. Wherever did you find her? I mean, is she safe?' Gareth adjusted the baby sleeping on his lap.

Isaac sighed. 'Safe? I don't know about safe. I think she may eat people alive, but perhaps not your four year old. He's probably having a wonderful time with her. I know I am.'

'How long will she last?'

'What, with him or with me, or with you, or with the rest of this planet? For ever, I hope, or at least until next Tuesday.'

'Oh, so you're going to show her off at the Folk Festival. Risky. She makes me drunk just to look at her, never mind listen to her. I don't think she's safe – oh, no, not with me, I don't want you to think that, I've got Sue. But I don't care to imagine what Sue will think of her. School finishes for the summer today, you know. I've got to take the boys to the concert this afternoon. Then I get Sue full-time at home, worn out and frantic about organising the Festival. Speaking of which, has Bryn Jones met Ainee yet?'

'No, thank God. That miserable old bugger. Do you know, he offered to buy the Glyn back from me yesterday.'

'Did he? Whatever for?'

'Forty thousand quid.'

Gareth gasped. 'Is that all?'

'All? Well, it's a hell of a lot of money for Bryn Jones to give someone.'

'And what is he planning to do with that filthy ballroom?'

'Give it to you.'

Gareth shuddered, and wrapped his head in his hands. 'Oh no, oh no, oh no. I don't want that bloody mausoleum. What will Sue say? Oh, no, oh no. What if she accepts? Oh, hell, I hate the place. We've carefully been living in the smallest possible house to prevent him coming to live with us, and now he wants to ... oh, no.'

'I don't think you'll have much say in the matter, knowing Sue. She's got your kids to think about now. She'll probably jump at it.'

'Only if you sell Bryn Jones the Glyn.'

Isaac thought about this.

'And what about Ainee? Will she stay here with you? It's about the safest possible place to keep her locked up, especially if you don't take her to the Festival.'

'Don't give me ideas. I thought it was you who was the liberated feminist new age wimp, and here you are suggesting that I keep a sex slave like her locked up in my bedroom.'

They both considered this over a rolled-up cigarette apiece.

'Anyway,' Isaac added eventually, 'no one else would be idiot enough to buy the Glyn off me. What if Ainee decides to go out into the big wide world? I'd have to get rid of the Glyn so that I could go with her. Think of what she could get up to out there!'

'How come you've only known her for – what – three days, and already you're dumping everything and doing whatever she wants to do? Where did she come from anyway? Has she no past?'

Isaac sighed deeply. 'Ah, well, not exactly.' He struggled for the words with which to explain, and found it easier, as usual, to lapse into silence.

Gareth glumly recognised that once again he was considered not worth the effort of speech. He tossed his roll-up tab into the stream and watched it float away. He stared and realised that, like the tab, all the many pleasures which he had once taken from life had disappeared.

They sat in silence, in the sun.

* * *

To his surprise Dr Keynes found himself enjoying a drink after lunch in the Golden Oak in the company of his survey team and the pretty barmaid, Lucy Goldhanger. He had foolishly been led into a rather bitter reminiscence about his school days during the second pint of Owd Roger, and this was the consequence. He had been praising Lucy's sticky toffee pudding, which led him into describing the blandness of the semolina and the appalling sliminess of tapioca pudding at his old grammar school – 'Frogspawn!' interjected Graham Ferris with glee, and they all groaned.

Keynes told them how on his first day at junior school, dinner was held in an enormous echoing hall, the big boys seated at the top of the hall below the battalion of teachers lining the dais. The new boys, feeling very small and lost, had been driven into the far end of the hall and made to sit on huge chairs with splinters in them. The scarred trestle tables were set with bent cutlery, shiny metal beakers and steel jugs filled with water. The nervous newbug Keynes had felt thirsty, and poured himself a mug of water. He had hardly taken a sip before the rustling hall hushed, and the vast voice of the Headmaster was hurled across the length of the hall, like a thunderbolt aimed at Keynes. 'How dare you! How dare you drink before grace is said, boy! Come to the front, this minute!' Keynes showed the group in the pub his wet palms, sweating at the memory.

He had to walk the terrible length of the great hall while every child and teacher stared at him, and was made to stand on a wobbly chair before the dais, facing the school for the duration of the endless meal. Every time he drooped or swayed on the chair, he heard the voice of the Headmaster behind him hiss 'Boy! Stand up straight!'.

Graham asked what the pudding was, but Keynes confessed that he didn't know, as part of the punishment was to go hungry. Whatever it was, he admitted, he fell off the chair while the school was eating it, hit his head on a table-leg, and passed out. 'I was only five,' he added, unnecessarily.

Lucy purred with sympathy, and laid her hand gently over Keynes's clenched fist. 'You poor pet, how dreadful. How cruel they used to be in the old days. How you must have suffered. Imagine being punished for not knowing the rules. Is that why you find it so difficult to relax these days?' Keynes found himself blinking back a tear. He could not remember a woman touching him so kindly, not since his mother died.

'Is that why you prefer to eat alone?' asked Richard Beavis.

Keynes considered this, and nodded. 'I never thought of it before, but I actually think that you're right!' The group nodded sympathetically, and Lucy squeezed his hand. He looked across into her face, and was surprised to see that her eyes were exactly the same colour as the toffee in her marvellous pudding. 'But I'm not as old as you seem to think I am, you know!' he found himself telling her earnestly. 'I'm only thirty-nine – well, forty on Sunday.'

They all exclaimed in surprise and pleasure. 'Oh, well then,' cried Lucy, 'we must arrange a very special day for you! And think of this – your birthday is going to be during the Folk Festival! How thrilling!'

Keynes, Graham and Richard looked back at her blankly. She let go of Keynes's hand, and clapped her own hands together in joy. 'You've never been to a Folk Festival! But we have one of the best Festivals in the world, here in Glasmaen, and it's happening this weekend! Did no one tell you? Oh, how wonderful! You lucky things! Your first Folk Festival! Just you wait and see!'

8

Gareth and Isaac took Ainee and the boys to the school concert that afternoon. With some difficulty they made Ainee promise to keep quiet, and just watch. To their relief, she even sat silently in the Hopkins-Jones 2CV, once they had briefly explained what all the stickers on the windows were about. Ainee was slim enough to squeeze between the child seat and the baby seat in the back, and the two little boys passed the journey holding her hands and grinning up at her in delight.

The school hall was almost full by the time they arrived, and every head turned to stare at Ainee. She smiled serenely and allowed Isaac and Gareth to lead her to an empty row of seats. Gareth smiled and whispered greetings to his many acquaintances, whilst Isaac nodded to the few people whom he bothered to know. Ainee's large brown eyes travelled slowly around the room, observing the multicoloured paper rainforest with interest. She swept her eyes over the audience, and her gaze made all the women avert their eyes. Most of the men blushed before they glanced away. Ainee recognised Keynes amongst the noisy crowd which arrived from the pub, and gave him a special smile which made him turn pale. Then she finally turned her attention to the stage, and settled back in her scooped plastic chair.

The stage was festooned with lianas and tropical flowers made from tissue paper. Even the upright piano had become a bush covered with lilies. The smartly-dressed elderly headmistress strutted onto the middle of the stage and made a crisp speech welcoming everyone to the school production. Emrys squirmed in his chair and giggled, pointing at his mother taking up her position by the side of the stage, ready to prompt the performers. Sue winked at Emrys, her glance lingering on Ainee sitting by his side. She raised one eyebrow delicately before returning to the script.

Ainee was as enchanted as the rest of the audience by the show. Tall trees moved in stately procession across the stage, chanting about the beauties of the rainforest. Tiny Kayapo

Indians danced long happy dances circling through the trees. Rainbow paper parrots flew squawking across the stage. Jaguars and lynxes prowled through the undergrowth, disturbing lively singing monkeys and swarms of fluttering butterflies. Jolly bees buzzed by, dancing the path to honey. An ant-eater lumbered across, tripping over his waving snout. Several stage-shocked infants had to be tugged onstage by their peers, and then cried, forgot their lines or sang the wrong song, but Sue Hopkins-Jones ruled them all with confident kindness, and the audience was keen to forgive. A number of costumes tore or were worn at the wrong time, but the magic of the attempt covered over these errors.

When the gang of lumberjacks arrived, everyone in the audience hissed fervently. They groaned as the loggers cut down the graceful trees and dragged them off the stage. The yellow cardboard JCB met howls of derision as it jigged onstage, but the poor farmers who arrived to settle the empty jungle caught the audience's sympathy. The vicious drunken gold miners who attacked and shot the settlers and the Indians met a shocked silence from the hall.

Everyone cheered when the Indian chief led his tribe to the edges of the forest and was filmed by a television crew. Letters of support from rock stars and foreign governments were read out. Eventually the chief shook hands with the President over an agreement to save the rainforest, and the Indians and animals jumped and sang with joy. Even the trees sidled back onto the stage, and the ant-eater waved its nose. No one minded when even the JCB reappeared to celebrate.

The audience stood to applaud and cheer. Sue and the headmistress bowed and grinned. The JCB shoved the ant-eater off the stage in the excitement, but there were no injuries.

Ainee was dazzled. Back in the car, she finally spoke. 'If being on a stage is such fun, what must it be like to be on this thing called television?'

They all went back to Gareth's cottage to drink tea and introduce Ainee to videos of the first moon-landing and 'Star Trek.'

*   *   *

Back in the pub, Keynes eventually asked 'What I don't understand, though, is why a schoolful of little children in rural Wales is so concerned about a tropical rainforest?'

'Ah,' replied Lucy, 'that's because of Sue Hopkins-Jones, old Bryn Jones's daughter. She's the teacher there, along with Miss Cobb, the headmistress. It's all down to those two at the school, really. They're the conscience of this village. They really get us all to care about green issues. It's the children who inherit all the problems which we're creating in the world, so they get us all fighting on their behalf.'

'That's right, love,' added Vin Goldhanger, Lucy's father, as he struggled behind the bar with a full keg of Owd Roger. Graham Ferris put down his drink and shot behind the counter to help him. Vin was thickset and very strong, but not beyond accepting help from an energetic younger man. 'She's a real green warrior is Sue, and good for her. Remember the time she led the campaign to stop the Sutherlands closing off the footpath by the Old Mill? She had us all out waving placards and cutting down new fences. She certainly knows how to organise a protest!'

'Oh, yes,' Lucy agreed, 'and Gareth, her husband, the drummer in the band, is such a nice friendly bloke that he even got the Sutherlands to forgive her and support her cause! That reminds me, Dad, do put plenty of that fancy white wine on to chill for when the Sutherlands come to the Festival. They usually bring quite a few of their posh London friends down.'

'So this Sue Hopkins-Jones is Bryn Jones's daughter?' mused Keynes.

Richard Beavis snorted into his Happy Hour half of bitter. 'So what do you think she'll get the village to do once she finds out what we're here for, eh?'

Keynes glowered at him, whilst Graham dropped his end of the barrel. Vin and Lucy both looked at Keynes.

'So what are you here for, then?' asked Lucy.

'Hang on, love,' broke in Vin. 'It might be none of our business.'

'Oh, I wasn't being rude, Dad. Just interested.'

Keynes swallowed another mouthful of Owd Roger. It might be a good idea to follow it with a mineral water, he thought. But he had to provide an answer of some sort. He looked at Lucy's smiling face, her eyes bright with enquiry. 'We're just here to survey some of Bryn Jones's land for him,' he explained. 'The valley they call the Glyn.'

Now Vin and Lucy looked at each other. Vin wiped his large red hands on his round belly, and stroked his greying beard. 'But I thought that Bryn sold the Glyn to Isaac Talboys, about – what – five or so years ago?'

'Yes,' replied Lucy, 'when Isaac first arrived, and started to do up his cottage.' She looked at the blank faces of Keynes and the survey team. 'Isaac is the fiddler in the band, absolutely brilliant. He's an artist as well, so he's a bit weird. He's the tall dark one who came to the concert with that strange blonde girl, you saw him! She smiled at you.'

Keynes turned pale again.

'So who is she, then?' asked Richard Beavis. 'She was an absolute stunner.'

'She was nothing compared to you,' murmured Graham gallantly to Lucy, who smiled and blushed.

'You know her then, Edward? Tell us who she is.' Richard looked expectantly at Keynes.

Keynes now regretted several things, not least that he had told these people to use his Christian name. He took another mouthful of the thick smooth beer. 'I don't know her, no. I just – er – saw her when I was out for a walk in the Glyn. I don't know anything about her.'

'So is she staying with Isaac in his cottage then?' asked Lucy.

'I didn't know there was a cottage, or that there was an Isaac, or that Bryn Jones had sold any land to him,' Keynes announced, bravely.

'So you can't have walked far into the Glyn then,' observed Vin Goldhanger, starting on another barrel.

'No, he might have missed the cottage, Dad, because it's well hidden by the trees. Even the gate is hard to find, unless you know it really well.'

Vin straightened up. 'How come you know the way to Isaac's cottage so well then, girl? I seem to remember telling you some time ago that I thought he wasn't suitable company for someone like you.'

Lucy flared up. 'I'm twenty-six now, father, and it's absolutely nothing to do with you who I visit or don't visit. How dare you say something like that –' she caught Graham's eye and blushed again. 'Anyway,' she continued, rather lamely, 'that was ages ago, and I only went for him to do that portrait of me playing the cello. That was your birthday present, remember. It was hard work lugging the cello down that track, too.' She pointed over to the fireplace across the lounge. The men all put down their glasses and moved over to study the picture.

'But this is an excellent painting,' exclaimed Keynes. 'I had no idea that such talent might be hidden in the countryside!'

'Oh, yes!' cried Graham, 'it looks just like you, Lucy. Can I have a copy?'

'Well, at least she's got her clothes on!' shouted Vin, coarsely.

'You can't make copies of an oil painting,' said Keynes. 'Not just like that.'

Graham returned to the bar. 'I'd rather look at the original,' he whispered to Lucy, who continued to polish glasses, coolly.

'I know he did quite a few sketches,' she remarked, 'so I expect he might sell some to you. That's how he makes his living, after all.'

'How much would he charge?' asked Beavis. 'Are paintings expensive?' They all laughed.

'It depends who did them, and whether the artist is dead or not!' Vin roared. 'How much did he charge you, Lucy?'

'It was a present, remember,' she replied stiffly.

Keynes continued to study the painting, then joined the others. 'I know something about art,' he said. 'I used to be invited to the openings of exhibitions in London and Cambridge. I never liked all that abstract stuff, but that is an excellent piece of work. It ought to be worth hundreds, perhaps even thousands.'

'Oh, never!' cried Vin. 'The bloke who did it hardly has two pennies to rub together. Always drinks halves, unless someone else is buying.'

'Like Bryn Jones,' added Lucy, sharply.

'But Jones owns that enormous mansion.' Keynes was puzzled. 'But then, I suppose that he does live in that squalid ballroom.'

'Ah,' said Vin, 'even so, Jones must be one of the richest people in the village. He sold off most of the land when prices were high, and did up the Knapp wing by wing. Then he sold off each wing, to city folk, mostly; a lot of them only come down for holidays, and the others commute to Birmingham or Cardiff. I did hear that he has a private income, too, from some book or other he wrote, and stocks and shares. He's loaded. No, the reason he never buys a round is because he's a stingy old miser!'

'I hope Sue and Gareth get it all soon,' said Lucy, sourly. 'They'd know what to do with it.'

Vin shook his head. 'Now then, Lucy. Bryn Jones is all right, once you get to know him. He might be tight with beer money, but don't forget that he's the one who organises the Folk Festival, and backs it, too, with his own money. He does a lot of good in this village. He paid for the repairs to the church tower, and for the new school hall, remember. And don't you go wishing bad things on him, neither! He'll be around for a long time yet.'

'But he's so old and smelly! He always tries to squeeze my bum when he's had a few, the dirty old man.'

'Does he?' asked Graham and Richard simultaneously, then glared at each other. 'Just you tell me, and I'll sort him out!' cried Graham.

'I'll do any sorting out that's required in this pub, thank you, young man,' said Vin sternly. 'Anyway, Bryn Jones only pretends to be old. He's really my age, in his mid-fifties.'

Keynes and Lucy both looked surprised.

'Well, fancy that,' said Lucy. 'So the Hopkins-Joneses will just have to wait for ever before they can move out of that tiny cottage. It won't be much fun, having two teenage boys lumping around in there, once the children have grown up a bit. Poor Gareth. He already has to do all his weaving in the shed.'

'Glad to get out of the way, I should imagine,' commented Vin. 'Now then, young lady, isn't it time you got the evening meal on? We've got the busiest weekend of the year ahead, so it's no good starting it off slackly!'

'It's all sorted out, Dad. Fresh Wye salmon and salad, followed by treacle tart. What do you think, boys?'

Keynes finished his last drop of beer, and thought about the snarling salmon in the naked blonde girl's arms. He felt a little bilious, suddenly. 'Not for me. I've got to get back to the hotel for my evening meal.'

'Oh, you poor thing!' Lucy looked sympathetic, but mischievous. 'The food is terrible up at St Briavel's. You ought to check out, and move down here like the boys did.'

'Don't be silly, girl. The pub is completely full up with bookings for the Festival, as you know quite well.' Vin turned to Keynes to explain, as he finished adjusting yet another keg. 'We get all the big stars staying here, you see. The lads were lucky to get a room, and they're sharing. You're much better off at the hotel; at least you get a room of your own. After the Festival, of course, it's a different matter, if you're staying that long.'

Keynes thought he detected sighs of relief from the survey team. 'Thank you, but I'd better be going. It's quite a walk.'

'No,' cried Lucy, 'it's not so far! You're still too citified. Anyway, you're well out of it. I was going to ask the boys if they'll help set up the Festival. We've got the marquees arriving tomorrow, and all the beer, and the Folk Club, and there's hundreds of jobs to be done. We need all the strong young men we can get. Oh, that's if you'll let them off whatever work they're supposed to be doing for you!'

Keynes looked at four faces filled with mute appeal. He sighed deeply and made a decision. 'From what you just told me, it seems that my job is going to be a lot more complicated than was expected. I've already had to spend the last two days going through the County Records in Newport. I daresay I can make it all right with the Department if we all stay here a bit longer.'

He left the pub quickly, but he secretly felt rather pleased with himself. He had just discovered new intricacies to the project, and he was relishing the thought of investigating them.

9

The sun was still fairly high in the sky as Keynes left the pub. He glanced back at the church and the ruined castle walls. The old red sandstone glowed with a golden hue in the early evening sunlight. A tractor rattled over the low bridge across the river. He could just see the bulk of what must be an old watermill downstream. Keynes decided that this must be the home of the 'posh' Sutherlands. An ant-eater hurtled past him, pursued by a battered JCB.

Looking ahead of him, the thatched roofs of many of the cottages gleamed in shades of amber. As he passed the Post Office, Keynes politely greeted the scowling old woman who was watering the geraniums in the window boxes.

Passing the surgery, a small, youngish woman with short dark hair, cut into a crisp bob, caught his eye. She was managing to lock the surgery door whilst removing her loose white coat to reveal sleek tanned arms. He greeted her, too, noting from the plaque beside the door that this must be Dr Celia Llewelyn. He had noticed no wedding ring. As she drove away in her sporty black Volvo he found himself rather hoping that he would make her acquaintance. Perhaps during this mysterious Folk Festival?

As he glanced ahead of him, Keynes stumbled and almost stopped short. The tall dark artist and the beautiful blonde girl were coming out of the driveway of the last cottage and entering the gateway of the thatched cottage immediately next door. They were laden with canvases and sheaves of drawings. Over her shoulder, the lovely pale girl threw him a disconcerting smile.

His eye caught some movement, and he looked up to see a man perched on the roof, waving to the couple. The man on the roof appeared to be adding the finishing touches to a straw cat. Keynes could just hear a shouted conversation between the artist and the thatcher, and walked very slowly indeed. The thatcher scrambled down a ladder with easy grace and shook hands with the girl, who had laid several canvases on the grass.

Then he exclaimed at the number of paintings and gestured the couple indoors.

As Keynes passed the last cottage in the village, a tiny cottage with a neatly-mown lawn but no flowers in the garden, he heard the sound of breaking glass and a woman's voice raised in rage coming through the open window. A small man with a short brown beard ran out through the door with a howling baby in his arms. He saw Keynes, turned sharply right, and ran around to the back of the cottage. Peering around the back, Keynes just glimpsed the man and baby disappear inside a shed. So that must be the Hopkins-Jones household, thought Keynes, proud of his deductions. And that must be – who was it? – Gareth's weaving-shed.

As he continued his stroll, Keynes tried a little faint whistling. He vaguely recollected a jolly little tune from Saturday night in the Golden Oak pub when the band had been playing, and soon found himself walking to the swing of the rhythm.

This pleasant bouncy walk took him along the thick, flower-filled hedgerows lining the dusty road. Keynes removed his jacket and slung it over his shoulder. He put his tie in his jacket pocket and rolled up his sleeves. He picked a small bunch of flowers as he walked, choosing the species which were new to him. He had borrowed a battered old book on wild flower recognition from the hotel lounge.

Keynes passed the turning to The Knapp, and revised his opinion of Bryn Jones again. The man did seem to be a force to be reckoned with, after all. This business about bargaining with land which had already been sold to the artist, officially or not, intrigued Keynes. Jones appeared to be playing a double game. With whom should Keynes discuss the matter next, he wondered, reviewing his acquaintance with the villagers. Perhaps not with Bryn Jones himself. Maybe with the Hopkins-Joneses, who ought to know something about their inheritance? Or with the Sutherlands, who sounded as though they were cultured people? With the attractive lady doctor? He thought again of the naked girl in the wood, and tried to push the thought out of his mind.

Undoubtedly, he should meet with the artist, evidently a man of great talent who was, after all, living in the middle of the supposedly uninhabited valley which he had been sent out here to investigate and purchase. Keynes sighed and picked another flower. He had almost reached the gateway of St Briavel's Hotel. He would have dinner first, and then decide what to do. But he did hope that it would not be salmon.

*   *   *

The interior of Don Craven's cottage was almost as untidy as Isaac's own cottage usually was. The ceiling beams were heavy and low, hung with an array of thatching hooks. Don boiled a kettle on the greasy Calor gas cooker and prepared a teapot, whilst Isaac sorted through his paintings on the stone-flagged floor. Don was as tall as Isaac, and also had long black hair, but his was caught into a pony-tail behind his head, and he was clean-shaven. His jaw and cheek-bones were sharply defined, his eyes almost as dark brown as Ainee's. As he stirred the pot, Don was very aware that Ainee was studying the exposed brown muscles of his arms and the firm lines of his back and thighs.

Isaac, too, was aware of Ainee's gaze, and kept calling her attention back to one or other of the paintings. She had coiled herself up at one end of the rather stained sofa, after brushing a pile of papers to the floor.

'So how do you take your tea, Ainee?' enquired Don. He still spoke with a soft Norfolk burr, from his youth in the reed-beds of the fens.

'You don't need to be so polite,' snapped Isaac. 'You aren't usually. Give her a straight cup of tea, and she can put in her own sugar if she wants it.'

After several unsuccessful experiments Ainee, it transpired, preferred tea weak with no milk or sugar. Don put the unwanted mugs back in the sink. He rolled a cigarette and passed the tin to Isaac, before leaning back against the dining-table and crossing his long legs.

'So is this a social call, Isaac, and if so, why have you covered my floor with your pictures?'

'Because I want you to frame them for the Festival.'

'Oh, come on, man, there's only two days left. Don't be ridiculous.'

Isaac pointed to one wall of the cottage, against which bundles of beading and empty picture frames were piled, five or six deep. 'We can fill that lot tonight.'

'They're commissioned.'

'Then uncommission them. You'll get paid for – what – two dozen completed frames, as soon as I sell one or two. We can choose them now.'

'Oh, yes,' sneered Don, 'so the price of your paintings has gone up, then?'

'It certainly has. Look at them. These new ones of Ainee are the best things I've ever done. Two, perhaps three hundred quid each.'

'At a Folk Festival? Don't be daft, Isaac. You can't charge those sorts of prices; no one who comes can afford that sort of money.'

'Yes they can, this year. I've got a gut feeling about it. I don't mean to sell the lot, just a couple. I've heard that some big London dealers may be down. It's time to break into the big time. These are good.'

'You need the money to buy pretty things for Ainee, eh?'

'What sort of things?' asked Ainee blithely.

Isaac stared at her. He felt a hot surge of desire for her slender cool body. He glanced at Don, who was also watching Ainee. He frowned.

'Wait and see. So you'll do it then, Don? We can start now – there's several we can reduce in size a bit. I can deal with the mounts.'

'And what about my thatching?'

'If you had any thatching jobs on, you'd not be putting new straw tomcats on your own roof. You'll get paid, don't worry. You've always been paid in the past.'

'Won't all this be rather boring for Ainee?'

'Not if you put the stereo on. Rock and new age music, Ainee, with a better sound quality than my old cassette machine? And perhaps Don will play his guitar for you later, if we get this lot finished quickly.'

Don grinned, and continued to gaze at Ainee.

Ainee yawned and stretched. A pile of glossy magazines slid to the floor, and she caught one between her feet. 'I can also look at these … photographs,' she purred. 'But I'm sure I'd like the music. Put it on.' She flipped through a few pages of the magazine. 'You've got some of these thin books too, Isaac, under your bed. You seem to like women wearing tiny frilly things. What's wrong with naked skin?'

Don and Isaac looked at one another. Both sighed deeply, and set to work on the picture frames.

*   *   *

The hotel seemed unusually clean when Keynes arrived. The windows had all been washed, and the brass doorknobs polished. The tiled floor in the entrance hall shone with a rainbow of bright colours, and the mahogany of the reception desk gleamed. The carpets had all been hoovered, and in Keynes's bedroom the bathroom was sparkling. Fresh towels hung on the rail, and there were new bars of soap. The bed which he used was freshly made. There was even a small vase of carnations on the dressing table. Keynes boldly put one in his buttonhole.

Before dinner Keynes bought the barmaid a sherry, after persuading her to join him for a drink and a chat. She enjoyed his courtesy, and giggled. He noted her wedding ring and asked her name.

'Oh, I'm Grace Mortimer. My husband Peter – well, we call him Morty – has Bryngar Farm, the organic orchards up on the hill, next to the Knapp. You're a doctor, aren't you? Dr Keynes. You married?'

Keynes shook his head graciously. He found the barmaid's faintly purring accent charming. 'I have not yet had the pleasure of meeting the right woman. So you know Bryn Jones, then?'

'Old Bryn? 'Course we do, the miserable old so-and-so. He's been there as long as Morty can remember.' She threw back her cloud of black curls. 'We heard you was up there the other day. Did you see that ballroom? A disgrace, isn't it? I don't know what Sue's thinking of, letting her old father live like that. She's a caution, and no mistake. Fancy calling herself by a double-barrelled name; it's something that she actually married poor Gareth. She goes off teaching and leaves him alone to look after the kids, you know. I bet he's glad it's the school holidays and he can put his feet up for a change. Don't you agree, Gwen?'

Gwen turned out to be the untidy, overweight maid who had been the first to greet Keynes at the hotel. Today her short brown curls seemed to be set hard with hair-lacquer, but her cheeks still flamed red. After unwrapping herself from a large flowered pinafore, which she thrust into a carrier bag, she heaved herself up onto the bar stool beside Keynes, and turned to look at him with her heavy grey eyes.

'Oh, it's my old mate Totterikins again!' she sniggered. 'What are you pestering him with now, Grace?'

'Oh, no, he bought me a sherry; here, you have one! This is Gwen Orgee, that cleans here on Wednesdays, and does the kitchen Saturdays. All done, then, Gwen?'

Keynes politely paid for another round of sherries, and complimented Gwen on the improvements which she had wrought.

'Well, it's a disgrace these days, is this 'otel. We remember when it was always spotless, doesn't we, Grace? Fresh flowers in every room, silver on the tables. But that there Manager, he don't care nothing about the place so long as the bar's well stocked for the lads.'

'I have not yet been introduced to the Manager,' pointed out Keynes.

'Nor you will, Doctor. He's gen'rally …'

'… resting,' added Grace.

'Dead dronk,' finished Gwen. 'He cut my cleaning hours down to next to nothing, and you can see the state of the place for yourself. We does our best, doesn't we, Grace, but I aren't had enough time to get things together proper-like for months now. It's like shovelling manure downhill.'

'At least us two have kept our jobs, Gwen, you mustn't grumble. The last chef, he got sacked, after a big row. He was good an' all. Not like this one now. Just a boozing pal for that Manager, this one, if you ask me. You ought to have your dinners down at the Golden Oak, Doctor, like those nice lads you arrived with do now. That Lucy, she knows how to run a kitchen.'

'That's right. I'm helping her out for the Festival, and I cleans there every morning, and you niver saw a spot of dust down there, I'll bet you, not in all your visits there.'

Keynes agreed, and asked about the Festival. Both women shrieked with laughter and drained their sherry glasses. He paid for another round.

'That Folk Festival! What a do that is! Best part of the year,' exclaimed Grace.

'Especially for the pubs. The Golden Oak gets a new carpet a year out o' the Festival, and holidays in foreign parts for Vin and Lucy. So much beer! So much drinking! But not like those discos or the Football Club, no fighting or glasses broken or anything. Well, except up here, p'raps, 'cos the village lads tends to come up here to hide out from all that lovely music. They're all right once you knows 'em, like my old man Davy Orgee, but some on 'em don't take to strangers, like that Spike Price.'

'Oh, no, you wants to stay away from here, Doctor Keynes. Stay down in the village. Morty and I help do the bar in the Oak. Though mind you, I daresay that the Oak'll be fully booked, isn't it?'

Keynes nodded.

'Never you mind. We'll keep an eye on you, won't we, Gwen?'

'Sure to. Hey, Grace, I don't s'pose that Manager has been on about shifting the Doctor here out into a smaller room, has he? I'll have something to say about it if he does, for sure.'

'He had a go, but I said no. There's some of the old folk booked in here, the ones that do that fancy dancing, but they all has early nights. The Doctor's young enough to be out late every night gallivanting, aren't you?'

'Like you did last Saturday, eh? You met Owd Roger, I heard from Davy. He said you was trying to dance with Lucy Gold-hanger!'

'Oh, whatever'd Vin say! She's been saving herself for the right man, you know. Well, except for that fling with the artist, I heard.'

'And that time with that thatcher. Scruffy-looking pair, both on 'em. Could do with a good bath apiece. Not good enough for Lucy, either on 'em, and Vin Goldhanger knows it. A proper Doctor might be different, though, eh?'

Keynes felt very awkward. 'I am a Doctor, but it's – well, just a title. I'm not a medical doctor, you see. Not like Doctor Celia Llewelyn,' he added slyly.

'Oh, she's such a love,' declared Grace. 'She's done wonders for Morty with his back, and for both my daughters.'

'And for my three little pests, when they was bad with shingles. Did you see my middle one, Darren, was an ant-eater in the concert? Lovely! 'Cept that Billy Banford was a JCB and pushed my Darren right off the stage. No, that nice Doctor Llewelyn, she deserves a good bloke. She works too hard, I reckon. I expect she doesn't eat properly.'

'Talking of which, Gwen, did you see that skinny blonde piece came in with that artist to the concert? Who's she, then?'

'I dunno. She's new. Barefoot, an' all. Though I don't s'pose that all the men was looking at her feet. Was you, Doctor?'

Keynes went pale, and shook his head.

'Oh, look, he's hungry, poor pet. Tell you what, I'll go and fix you a nice salad in the kitchen, better'n what that chef could do. You stay here and lay the table for him, Grace. Shan't be long.' Gwen Orgee slid off the barstool, and bustled off towards the kitchen.

'No salmon!' called Keynes, inspired by sherry. Grace grinned, and went to set the table for him.

'You have a nice quiet early night, Doctor,' she said. 'There's a lot of fun ahead for you in the next few days.'

10

As Don Craven drove back home, having dropped off Isaac and Ainee at the top of the lane to the Glyn, his thoughts were not on the road. Ainee had sat in the back of his old green van, curled up on the bundles of straw and reed. As Don made polite conversation with Isaac, she had tugged very gently at his pony-tail. She had even run her fingers along the rim of his earlobe several times. He shuddered involuntarily, and shifted in the driving seat. She was delicious, and he wanted her.

Don had no idea where she came from, except that she seemed startlingly naïve as well as very sexy. He decided that he didn't particularly care about her past, even if she had escaped from a mental asylum. But she should not be with that boor Isaac Talboys.

Isaac and Don had always got along well together until that business with Lucy Goldhanger, some years ago now. Don would have married Lucy, despite some resistance from her Dad. Lucy was a lovely girl, pretty and gentle and charming. She would have made a good mother for Don's children. She could have made Don's cottage very comfortable. She ran an excellent pub. He had written some of his best love songs for her. But she had only been – what? – twenty-one or so, and Don had been prepared to wait for her.

Until Isaac came along, and swept her off with all his arty ways, painting her and sneaking her off to the Glyn. And then dumping her after a few months. Don swerved sharply to avoid what looked oddly like an ant-eater, but must have been a large badger, and almost ended up in the hedge. He tried to concentrate on the road ahead.

Slowing as he passed the Hopkins-Jones's cottage, Don noted that the light in Sue and Gareth's bedroom was on, and there was another light on in the weaving shed. Poor old Gareth, he thought, as he pulled into his own drive. Still, it was the last day of term, he remembered. Isaac had praised the school concert, most of which must have been Sue's work. Sue would be absolutely shattered, and probably in a filthy mood. She usually drank an entire bottle of wine on the last day and then slept for eighteen hours. And this time she had the Festival to organise, as well. Don wasn't particularly worried about them. Gareth could cope. They seemed to have a pretty sound relationship, despite the rows.

His own cottage was in darkness. He sighed deeply. How lovely it must be to come home to a welcoming woman, someone like Lucy, or perhaps Ainee ...

He sat in front of the first framed drawings and studied Ainee. Grudgingly, he had to admit that Isaac's new pictures were superb. His drawing skills had always been excellent, but Ainee seemed to have inspired him with real genius. Don had to agree with Isaac that these pictures should sell for very large sums of money indeed. It might seem almost a shame to take Ainee away from him. Don grinned, his eyes and teeth sparkling in the light reflected from the spotlamp which he had trained on the pictures. He made a decision.

Ainee was worth trying for.

*   *   *

Gareth crept into the kitchen and shut the door as gently as he could, his arms burdened with sleeping baby. Skip the dog raised a lazy head from his basket, and wagged his tail cautiously. Sue had swept up the broken jug, Gareth was pleased to see. He tiptoed upstairs and laid Berian in his cot on the landing. Emrys was fast asleep and Gareth adjusted the covers over his small body, then undressed silently. He pushed the bedroom door open very carefully, and slid across into bed. There was no movement from Sue, and Gareth gratefully relaxed and closed his eyes.

Then Sue stirred. She rolled over towards Gareth. He turned his head and opened his eyes. Sue was staring at him, her face pale and her eyes bright in the moonlight. Gareth grinned weakly.

'I'm sorry about the jug,' whispered Sue. 'Did it hurt you?'

'I'll have a bit of a bruise on my shoulder, but the jug's gone

68

for ever. Still, I never liked it much. At least you chose the cracked one.'

'I might have hit Berian.' Sue brushed away what might have been a tear. 'Thank the lucky stars that I didn't.'

'You did hit me,' Gareth reminded her, hoping for sympathy. He pulled the duvet back slightly. 'Shall I show you my bruise?'

Sue peered at his chest in the dimness. She prodded the bruise. Gareth winced dramatically. 'Sadist!' he whispered cheerfully, and reached out for Sue's warm body. Sue pushed his arm aside, and sat upright.

'First tell me how that dumb blonde girl came to be wearing my old black dress.'

Gareth groaned. 'Because it was old, Sue. It was in the jumble sale box. Isaac asked if we had any old clothes for her …'

'So you gave him my black dress! Gareth, that wasn't ever jumble sale material! Just because I can't fit into it since I had the boys!' She glared. 'Gareth, I was wearing that dress the night I met you, and you gave it away to some … some … some floosie!'

Now Gareth really groaned. He thought hard. He remembered Sue smiling and laughing at his jokes at the student party all those years ago, but he couldn't remember anything about what she was wearing. Had it been that dress? Certainly it had looked stunning on Ainee this afternoon.

'She's not a floosie, Sue, you're not being fair. She's really interesting. She doesn't say much because she's trying to find out all about how we live. You won't believe this, but Isaac says that she's …'

Sue gave one push with both feet and both hands. Gareth yelled as he tumbled onto the floor with a crash.

'Isaac says! Isaac says! Anything that filthy drunken old goat says, you think it's a bloody oracle speaking! Now it's his girlfriend prancing about, flashing her skinny legs, great big googly eyes, that's what's so bloody interesting! No thought for me, working my guts out, mother of your children, oh no. Just have a party any time I'm out, let complete strangers play with my children, invite in any weird wild men and half-naked women you can find! The last day of term, and you just don't care! You don't even say anything about all the hard work I put into the concert, and the bloody Folk Festival, and earning the money around here, it's just all Isaac this, and now it's Any Fishfingers that! Piss off! Go and sleep on the sofa or in your precious weaving-shed, or up a pole as far as I care. Out!'

The pillow thudded against the door as Gareth closed it behind him. Perhaps Sue would feel better after a good night's sleep, he thought. Perhaps she wouldn't. Perhaps the entire Festival would be like this. Perhaps the entire summer holidays would. Perhaps the rest of his life would be like this.

He descended the stairs slowly. At least the boys hadn't woken up. He would sleep on the sofa, and tend to them all in the morning, as he always did, with no thanks from anyone. Especially Sue. Gareth cried himself silently to sleep.

*   *   *

THURSDAY 25 JUNE

Keynes woke early, brilliant sunshine filtering through the thin grey curtains into his bedroom. He felt rested and energetic. As he dressed, he browsed through the colourful modern books on wild flowers and healing herbs which Grace Mortimer had produced for him when she had discovered him reading the limited supply of dog-eared books which the hotel possessed. He compared his wilted specimens from yesterday with the illustrations in her books. He found the processes of identification fascinating. For once, his schoolboy Latin was useful, and his brain stretched and creaked under such novel exercise.

He had intended to visit the Glyn again today anyway, seeking this mysterious cottage. He leaned out of the open window and decided that it was going to be too hot to wear a jacket. He packed a selection of nature books into a small knapsack which he had bought in Abergavenny. Then he went downstairs and ate a heavy breakfast under Grace's smiling eye. The heat of the day was already oppressive, and he felt that perhaps chilled fruit juice and a slice of toast would have been more suitable.

Once out in the meadow leading to the Glyn he heaved a sigh of relief as he passed Glyn Tump and entered the cool shade of the woodland. He had been sweating all through breakfast.

Keynes dipped his hands in the clear stream and wiped the cold water over his face and arms. Refreshed, he followed the path of the stream into the wood. He was startled to come across an enormous white-and-brown striped bird wading in the stream and dabbling in the mud with its long, pointed beak. The bird turned and regarded him coolly when it heard his approach. Its eyes glittered with a malevolent intelligence. Keynes and the bird stared at each other for several minutes before the bird spread vast rattling wings and launched itself into the air, flying through the trees like a dart.

Pulling open his knapsack, Keynes ruffled through the bird book which he had borrowed from the hotel and eventually identified the bird as a grey heron. But it was so big! He was amazed that birds as large as this heron populated the Welsh countryside. And seemed so – well, wild. That heron could have easily pecked out his eyes if he had alarmed it.

A flicker of movement made him jump. A large brown blackbird-looking bird with a flash of brilliant blue on its wings flew past his head. The book eventually revealed it as a jay. Keynes had never heard of jays before. How did people learn about these things? The schoolchildren in yesterday's concert obviously knew all there was to know about tropical rainforests, and they had only been eight or nine. Did children learn about the flora and fauna of Britain even earlier? Certainly school today must be a lot more interesting than even the Latin and algebra lessons of his youth. More relevant to the environment in which the children would grow up, certainly.

Keynes felt a sudden dizzying pang of inadequacy. He was in a place where things that he had never imagined before existed. He felt lost, alienated. Peculiar creatures like herons and jays, flowers which he did not recognise. Secret cottages. Schools which taught exciting subjects. Dangerous beer. Witches whom no one would admit to knowing about. Naked girls with salmon. And gossip! Everyone knowing intimate details about everyone else.

He rolled his eyes, looking all around him. The trees rustled and waved. Their leaves glowed with many tones of green. The brook chattered. Hidden birds sang soft and liquid songs. The air was hot and damp with woodland scents. Keynes inhaled.

He seemed to smell the very greenness of the wood, the smell of growing. He grinned. It was as though he had been transported to another planet. He realised that he had not missed his dark, tidy office, or his sterile and gloomy flat once. He had never before realised that life could be so interesting. He felt alive, perhaps for the first time ever.

About to burst out whistling, Keynes stopped himself. He would listen to the bird-song instead. He continued into the wood.

When he reached the emerald-green lawn in the loop of the stream, Keynes glanced about cautiously, half hoping to see the girl again. Startled, two brown rabbits with bright white tails ran across the oval lawn, disappearing into the cascade of brambles and dogrose covering the valley side.

Keynes wandered amongst the tall green grasses and looked at flowers. He carefully picked a small bunch and compared them with his books. The common names enchanted him just as much as the colours; delicate white meadow saxifrage and pignut, oxeye daisies and the glittering yellows of cowslip, balsam, buttercup and dyer's greenweed; bright blues of devil's-bit scabious and meadow cranesbill; the reds and crimsons of saw-wort, knapweed, campion, and great burnet; pale purples of violets, forget-me-nots, wood bitter-vetch, milkwort and milkmaid.

He was delighted by the discovery of the greater butterfly orchid and the green-winged orchid, as he had always thought that orchids were rare. He could not identify one colourless and particularly fragile orchid. He sniffed at the bunch and enjoyed the elusive perfumes. He felt a sudden comforting kinship with the generations of country folk who had picked these flowers for their lovers, tasted them in times of hunger, dyed their clothes with them, and passed on the pretty names to their children.

Keynes dipped his clean handkerchief into the cool water of the stream, and wrapped it around the stems to preserve them. He slotted the bunch through the straps of his knapsack and set off upstream amongst the ancient dark trees. He identified the heavy joists of oak from which great tufts of berryless mistletoe sprouted, the smooth silver trunks of beech, brightly-leaved hazels and the shivering leaves of ash. Morning-glory and wild hops wound around stems and branches. Dog-mercury, docks, comfrey, and dramatic lords-and-ladies sprang up from the leaf mould underfoot. The shining star-like flowers of brambles and guelder-rose promised an Autumn laden with fruit.

Keynes continued deeper amongst the trees, carefully jumping the stream several times. Once he got his feet wet, but only smiled, actually taking pleasure in the cool dampness. Then he pulled up short. In front of him was a gate.

The small gate spanned the narrow gap between two trees, under an arch laden with wild – Keynes checked his book – honeysuckle. There didn't seem to be a fence or hedge; the gate seemed more symbolic than practical. Nevertheless, Keynes walked up and peered over it.

Between the bushes and trees, a path wound into the distance, the first path which Keynes had seen in this wood. He bravely unlatched the gate, and pushed it open.

The path was faint and rather overgrown in places, perhaps more of a track than a path. Keynes had to push aside several brambles and fern fronds to follow its route. Eventually he looked up, and stopped dead in surprise.

In front of him was the prettiest cottage he had ever seen in his life.

The long low slate roof gleamed in the dappled sunlight like tarnished silver. A pair of jolly red gables lifted above small dark windows, like amused eyebrows. The door was striped red and blue, like a clown's trousers. A wisp of smoke from one of the stubby stone chimneys hinted at kettles boiling and toast browning. The sunlit terrace was decorated with curious objects which Keynes peered to identify. A slab of stone formed a bridge across the stream, which bordered the terrace and shone as it gurgled by. The upper and rear windows must open straight out into the trees, thought Keynes. He stared at the cottage, entranced.

Then the front door jerked open and a procession of people emerged. Keynes dodged behind a tree, and identified each one; Gareth Hopkins-Jones with his baby in his arms, and a toddler trailing behind; Isaac Talboys, the artist, carrying several large objects wrapped in a blanket, probably framed pictures; and then the blonde girl. She was thankfully not naked now, but wore a floating dress of pinks and greens. Her long hair was bound up with a matching scarf, into a pony-tail which waved and swayed as she walked. Her feet were bare, but she walked with a light, almost dancing step. Keynes found himself licking his lips as he studied her.

For a moment, Keynes panicked as he thought that the group was going to walk towards him, but they turned and climbed a winding path up the side of the valley, disappearing into the thicker woodland beyond the cottage. The small child had seized the hand of the blonde girl and was gazing up at her in adoration as they walked. The child stumbled over roots or rocks several times, and the girl pointed to the track, laughing. Suddenly Keynes envied the child. As they vanished into the distance, Keynes' gaze returned to the cottage. Perhaps his admiration of the charming house had been sharpened by his desire for the blonde girl, but his stomach convulsed with a twinge which made his eyes water. As his vision cleared, and with growing horror, Keynes identified the sensation as lust. Was he going mad?

Keynes realised that, even more than he wanted to possess the beautiful blonde girl, he wanted to possess this beautiful house.

* * *

11

Once the framed pictures had been loaded into the van outside Don Craven's cottage, there was some trouble about which vehicle Ainee should travel in.

'Come in with me, Ainee,' grinned Don. 'Isaac'll only make you walk otherwise, and you'll hurt your pretty feet.'

'Certainly not,' announced Isaac firmly. 'I want to keep an eye on the paintings. These pictures are our investment in the future. The way Don drives, he might smash them up between here and the pub.'

Gareth prevented Berian from tugging his short beard with his free hand. He frowned as he remembered the bitter jealousy between Don and Isaac over Lucy Goldhanger, when Isaac had first moved into Glasmaen. It looked as though it was about to start again with the lovely Ainee as the cause. He wondered whether to invite Ainee to travel with him and the children, and whether this might make both the other men suspicious. Fortunately, little Emrys came to the rescue.

'Come with me, pretty Ainee!' commanded Emrys, pulling at her hand. Ainee smiled, and helped strap the boys into their car-seats before climbing into the front seat of the 2CV. Gareth shrugged his shoulders helplessly and leapt into the car, reversing out of the gate before there was any more argument. He just missed hitting a dark green Range Rover which was driving slowly down the lane. The Range Rover honked loudly but Gareth tried to ignore it as it accelerated towards the village. Gareth followed it in the 2CV at a more sedate pace.

Outside the Golden Oak, Vin Goldhanger was watering the tubs of geraniums. He called out a friendly greeting to Gareth as he settled Ainee and the boys at one of the picnic tables in the sun. Gareth followed Vin into the empty bar and ordered beers and fruit juices all round.

'Nice-looking babysitter you've got there,' Vin remarked as he gave Gareth his change.

'Yes, isn't she?' Gareth grinned. 'Isaac Talboys's new lady friend. She's very good with the children.'

'I thought she was new around here. Is she over for the Folk Festival?'

Gareth picked up the tray of glasses. 'Yes, I suppose she is. Her name is Ainee Sealfin.'

Vin raised his bushy eyebrows. 'Unusual,' he remarked.

'She certainly is!' Gareth carried the tray out into the garden, nodding at Isaac and Don as they passed him. 'Yours are on the counter.'

Isaac scowled, but Don was still grinning at Ainee. He thanked Gareth absently, and walked hard into the doorframe. Isaac gave a scornful laugh as Don rubbed his bruised arm, then crossed over to the bar. He took a deep drink of beer before turning to Vin.

Vin nodded briskly at Don. 'Nice to see you, Isaac. The band missed you on Saturday, I hear; busy with your charming new girlfriend, were you?'

Isaac glanced at Don, who was studying his beer. 'I've come to claim a favour, Vin. Remember you said I could exhibit some of my paintings in your pub?'

Vin scratched his balding head. 'I do. But that was months ago!'

Isaac shrugged. 'Well, I've brought them over.'

Vin looked around the lounge and the bar. 'Well, there's space enough. But it's the Folk Festival; the place will be packed. Mightn't they get damaged?'

'Nah. It's the best time to show them; plenty of customers about. They'll be all right.'

'Well, I hope you brought a hammer and picture hooks with you. I'm much too busy to do it.'

'Don has. We'll bring the pictures in, then.'

They both put down their drinks and went outside. Ainee was singing softly to the boys as she bounced Berian on her knee. Don and Gareth wanted to stay and listen to the song, but Isaac pushed them away, in the direction of the car park and the loaded van. Before long the lounge looked like an art gallery.

Vin was impressed. 'I like it. They're good pictures, Isaac, the best I've ever seen, especially these ones of Ainee. I might buy one myself. How much?'

When Isaac told him, Vin gasped. 'I can't afford that kind of money – well, not before the Festival anyway. Perhaps afterwards, at a special rate for letting you hang them …?'

Isaac shrugged. 'We'll see. They're worth the money, I reckon. I'll bring in a couple more tomorrow for the bar.'

Vin pointed at the painting of Lucy over the fireplace. 'There was a bloke in just yesterday was interested in that one. Quiet bloke, a stranger, Dr Edward Keynes. Seemed to have plenty of money. Arrived in a new BMW. Got ratted here on Saturday – you saw him, Don.'

Don broke off studying one of the pictures of Ainee, and adjusted its hang on the wall. 'I did. But I thought this one wasn't for sale.'

'Certainly not! That's my present from my little girl.' Don did not miss the protective note in Vin's voice, and grinned pleasantly before sauntering outside to chat to Ainee. Isaac paid for another round, thanked Vin gruffly, and followed Don outside, balancing the heavy tray of drinks as he crossed the flagstones.

Isaac sat down on the bench next to Ainee and put his arm heavily around her shoulders. Gareth reclaimed the sleepy Berian from her lap, and Don sat next to him, gazing into Ainee's deep brown eyes. Little Emrys fidgeted.

'Sing another song for us, Ainee, now that we can sit here and listen to you,' said Don, passing his tobacco tin around the men.

Ainee smiled, and raised up her head. Her voice was cool and clear, and the ancient language lilted and rippled in her song like the music of a flowing stream. Even the birds in the trees on the castle mound fell silent as she sang.

'Hey, I recognised some of the words there!' cried Gareth when she finished. 'It was something like Welsh. Was it some sort of Celtic language?'

Ainee shrugged. She turned and watched Lucy Goldhanger cross the terrace from the back of the pub. Lucy wore tight white jodphurs, a small sun top, and her hair tucked under a riding hat. Two large black labradors ran at her heels.

'Hi there!' cried Lucy. 'Isn't it a perfect day? I hope the whole Folk Festival will be as sunny as this!'

Gareth and Don called out a greeting to Lucy. Isaac continued to study Ainee, gently twisting and tugging at her pony-tail.

Lucy smiled sweetly at Ainee, and removed her riding hat. Her own long blonde hair tumbled over her shoulders, gleaming golden in the bright sunlight. Gareth hurriedly introduced the girls to each other.

'Was that you I heard singing as I was stabling Merlin?' asked Lucy. 'You've a lovely voice. Are you performing at the Festival?'

Isaac shook his head, but Ainee smiled and laughed. 'On a stage, like the school concert? Yes, I'd love to!' Then she glanced down at the dogs. Both stood silently, staring at her, the hair along their backs slowly rising. One growled faintly, and the other whimpered softly. Both dogs backed away from Ainee. Suddenly, they turned and bounded away around the corner of the pub.

Lucy stared in amazement. 'Demon! Dil!' she called, but neither dog reappeared.

'You did the same thing to Skip, yesterday. I've never seen him react to anyone like that before,' observed Gareth.

Ainee shrugged again. 'I don't like dogs,' she stated calmly.

'Well, that's quite some trick you have with them,' said Lucy. 'I've seen customers back off from them like that, but never the other way around. They're supposed to be guard dogs; we usually keep them upstairs. I hope you're not a burglar!'

Ainee frowned in puzzlement, and was about to ask for an explanation when little Emrys spoke up. 'Can I see your horse please, Lucy?' Lucy grinned, and held out her hand for him. Emrys struggled across the bench, and ran over to her. He turned back to Ainee. 'Ainee come too, and see the pretty horse!'

'Only if your new friend doesn't frighten my Merlin!' added Lucy, half-joking.

Ainee smiled at the pair. 'No, only dogs,' she promised. Then she swung herself over Isaac's lap and followed them to the stable, which lay amongst the outbuildings at the back of the Golden Oak. A few moments later came the sound of faint yelping. Demon and Dil hurtled around the opposite corner of the pub, and raced inside through the open door.

'She scares me, too,' observed Isaac, 'but she can't half sing!'

'I could get up some duets with her over the Festival,' offered Don, slyly.

Isaac glared. They were interrupted by the arrival of a noisy group walking up from the village. The woman who led the

78

way shrieked and waved when she saw the three men sitting on the terrace. She was a tall, angular woman in early middle age, with striking silver-grey hair, cut short. She was dressed in an exotically embroidered sun-dress and high-heeled sandals.

'Oh, look! It's our friends from the village.' She turned to her companions. 'Oh, you must meet these people! Such talented craftsmen, all of them.'

'Artist,' growled Isaac, but he stood up to shake hands with the woman nonetheless.

'Darlings, it's so nice to be back in this wonderful village again! How I've missed it in grimy old London! Look, this is Isaac Talboys, that marvellous artist I told you all about. And Don the thatcher, very clever guitar player too. And dear Gareth, who wove all those superb fabrics I showed you at the Old Mill. And his baby. Emrys, isn't it, sweetie-pie? Such a New Man! Do meet my friends from London!'

'Textiles,' corrected Gareth, smiling, as he adjusted the baby to shake the woman's hand. 'And this is Berian – Emrys is his big brother. Lucy's showing him her horse.'

'Oh, my, how time flies! We really don't get down here often enough! But wait – we must order some drinks, and come and join you. This is such a perfect place to sit, out in the sun with all these flowers and the castle ramparts looming through the trees! Isn't it just unreal! Pull over a table, darlings. Can we get you some drinks?'

Three empty pint mugs were instantly placed before her, and three fruit juice glasses were identified. The woman swept her party before her into the pub, shrieking for Vin. Lucy peeped around the pub corner before coming over to the table, followed by Ainee and Emrys.

'Was that the Sutherlands I heard arriving?' asked Lucy. The men at the table all nodded. 'Just Ellen, with four strangers down from London,' explained Gareth. 'She didn't say where Jeremy was.'

Lucy nodded. 'I thought so. I expect they'll want lunch, even though it's – heck, nearly two o'clock.' She disappeared into the pub. Whoops of rapture from Ellen filtered out through the open windows.

'She's spotted your paintings,' noted Don.

'Let's hope she'll buy some,' Isaac said drily. 'They all look as though they've plenty of money.'

'Mmm,' agreed Don. 'Perhaps some of them have thatches that need redoing on their holiday cottages.'

'I've got a lot of new textiles to show her,' Gareth added. 'Come on, Don, let's be polite and pull another table over for them.'

Emrys tried to help, but got in the way. 'Did Ainee like the horse?' Gareth asked him.

Emrys nodded fervently. 'And the horse liked her. I like her too, Dad. She sings such pretty songs, and she showed me wonderful things in the woods.'

'What kind of things?' asked Don.

'Oh, tiny little fairies and elves dancing about inside rings of mushrooms.'

'Toadstools?' suggested Gareth, glancing at Ainee.

'Them as well, and green men and ladies inside trees.'

Ellen Sutherland led her group back onto the terrace, laden with drinks. 'Isaac!' she shrieked, 'Your paintings! They're just marvellous! Dominic just adores them! Oh!' She stared at Ainee. 'And this must be your new model. She's even lovelier in the flesh.'

Everyone looked at Ainee, who smiled and tossed her pony-tail. Emrys stared at Ellen's sunglasses, which were magically turning black in the bright sunlight.

'Wait till you hear her sing,' said Don.

'Oh, such talented people!' cried Ellen. She handed out the drinks. 'But meet my clever friends from London – and Lyndon Cotton from Hollywood!' She lowered her voice. 'He's a film director!' she whispered. Lyndon bowed, and took Ainee's hand. He kissed it, not releasing her from his gaze. He was tall, balding, muscular and bronzed, wearing a crumpled beige linen suit and a short sun-bleached blond pony-tail. 'Lovely!' he murmured, in a faintly transatlantic accent.

'And this is Dominic Batista, Isaac, you must meet him,' added Ellen quickly, pushing forward a small thin man with dyed black hair curling over the collar of his elegant plum silk cossack shirt. He wore a small goatee beard, which he kept tugging, and ridiculous moustachios, which he twirled every five minutes.

'Dominic has a wonderful art gallery in Kensington, often puts on entire exhibitions in the Serpentine!'

Dominic, too, kissed Ainee's hand with a flourish. 'Charming!' He turned to Isaac and shook his hand. 'Fascinating pictures. Such brio! We must talk.' Gareth winked at Isaac.

Ellen pulled her other two guests forward. 'This is Ambrose Fisher and Sonja Barnaby. They're into anthropology, would you believe. Quite fascinating!'

Ambrose took his cue from the others, and kissed Ainee's hand. Sonja shook hands all round, and tried to ignore Ainee. Both were slim to the point of emaciation, with haloes of curling blond hair, and identically dressed in black jeans and t-shirts, with lots of chunky silver jewellery. They smoked thin black cigars. Ainee and Emrys stared at Sonja's tinkling earrings and pendants in obvious admiration. 'Where can I get a necklace like that?' asked Ainee, pointing across the table.

'Somalia before the war,' replied Sonja crisply, and turned to pick blond hairs off Ambrose's black-clad shoulders.

'Wasn't that you who tried to reverse into Ambrose's Range Rover, Gareth?' declared Ellen when they were all sitting down. Before Gareth could answer, she waved her hand. 'No harm done – it rather got our adrenalin flowing, though!'

'Is Jeremy coming down for the Festival?' asked Gareth.

'Oh, yes, yes, with a few other people, but they can't make it until tomorrow evening. Quite a house party, don't you think!' Ellen sipped her white wine and stretched out in the sun. The others nodded obediently. 'Oh, isn't this heaven!' she trilled.

Lucy made a welcome appearance with several plates covered with salad and miniature cottage loaves. 'Ploughman's for five!' she sang out. 'One Stilton for Ellen, two Brie for the couple in black, two Cheddar to follow!' She handed Emrys a packet of crisps, before briskly clearing away the empty glasses and used ashtray.

The visitors ate solemnly, while Ellen chattered and the villagers drank.

12

Once the inhabitants had vanished up the track and their voices had faded away, Keynes crept along the path. Nearing the cottage, a faint memory twisted in the back of his mind. As he carefully crossed the slab of slate which served as a bridge over the chattering brook he glanced down.

The water sparkled and wriggled across the bed of the stream. This was roughly paved with odd flat rocks gleaming like pewter, and garnished with delicate fronds of jade-green weed. Pebbles glittered underwater with many different shades and textures; rose quartz, agate as iridescent as opal, amethyst, garnet, amber and glowing topaz; there were lumps of emerald green, ruby and lapis-lazuli glass, like the molten residue from church windows. Tiny silver fish flickered amongst the splashes of colour. It was like peering into a casket of jewels.

The soft grey stones of the terrace were patchworked with panels of creamy gold and saffron-yellow cobbles, and set with the upturned bases of old brown, cobalt blue and dark green bottles. Inside many of these tiny carboys miniature mosses and fragile ferns thrived. Keynes marvelled at the collection of pre-war enamelled advertising and street signs which were propped up around the walls of the house. An axe was embedded in a tree trunk, the surface scored with years of wood-chopping. Neatly cut lengths of firewood were stacked in a great pyramid in a corner.

A sudden tinkling noise made Keynes jump. He had accidentally caught the dangling wind-chimes with his shoulder. He tapped the discs of translucent shell again, taking pleasure from the sound.

When he peered into the small windows of the cottage, the interior was too dark to make out any details. Keynes glanced around, then knocked firmly on the striped front door and waited. There was no reply. His stomach churning with excitement, Keynes took a deep breath and lifted the latch. The door swung slowly open, and Keynes, amazed at his own daring, tiptoed inside.

*   *   *

'And this is our room, mine and Jeremy's,' announced Ellen, sweeping her party through double doors into a sunny room which took up half the third floor of the Old Mill. The mellow red brickwork and golden pine floor glowed in the afternoon sun. The bed was one dazzling cloud of pure white cotton. The bedhead was an expanse of gilt-framed mirror, which immed-iately caught Ainee's attention. For several minutes she stretched and turned and studied her reflection, while the others watched her in silence.

Finally Lyndon spoke, almost gruffly. 'You might as well have a bank of cameras watching you, Ainee Sealfin.'

Ainee turned to him, lifting her streaming, sunlit, pale gold hair in both hands, and smiling. Then she cried out in surprise. 'Oh! Dresses! And so many! So many colours!' Everyone turned to look at the confection of Ellen's dresses, spilling out from a pale cream leather suitcase over the ottoman and onto the floor. The doors of the vast pine wardrobe hung open, a treasury of fabrics within. 'And I have only three dresses,' Ainee added, her voice resentful and awestruck all at once.

Ellen glanced at Ainee, clad only in Sue's slightly tattered and faded old cotton dress, and then peered into the cavern of the wardrobe. 'Well, then, we must do something about that, my dear. Someone as pretty and charming as you should have clothes to match. Let's see ... what have I got that will fit you?' She began to select clothes, layering them over her shoulder, and then casting the multicoloured package onto the bed.

Ainee silently held each dress up against her body and studied it in the mirror, swaying out the fullness of the skirt, seeing how it would move in the dance or the wind. Then she turned to the assembled group for approval, her face serene. Dominic squinted at the colours, Gareth made observations on the flow and movement of the fabric, Lyndon commented on the image which each garment portrayed, Ellen described the origins and labels of each dress, and Emrys giggled and clapped his little hands whenever one was unanimously accepted. Ainee smiled and laughed to see the pile of chosen dresses. 'How kind, Ellen,' she curtseyed with grace. 'You are very generous.'

'I just hope that your Isaac won't mind me giving you these,' Ellen observed, glancing anxiously from the window. Isaac and Don had been sent off in the van to collect Don's guitar, Gareth's textiles, and Isaac's sketching equipment. Sonja had tugged Ambrose away for a walk around the village.

'Are you quite sure you should, Ellen?' Gareth enquired quietly, loath to interfere. 'This little lot must have cost you an absolute packet, with designer labels and all.'

Ellen, surprisingly, blushed. 'Oh, it's all just shopping. These are all old things I've worn to every party in London. They ought to be passed on, really. What's the point in being comfortably off if our friends can't share in the benefits? I just want to share my good fortune around a little ... Oh, no, I think not, dear!'

Ainee had been ruffling through her trophies. She had selected one particularly lavishly embroidered blue silk garment, and was about to strip off the dress which she was wearing and try the new one on. None of the men moved, all suddenly rigid. Ellen caught the skirt of the dress just as Ainee slipped it up over her slim pale legs. 'Later, darling, let me just finish showing everyone around the Mill first!'

As they departed the amber-and-pink room in the eaves which had been delegated to Lyndon, the tanned American caught Ainee's hand softly. He leaned down to whisper into her ear. 'Remember the way to my room, Ainee. I want to ... talk ... to you – alone – sometime this weekend, about getting into the movies. You are so special.' He sighed as his grey eyes slid over Ainee's face and body.

Ainee merely gazed up at him for several moments. Her eyes were dark and hollow. She slipped her hand from his grasp. Then she turned and walked lightly along the corridor, which still smelled faintly of flour. She descended the wide staircase, in which each step was a smooth pine plank hanging from iron straps. She collected her prizes in Ellen's room, then continued to descend the next flight into the vast living room which took up the second floor. Gareth was pointing out the path of the millrace to Emrys as they stood in one of the tall windows. Berian was fast asleep, collapsed limply over Gareth's shoulder like a bag of sand. Ellen was displaying her paintings to Dominic.

'... and a wonderful little woman from the village, Gwen Orgee, comes in once a week to water all the plants and dust around, sort out the post, that type of thing. She even stacks the fridge for us before we arrive! We're so lucky! Oh, there you are, Ainee, Lyndon. Do please help us carry out a tray of glasses and lots of wine bottles. Would little Emrys like lemonade or fruit juice, Gareth, dear? We'll all go and lie in the sun in our garden, won't that be just glorious!'

Ellen spread out multicoloured pastel rugs on the grass, and was handing round glassfuls of chilled white wine when Isaac and Don arrived. 'Over here, darlings! Oh, this is the life! Sunshine, countryside, water, wine, music and art! Heaven! Now, Isaac, you promised to draw my Mill for me years ago, so now is the perfect opportunity. Just look at it all: a cloudless sky, the willows all green and weeping, the mill pond like a mirror, mellow old brickwork, and such beautiful people lounging in the garden! Inspiration for whom – Monet, do you think, Dominic?'

Dominic had stripped off his dark silk shirt, and was sunbathing his rather pale and bony body. He rolled onto his elbows and studied Isaac. 'I think that we may have a new Courbet here,' he announced. 'A natural being with an untamed appetite; a man of the country. Individualism and realism so closely connected that you become anarchic; wishing to create a classless society of free individuals. You can only realise yourself through an immersion in the physical world. Nothing abstract for you; loose brushwork and sweeps of the palette knife. The primacy of the eye over the conventions of academic art.'

There was a long silence. Isaac and Dominic stared at each other. Isaac cleared his throat.

'So will you buy the paintings, seeing as you've already written the catalogue?' Isaac asked.

Dominic smiled and twiddled his moustaches. 'Of course I will. We just need to discuss prices.'

Everyone relaxed. Ellen giggled with delight. Ainee, sitting in the dappled shade of a willow, stretched out her arms to Isaac and laughed. 'Now you can buy me those pretty things you promised!' she cried. Isaac glared at her.

'You're drinking alcohol!' he hissed. 'I said no alcohol!'

Ainee gazed at him, her eyes cool and dark. She raised the wineglass to her lips, and took a sip. 'Congratulations,' she said quietly. Then she turned away, and watched a pair of iridescent dragonflies as they courted over the mill pond.

Lyndon had occupied the rug overlapping hers. 'I'll give you pretty things,' he whispered to Ainee. 'Or better, I'll show you how to earn them yourself.'

Ainee shrugged. She set her glass down in the grass, and began to plait her hair, her fingers deft. Strained chords rang across the garden as Don began to tune his guitar.

Isaac drank down a glass of wine in one angry gulp. Gareth warned Emrys against going too near the water. Baby Berian whimpered in his sleep. Ellen fretted. Ainee twisted up the flat wide plait around her head.

Then Ainee began to sing, and everyone listened. Her lilting melody was strange and sweet. She stretched out her hand as she sang. A mist of glints of colour rose from all the flowers of the garden, like tiny vivid ghosts, and hovered in the air around the singing Selkie. One after another, butterflies landed on her outstretched palm. She delicately placed each butterfly on the silvery blonde braid. They formed a coronet of trembling kaleidoscopic colour; Brimstone yellows, Tortoiseshells, Emerald Moths, Purple Emperors, Red Admirals, and Peacocks with winking blue eyes. Each one seemed unwilling or unable to depart from its small enchantment.

The watchers crept closer, unbelieving, and sighing with the beauty of it all. Isaac forgot his anger, and sketched frantically.

Ainee finished her song and turned to regard her audience. She bowed her head on her long and slender neck, crowned as regally as any queen. She smiled, and then clapped her hands. The butterflies flickered away into the hot summer air.

'I didn't have a camera ...' breathed Ellen. Lyndon nodded, baffled.

'What is that song?' asked Don. 'I want you to teach me that song.' He caressed his guitar as though it were Ainee reclining in his lap.

'Oh, it's just an old fishing song,' Ainee said. 'It calls a shoal of fish into your net or your hand when you are hungry.'

Dominic spoke. 'I once read a story in which the Japanese goddess of beauty tied living fireflies to strands of her hair, so that they flew around her as she danced in the darkness of chaos, and became the stars. This is just as marvellous.'

Ainee pursed her lips and considered this. 'What exactly do fireflies look like?' she enquired. 'I think that they might be entertaining, too.' She smiled again, and sipped her wine.

Isaac, frowning over his drawing, murmured in a voice which only Gareth could hear, 'Now it starts. She has begun to fish for the souls of men.'

* * *

The cool dark interior of the cottage was a complete surprise to Keynes. It was filled with garden flowers; vases and jam jars top-heavy with huge, scented blooms. With their unexpected fragrance, the memory which had been twitching in the back of his mind flooded out. For the first time in a quarter of a century, Keynes remembered visits to his grandparents' house.

He had spent most of his holidays there, since his own parents were always too busy to bother with him when he returned from boarding school. Happy homecomings – how could he have forgotten? – were always to his mother's parents on their small-holding on the flat black plain of York. Unlike suburban Esher, there was little to read but a great deal to see.

The Yorkshire horizon sprouted cooling towers, creating a rim of clouds from power-stations. Those innocent white mountains blew away airily, he now realised, journeying to poison Scandinavia. That limitless landscape was so different from the cosy confines of these lush valleys. In Yorkshire, there were no hedgerows, no woods. A vast oozing river ran sluggishly, banked up high above the surrounding land. The prows of boats floated through the sky. There was no fresh paint and golden thatch there; it was a landscape of rusting iron and cracked pantiles.

But when the child that was Keynes looked down from that vast bleached sky, he discovered a wealth of sensations and wonderful smells on his grandparents' smallholding. There was the dry, warm sweetness of the hessian sacks of pignuts stored in an old railway van, and the milky mustiness of the farrowing sheds, where piglets joggled like sausages strung from their mothers' teats. There was the sharp wholesomeness of chicken feed to be scattered over the chickweeded earth. Keynes had helped his busy, bright-eyed grandmother collect the warm eggs into straw-filled pails. At Easter, the eggs were hard-boiled in onion skins lined with flowers. Unwrapped, the shells bore magical patterns of primroses and ferns, outlined in ruby and amber.

When the weather was hot, there was the golden dustiness of ripe wheat, which clogged the nostrils with goodness and sunshine, and huge, spiky gooseberries painful to touch, but purple-green and luscious within, and fragrant with summer. In the cottage garden brilliant flowers were staked to attention in rows, parading their colours until market-day.

Richest of all was the tropical green fruitiness of the glasshouses. Here Keynes's big, gruff grandfather fed him tiny, living scarlet tomatoes, plucked warm from the vine. Too small to sell, these were the true taste of paradise; no wonder the Elizabethans called them 'love-apples'.

There were mewling kittens to be played with, and the musk of a wet and happy dog towelled down after a rainstorm walk. And at nightfall, the pleasure of being tucked up in blue flannel sheets, fresh from the line, in a bed with feather bolsters. As the child Keynes slipped into exhausted sleep, he remembered listening to the gentle gurgling of the water tank in the cupboard. It was like holidaying in childhood, a childhood from which term-time at his harsh boarding school had deprived him.

Now Keynes understood why he wanted the cottage. The sound of the stream running was the sound of the water tank at night, and that had been the only time in his life when he, that lonely little boy, had felt secure and loved. But there was more; there was the fragrance of the promise which scented flowers. There was the sense of growing things all around him; there was countryside. And such countryside! Unlike the regimented rows of weedless vegetables in Yorkshire, this corner of Wales seemed to have cast aside any control by the farmer. The soil seemed to bubble with the energy of Nature, like a rich red cauldron.

Keynes brushed away the tickle of tears as he remembered the loss of his grandparents. Two sudden funerals which he was not told of until the beginning of the summer holidays; the smallholding already sold to pay for his schooling. To sell such a treasury of pleasure so that he might continue in the torment of school! No wonder, he realised, that he had locked away such happy memories from his mind. The pain of recalling them was too sharp.

Swallowing the bitter lump in his throat, Keynes's bleared eyes travelled slowly around the cottage. This was an extraordinarily special place. This was a place where he could regain happiness; something which had eluded him for almost the whole of his life. His task as a professional civil engineer was to purchase this valley and this cottage which was supposed to be an empty ruin on the map. Instead, he had discovered a place so warm and alive and beautiful that he no longer had any choice but to possess it; to have it for himself, not for the Department of Energy to despoil.

Keynes shook himself, stiffening his shoulders, which had relaxed during his reverie to the most surprising extent. He did not know how he would achieve his aim; but he had an entire Folk Festival – whatever that was – to contemplate ways and means. He strode out into the dappled sunlight and firmly closed the striped door behind him. Crossing the slab bridge, he struck out along the steep path which climbed up above the cottage.

As he walked, Keynes set his jaw in resolution. The Glyn would be his.

13

'Coffee for eight, and brandies on the house!' announced Vin Goldhanger as he set down the large tray on the table in front of Ellen Sutherland. 'I thought I might join you myself for a while – in the lull before the storm. Cheers!' Vin pulled across a chair beside Ellen's, lowered his bulk gently into it, and raised his glass.

'How kind!' replied Ellen, raising her own glass graciously. She sat like a queen at the end of the table, surrounded by her London companions and their village guests. But it was Ainee, silent and silvered in the candlelight opposite her, to whom the assembled party drank their toast. She sat as though reflected in mirrors, so many portraits of her hung around the lounge bar of the Golden Oak Inn. Her coronet of braids now had bright garden flowers twisted into it. Isaac glowered beside her, drinking in her eerie beauty and quantities of dark red wine, and paying little heed to the desultory conversation over dinner.

Lyndon Cotton, the other worshipper by Ainee's side, leaned behind Don and Dominic, and flipped a gleaming plastic card into Vin's capacious aproned lap. 'My treat, mine host!' he drawled.

Dominic looked affronted. 'Oh, you New Worlders!' he returned to Lyndon. 'Columbus went over so recently, seeking gold and glory, and all you can bring back is a gilded charge-card. What price all our ancient history now?'

Ellen giggled. 'Now, gentlemen, please don't compete to pay for our pleasures! We have a long weekend ahead of us, and I'm sure that most of our cash will end up in dear Vin's lap. Thank you, Lyndon, darling, we accept most gratefully, I'm sure! Now, Vin, do tell us about the history of your delightful pub. Don and Isaac tell us they're newcomers to Glasmaen, and so we have to ask you all about the village.'

Vin roared, and stretched out. 'Well, the Golden Oak was damn old when Columbus went sailing. Us Goldhangers have only been here for five generations, since we came over from

Essex. We liked the sound of Glasmaen, so we settled down here, very comfortable-like. My Lucy will be the last of the Goldhangers; so all that glisters is not gold, you see!'

Sonja winced visibly. 'Ellen said her mill was mentioned in the Domesday Book; was your pub there too? And the castle?' Her voice was sharp and brisk, like her pale blue eyes. She had spent the meal in growing irritation at the attention which Ellen demanded and Ainee received from the assembled men. These included Ambrose, whose hand and shoulder Sonja constantly touched and stroked, establishing possession.

'Oh, bless you, yes. Them Normans were the lads around here! There's a great deal happened as soon as they turned up, and not a lot since. And you can forget your 1066 and all that, 'cos our Normans came over here well before old Harold got an arrow in his eye. Mercenaries, they were; big hard Norsemen in tough armour on good horses, bribed by good King Edmund to come over and kick out the rampaging Welshmen from the Border lands, with promises that they could help themselves to as much land as they could win. And they did. Castles all the way from Monmouth to Chester, dug up by slave labour, all in a dozen years or so. And then there was no stopping 'em! Ruled this stretch of land for five hundred years, they did, until old Henry the Eighth settled 'em down, being as he was a Tudor king, and came from these parts himself. Tough old boys, them Normans, them Marcher Lords! They're still here, as well,' Vin pointed behind him.

'You just take a look at our Morty, behind the bar. Peter Mortimer, he is, and the Mortimers ruled round here for all that time. His ancestors seduced Queens of England, and married a few of 'em, and helped to father the Tudors themselves!'

The group turned to stare at the barman, who had been listening and grinning as he polished glasses. Peter Mortimer was tall, muscular and stocky; his straight brown hair was cut short into a cap around his square shaven chin. Red patches flamed on his flat cheeks, and his bright blue eyes glittered under heavy eyebrows.

'Oh!' breathed Sonja. 'Look, Ambrose, if he was dressed in chain mail and helmet he'd be straight out of the Bayeux Tapestry! Living history!'

'And he's not the only one. There's Vaughans and Talbots and Presseys alive and well and living in the village. Corbets, too, only they've all got hair as black as the ravens they were named for. And you look at our Gwen Orgee, who served your dinner. She's got Norman blood in her, with those red streaks on her cheeks, even if hers has gone a bit sideways from the Marcher Lords. Oh, yes, there's real history living here, alright.' Vin nodded sagely.

'But this is fascinating!' trilled Ellen. 'Who'd have thought that families could survive so long.'

'And some for much longer,' came a quiet, lilting voice from the window seat. A slender, dark young woman emerged, a glass of mineral water in her hand, and stood beside Vin. She nodded to Don and Isaac.

'Ah, I hadn't forgotten you, my dear. Doctor Llewelyn, I presume! Ellen Sutherland and her friends from London.' Vin waved his hand around the table in introduction. 'The Llewelyns were Princes of North Wales a long time before Morty and his mob came over. Royalty, compared to his barons and earls!'

Ellen gestured to a chair, smiling, and Dominic dutifully leapt up to pull it over to the circle. 'A sorry throne for a Welsh princess,' he apologised.

'Celia, please, and we're only a minor branch!' laughed the doctor as she took the offered chair. 'I know Don and Isaac, but the rest of you are visitors, I take it?'

'Dominic Batista at your service! Descended from a race of unimportant Italian Renaissance bankers, I'm afraid. Ambrose Fisher and Sonja Barnaby ...'

'Anthropologists,' Sonja nodded, grateful for the addition of an obviously professional and intelligent woman. 'That's why we're so fascinated by these family histories, which are so evident in the physiognomies we see in – ah – Mr Mortimer and yourself.'

'Lyndon Cotton, Monterey, California.' Lyndon bowed. 'I'm honoured, Ma'am. Do all Welsh people look as fine as you?'

'Ah, black hair and eyes is not necessarily our insignia.' Celia Llewelyn studied Ainee as she spoke. 'This young lady here could well be a Llewelyn, for example. We have a family heritage of striking pale skin and white-blonde hair, which I missed out on, of course.'

'Ah, this is the mysterious Ainee Sealfin,' explained Ellen, 'whose portraits surround us.'

Celia Llewelyn's gaze returned to Ainee. 'What an unusual name. It has Celtic origins, doesn't it?' she enquired softly, trying to prompt a response.

Ainee watched her silently, a small smile flickering on her lips, then spoke for the first time for hours, except for ordering half a pint of prawns – which she had crunched up, heads, shells and all – and to express delight that steak tartare should be made from raw beef. Now she picked at a sprig of green grapes. 'Descent from royalty will always mark the bearer with name as well as looks and bearing. But my descent is through the female line, and you are all talking about the families of men. And such recent families you have, too! My mothers have descended from the dawn of time, not mere centuries.'

Everyone stared at her. Celia Llewelyn's eyes were as dark as Ainee's, and shared some elusive quality of mystical depths, but Ainee's suddenly appeared fathomless. No soul shone from her eyes; they were bottomless pools. For a long moment her audience sat hypnotised.

Isaac bristled. 'They don't want to hear about you, Ainee,' he growled. But the fascinated eyes of everyone at the table silently contradicted him.

Ainee turned to face him. 'Since these people have been so kind as to serve us with this delicious food and drink in exchange for our company all afternoon, I think that you should follow the custom here and go and purchase some more bottles of wine. As Dominic Batista will be paying you a great deal of money for the paintings which you have made of me, you may spend some of it in this way.'

Isaac's already dark face blackened with anger, and his hands became fists. He glanced around the table under hooded brows, then stood, his chair scraping harshly across the flagstones. He stepped stiffly behind Ainee's chair as he made his way to the bar.

Dominic quickly caught his sleeve as he passed, and pressed a small bundle of notes into it. 'Advance,' he whispered.

Ainee's dark eyes slid around the circle of watchers.

'I am a Selkie Princess,' she announced proudly. No one moved. A few local witches grinned in the shadows.

'Well then,' said Ainee, 'you want me to tell you about Selkies. There are not many of us any more, I must admit. We are Faery children, cousins to the seals, and we usually dress in their image. I have eleven older sisters, and we live in a cavern lined with mother-of-pearl. The cavern is under the ice, so it is filled with cool, fresh air, and the light filtering through the ice is of a deep dark blue, bluer than the sky. The ocean around the cave is green, deeper and darker green than the green of your trees. The sound of the sea is around the cave, like the sound of heavy sleepers breathing. The ice cracks and tinkles overhead. The entrance to the cavern is hung with strings of pierced abalone, which shimmer with the blues and greens of the ice and the sea, and clitters and rings with the sound of bones. There is a fragrance like the wind over the ice, and the stench of decaying seaweed.

'The floor of the cavern is white sand which shifts underfoot. The sand catches, look, in the webs between our toes,' Ainee gracefully lifted her naked foot onto the table, Ellen's blue silk dress sliding along her thigh to expose her long slender leg. She spread her toes, and small translucent films of skin glistened in the candle light. She replaced her foot on the cold stone floor.

'Around the pearly walls of the cavern we store the casks of silver and the tubs of gold which we have collected from wrecked ships. There are many different faces on those coins, and we pass the time by studying the faces and telling one another stories about them. There are pictures of ships and birds and ears of wheat on the reverse of the faces. We compare the crowns on the heads to the crowns and coronets which we have collected, and which hang on the blades of knives which we have driven into the walls. For our table, we have a slab of clear ice which rests on the four lovely yellow drums which we found not long ago on the sea bed. The drums have a strange mark on them, three triangles inside a circle, and they are very useful. They make our skin tingle.' She stretched the webs between her toes again.

'But our pearls are the prettiest things. Precious, deep sea pearls, as large and white as eyes, or strung like teeth. We tore them with bleeding fingers from the oysters and clams in the warm places of the ocean. The pearls are caught in slithering piles by fine nets woven in Ancient Greece from the beards of mussels. These are our couches. When we sleep, we curl up amongst the pearls, which slide around us to give us comfort.'

Ainee caught Lyndon's glistening eyes, and smiled. 'Comfort? I see that you want to know about sex. Well, we do it occasionally, but it's not very pleasant doing it under the sea, or with a male Selkie. They're so gross. They have enormous tusks which they like to dig into your neck. And they stink. They smell like rotting corpses. They have bristles and long trunks, which they snort into. Ugh. And they live such a long way away.' She sighed, and the shudder ran around the circle of listeners like cracking ice.

'No, the only time we touch is when we join our hands into a circle when we dance. As you know, Isaac.' She pouted and frowned, remembering.

Isaac grunted, and thumped the new bottles onto the table. Everyone shushed him, and continued to gaze at Ainee.

'Isaac captured me on Midsummer's Eve, before I could escape back into the sea. I was in seal-shape in our palace, and I had been studying the moon's patterns, which is my duty as the youngest. It was a full moon on the shortest night, and the sands would be bright and warm for dancing. I clapped my flippers and barked to summon my sisters.' Her sharp clap and sudden wailing cry echoed around the bar, which was gradually filling with silent people.

'They swam in through the shell-hung arch at the entrance to our gleaming cavern, spinning and nudging each other with their long silky noses.

'It is Midsummer's Eve tonight, sisters,' I cried, 'and the full moon shines to light up a path for us over the tips of the waves.' My grey and silver sister-seals twirled and clapped with excitement.

'Come with me and dance in circles on the wet white sands,' I whispered to my sisters. 'For tonight we can throw aside our sealskin caps, and dance with the slim white legs and thin pale skin of humankind. Our long fair hair will swish and float about us, alight with the sheen of moonlight, and our eyes will glow like a necklace of pearls, as we weave hand in hand over the shores of the earth.'

'My sisters hissed with joy, and I rose up from my couch. They followed me, already singing softly to themselves with delight, back through the wavering archway. Once we had gained the edge of the ocean, we flipped our long tails and sprang away, up towards the faint light of the rising moon, seeking the silver path across the sea to the dancing-beach.

'And there, as we were singing and dancing naked under the full moon, Isaac wove the music of his fiddle into the rhythms of our song. He made us dance until we collapsed on our unaccustomed legs, and then he leapt down from his hiding place and caught me, me – the youngest and lithest of all my lovely sisters. He caught me and tore my sealskin cap from my head, before I could escape to the freedom of the water. And he almost drowned me before he lifted me and carried me onto the land. And there he crushed me under his body and forced me to become his possession. He has few enough possessions, but he calls me his treasure. And I have been stolen from my sisters and from my empire in the sea.'

Ainee looked slowly around the room. Shadowed faces were everywhere turned toward her, enchanted by her tale. She glanced down at the table before her, littered with the debris of food and drink. She raised her wineglass and turned it in the candle-glow to see the refractions of golden light.

'But this is a different world. At home, we drink fresh spring water from polished skulls.' She smiled.

'And what do we eat? Well, we don't eat very often. Only after a storm, when the drowned sailors sink down to us. But they do taste very good.' Ainee sighed, and drained her glass, before holding it out to her audience to refill.

The room was silent for a long time. Then Lyndon began to clap softly, and gradually applause began to ripple around the room. It grew louder, becoming fervent, before fading away into a welling murmur of astonished voices.

Lyndon was the first to seize a bottle and refill Ainee's glass. No one else moved as they watched her toast Isaac silently, before drinking the crisp white wine with relish.

Vin spoke first: 'So you'll be entering the storytelling competition at the Festival?' he asked.

Ainee smiled and raised one arching eyebrow, but said nothing. Amongst the crowd, someone began to sing loudly, in a hissing and cracking voice, a long and complex ballad about an old battle. It was Bryn Jones, introducing the start of the Folk Club. The audience hushed to listen politely, already shaken and puzzled by Ainee's peculiar story.

Someone leaned over the table and passed her a torn beer-mat with a pattern scribbled on it in biro. It was Graham Ferris, one of Dr Keynes's survey team. 'Excuse me,' he whispered, 'this is a daft question, but these yellow drums. Did the marking on them look like that?'

Ainee took the card and glanced at it before nodding serenely.

Graham thanked her and made his way back to Richard Beavis and Dr Edward Keynes, who were both standing at the bar. He handed the beer-mat to Keynes, and spoke into his ear.

'Yes, she says. The yellow drums are marked like that. High-level nuclear waste. Dumped into the Atlantic fifteen or twenty years ago. She doesn't look much older than that herself. She obviously made it up – but how did she know?'

Keynes stared across the crowded room, where Bryn had finished singing and Vin Goldhanger had begun to roar a rousing drinking song. He met Ainee Sealfin's dark eyes looking back at him. She gave him a smile which made his fingers tingle.

'I don't know,' he stated. 'I don't know anything at all, any more.' And he shuddered.

14

During the interval the band set up their instruments, and the audience milled around, chattering and gossiping. Keynes sipped from his third pint whilst perched on a stool at the corner of the bar. The long succession of folk-songs gave him an excuse to remain silent, apparently listening. He stared across the room at the noisy group around the far table, at the objects of his desire. The cool dark Welsh lady doctor; the mysterious pale blonde; and the reputed owner of the house of his dreams.

Graham Ferris took every opportunity of engaging Lucy in whispered, giggling conversation, whilst Richard Beavis attempted to join in every few minutes. Rebuffed, he tried unsuccessfully to get Keynes to offer explanations about the drums of nuclear waste.

'This all sounds very interesting. Are you experts on this subject?' enquired a clear lilting voice.

Keynes and Beavis turned suddenly to see the smiling face of Doctor Llewelyn as she ordered a fresh drink.

Richard Beavis grinned. 'Well, yes, we do know a bit about it all. But please, let me pay for that drink.'

Celia Llewelyn shook her head, the sharp cut of her hair swinging around her face gracefully. 'No, but let me order a refill for you and your friend.' Her black eyes glittered as she looked at Keynes. 'I've been hoping to meet you. I hear that you're a doctor too.'

Keynes slid from his stool and gave her a half-bow. 'Applied Physics, Cambridge. Dr Edward Keynes. Call me Edward. Pleased to meet you – Dr Llewelyn, isn't it?'

'Celia. Oh, thank you.' She accepted her drink from Beavis, and the stool from Keynes, but insisted on paying for the round. 'My cleaner, Gwen Orgee, told me about you, and I've seen you and your survey team around the village. I'd love to know what you're doing!' She leaned forward confidentially and gazed into Keynes's eyes over the rim of her glass of white wine. Beavis, realising that he had been excluded again, turned away. 'Do tell!' she whispered.

Keynes tried to change the subject, but was secretly thrilled to be speaking with this graceful woman at last. 'Ah,' he smiled stiffly. 'Gwen! She seems to have a great many different jobs. One of those rare 'treasures', I suspect. I wish the cleaning lady my Cambridge flat were as efficient!'

'The surveys?' repeated Celia Llewelyn, her smile unwavering.

'Oh, just the preliminary enquiries before our company purchases land on behalf of a Government Department.'

'Which Department would that be?'

'Ah, Energy.'

Celia arched one delicate eyebrow. 'How fascinating! And which piece of land are you interested in?'

Keynes felt distinctly uncomfortable, but her questions were so direct and her attention so complete that he felt compelled to reply. He drained his glass and turned to the next pint. Celia crossed her legs slowly. He swallowed again, and forced his eyes upwards from her smooth brown knees. 'The valley called the Glyn, actually.'

'Oh! Where that artist lives, Isaac Talboys. Lovely place.'

'It certainly is,' agreed Keynes with feeling. 'We had thought that the valley was uninhabited, so his cottage came as rather a surprise. Isn't the valley owned by Bryn Jones?' He nodded towards Jones, who was now hushing the room to introduce the band.

'I don't think so,' whispered Celia, leaning closer to Keynes. Her naked shoulder brushed Keynes' shirt sleeve, and he repressed a shiver of pleasure. 'I'd heard that he bought the ruin and the valley from Jones about – what? – five years ago.'

Keynes considered this. The band launched into a bouncing, rippling melody which made his toe tap on the stone floor. 'If he did so, there's no record of the transaction in the county records.'

Celia sipped her wine and licked her narrow pink lips. 'Well, Edward, just look at the pair of them! Not the sort to follow regulations, either of them.'

Keynes glanced at the two men across the room. Bryn Jones was accepting another pint, his hooded eyes glittering. Whilst he sat in the midst of his folk club cronies, no one sat very close to him. Keynes sniffed, remembering the smell of damp and mould in his cold and dusty ballroom. Isaac was tuning up his fiddle in the very corner of the room, frowning at the slender blonde beside him as he concentrated on the strings. Both men wore clothes which looked distinctly grimy and frayed. Keynes nodded slowly. 'You may well be right.'

'Compulsory purchase, is it?' enquired Celia.

Keynes turned back to her and shook his head. He took another large gulp of the smooth and bitter beer. Was it too much beer which was edging him into this corner, or just the astute questioning of this undeniably attractive woman? Why was he so unused to talking with women, anyway? The ones he had met recently all seemed very clever, and considerably more in control of every situation than he was.

'No, we try to do these things rather more discreetly than that.' He had attempted to close the subject; instead, admiring her slow smile, he realised that he was in fact sliding into a complicity with her. A little hope wriggled in the back of his brain: as a responsible local professional person, perhaps she could help him to bargain with Bryn Jones or the artist, whichever of them turned out to be the owner of the Glyn? Her perfume was a crisp light citron fragrance. He leaned closer to her. 'I've been empowered to make an offer to Bryn Jones for the land, which he's considering. Whether he rents it to this artist or whether he's sold it to him, he was careful not to let me know, so I really rather need to find out the true position.'

Celia's eyes went wide and black. 'How extremely interesting. You've discovered that the land is suitable for your plans, then?'

Keynes nodded. 'Geology's perfect; fault line in the old red sandstone with impervious rocks beneath. Access wouldn't be a problem, even though it is very out-of-the-way.'

He could feel Celia's fresh breath on his chin. 'So there wouldn't be much in the way of local opposition to your plans, then?' she asked in a low tone.

'I certainly hope not! Our sort of work does seem to upset the ill-informed and trouble-making element of a population, but Glasmaen seems to be small enough and quiet enough for that not to be a problem, thank goodness. Yes, it seems a very promising site.'

'So you'll be drilling in the valley, along the fault line? Soon?'

Keynes shook his head. 'That depends entirely on the Department, and on future energy demands. Everyone needs electricity, after all, and we all use more and more of it all the time!'

'Except Isaac Talboys,' put in Celia, quietly.

Keynes frowned, puzzled. She sipped her wine and smiled again.

'No electricity in his cottage in the Glyn. Paraffin and oil lamps. No central heating, or hot water. No telephone. No mains water, or mains drainage, come to that. Not even a septic tank, I suspect.'

Keynes was surprised. 'I hadn't noticed – how extraordinary!' However had he missed these details? He took modern facilities for granted, he supposed. Then he paused in his train of thought. His visit to the cottage had been entirely illicit, but he had just admitted to having been inside. And, anyway, how did Celia come to know so much about the lifestyle of the artist? Gwen and Grace had hinted darkly at his baffling success with the attractive women of the village. Was Celia another conquest? Did this man possess everything that Keynes desired, the lucky bastard? A hot shudder of jealousy ran down his spine and curdled in his stomach, on top of the pints of bitterness already there. He glared at the artist, suddenly aware that he was holding the room spellbound with the glories of a solo on the violin. Was there no limit to this man's talents?

Then the blonde girl reappeared; she had stood up, and was singing with Isaac's music. Her voice, thin and sweet, was as clear and piercing as the crescendos of the violin, and as they concluded their silvery duet sighs of appreciation ran around the crowd, followed by gusts of enthusiastic applause.

Beside him, Celia sighed too, her gaze still on the fragile blonde girl. 'Isn't she enchanting? A voice to match all that ethereal beauty. Ainee Sealfin ...'

Keynes winced in surprise. He had never imagined a woman praising another woman's looks, unless ... he suddenly felt very hot, and swayed. 'Excuse me, I have to ...' he muttered, and stumbled for the door, pushing past yielding bodies as he hurried towards the men's toilet, where he was violently sick.

*   *   *

Sue Hopkins-Jones was adjusting her candy-stripe dungarees in the mirror of the ladies' toilet when Celia Llewelyn walked in.

'How are you, Sue? You must be worn out, what with the end of term, *and* the Festival to organise.'

Sue grimaced at her reflection, and traced the dark bags under her eyes with a fingertip. 'Do I look that bad? God, I suppose I do.'

Celia grinned and shook her head. 'Nothing a good night's sleep won't fix. Have you got Gareth doing his share of dawn feeds yet?'

Sue replied with a scornful laugh. 'Not without him creating hell before he does help out. But at least the baby seems to settle down sooner with bottled milk. So perhaps it'll work out okay, after all. I do wish he wouldn't rattle on about Isaac's new dumb blonde floosie all the time though. Any Fishfingers, I call her.'

'No!' They giggled together. 'She's a stunner, though, and not as dumb as you might think. I just met her. Perhaps you ought to take her a bit more seriously. She seems to attract men like jam does wasps. She's also got the gift of storytelling, and the voice of a diva. You should get to know her. I'd certainly like to get to know her better.' Her voice had taken on a purring quality.

'Now then, Ms Respectable Lady Doctor, keep your wicked inclinations under control. We're not in the Coven now.'

Celia shrugged, and lent Sue a lipstick to redden her pale cheeks. 'By the way, I think you ought to know, Sue. I just had a very interesting conversation with a guy from the Department of Energy – the one in stiff clothes who's been wandering around the village all week. He's trying to buy the Glyn from your father.'

'Whatever for?' Sue swung around from the mirror to face Celia, her eyes narrowed in puzzlement.

'So that they can drill along the old red sandstone fault in the valley, because it has impermeable rock under it. They're particularly interested because the Glyn is – they think – uninhabited, and in an area of low population. And they're trying to keep it all secret.'

Sue gaped. 'What's it all about, Celia?'

The graceful young doctor brushed her already shining hair. 'I can't be certain, but I can take an educated guess.' She took a deep breath, and met Sue's eyes. 'They want to dump nuclear waste in the Glyn.'

They stood in silence for a moment, then simultaneously turned back to the mirror. Their reflected faces, left side now predominating over right, gave them each a harder expression, and their eyes clicked in the glass, glittering and cold.

'Right then,' declared Sue. 'I'll get Glasmaen Environmental Action Party together. And the Women's Group. And the Coven. They'll all be at the Festival, anyway.'

'And I think I might entertain myself by slowly screwing more information out of our elegant new friend, Dr. Edward Keynes.' Both women laughed sharply. 'Although I have a suspicion that just now he's puking up all his beer into the Gents' loo.'

'Well, Celia, it sounds as though he may need a ministering angel, and I'm sure you're just his type. Be gentle with him. Catch you later.'

Both women giggled as Celia retreated into one of the cubicles and Sue returned to the Folk Club, intent on whispering her new information into a dozen interested ears.

*   *   *

Edward Keynes sprawled against one of the tables on the terrace outside the pub, breathing deeply in the flower-scented evening air. Wisps of melodies and snatches of songs drifted out through the open windows. Hearing someone walk briskly towards him, he sat up stiffly.

'Dr Keynes,' came a resolute voice. 'I wish to register a complaint about your professional attitude.'

Keynes looked up in surprise to see Richard Beavis standing beside him, arms folded. His steel-rimmed spectacles glittered coldly. Keynes scowled. 'Have you been drinking, Beavis?' he asked sternly.

'Not as much or as often as you have, sir.'

'Nonsense,' lied Keynes. 'I really can't be bothered with any silliness from a junior member of staff during off-duty occasions …'

'With you it's been all one long 'off-duty' occasion, Dr Keynes. Graham and I have been working all day and every day to com-

103

plete our surveying assignments, and you've entirely failed to supervise our work, because you're constantly in one pub or another, or taking nature rambles whenever the pub is shut, and chatting, sir, chatting to the locals about our aims. We're here to survey a confidential project, and yet here you are telling women in pubs all about our plans.'

'Eavesdropping, too, as well as insolent nonsense. I shouldn't have to remind you, Beavis, that I am your professional superior and that you are taking the greatest liberty in interfering with or commenting in any way whatsoever upon my system of research ...'

Beavis sniggered.

Keynes glared at a spot six inches behind Beavis's head, but felt distracted from the issue. He remembered all these techniques of oppression from his schooldays, used with great effect by his teachers to make their pupils writhe with humiliation. So why wasn't this working on Beavis? Lack of commitment, Keynes realised, and inadvertently he sighed. He couldn't be bothered to be angry. He rubbed his eyes, and suddenly felt extremely tired.

'Sit down, Bea ... ah, Richard. Or is it Rick, or ...? Sit down, please.'

Beavis looked warily at Keynes, but sat down on the opposite side of the wooden bench. 'Richard,' he replied firmly.

'Richard, in your lengthy university training course or during any of your several years working for our company, did you ever permit yourself a working holiday?'

Beavis stared for a few moments. 'I don't know what you mean, sir.'

'Edward. No, I didn't think you would. Well, consider this project as a working holiday. I've never taken one before, and I see that you haven't either. Ferr – ah, Graham, back there, flirting with the landlord's daughter, seems to be a great deal more proficient than either of us at – well, enjoying himself.'

'Isn't he just,' observed Beavis sourly.

Keynes paused and looked at the younger man carefully. Was this a trace of jealousy, he wondered? He reconsidered Beavis's behaviour recently: working long hours in the field and then sitting silently whenever in company. Then trying to include himself tonight in the conversations between Graham Ferris and Lucy Goldhanger, and then his own with Dr – Celia! – Llewelyn.

'I thought I had suggested that you and – ah, Graham could take things more easily for the next few days. I have been entirely satisfied with your work – so far, that is. Weren't you going to spend today helping put up marquees and beer barrels and what not for this festival business?'

'From nine this morning until nine this evening, that's exactly what we have been doing. I don't see that as 'taking things easy'. Nor do I consider it suitable work for someone with my qualifications, or Graham's for that matter – sir.'

'Didn't Graham enjoy the work?' asked Keynes slyly.

'I expect he did. But then, he's not as committed to his career as I am. And if you're giving us time off then I'd rather be out windsurfing this weekend than carting barrels and setting out chairs.'

'Then your windsurfing will be done in your own holiday time. This is work.'

'How can it be? You're completely under-using our abilities …'

'Not so. Liaison with the locals is a key aspect of our assign-ment.' Keynes straightened his spine and glared at Beavis. 'You should be grateful that the locals at least speak the same language as us, and that alcohol is freely available, and that women are visible, never mind willing to have conversations with us. If you don't like what seems to me to be an entirely idyllic situation, perhaps I should arrange for a transfer for you; to Riyadh maybe, or Kuwait, where I have spent most of my working life.'

Beavis stood up stiffly. 'I'll consider that option, sir. I'm certain that it would be more beneficial to my career than acting as a – a labourer for a bunch of yokels.'

Keynes, unaccountably, blazed with sudden anger. 'You young idiot!' He jumped to his feet, and became entangled with the leg of the table. He cursed loudly. Beavis began to snigger again.

Freeing himself, Keynes swayed toward Beavis and caught his left wrist. 'You've no idea, have you, you blasted idiot, what it's like to spend your youth working out there. This place is a bloody paradise after Riyadh! Dust and mosquitoes and heat and thirst and complete bloody loneliness! Nothing but work, work, sodding work. You're bloody lucky to be here, paid a damn good salary to take things easy! You should damn well start to enjoy yourself! That's an order!'

Beavis angrily shook himself free of Keynes's grip and pushed his boss away from him as he turned and hurried back into the pub. Keynes's foot caught again in the table leg, and he twisted and fell hard against the stone paving. He put out his right hand to save himself. As he did so, he heard a sharp snapping sound, and excruciating pain shot up his forearm.

15

Celia Llewelyn, a light jacket draped elegantly over her shoulders, found him first. 'Edward!' she declared. 'Whatever are you doing? I don't expect you to go down on your knees to me on first acquaintance!'

His eyes clenched against the pain, Keynes glanced up at her. 'Oh, God …' he moaned. He struggled to his feet, and sat down heavily on the bench, gripping his right hand with his left. 'This is so embarrassing. I'm so sorry …'

'What's the matter?' Her voice was crisp.

Keynes limply held his arm out towards her. 'I'm so sorry, but I seem to have, er, broken my wrist.'

Celia sat down beside him, feeling his wrist with a light professional touch. She bent his hand and manipulated the bones until he yelled. 'Hospital for you, Edward. You obviously can't drive, so I'll have to run you over to Abergavenny. No point bothering the ambulance service. Wait here. I'm going to ring the General, fetch some bandages. No more beer for you tonight.'

'I wasn't … I didn't …'

She stood up, wrapped her jacket around his shoulders, and walked quickly back into the pub. Keynes bowed his head in pain and shame, as he sensed other people walking by.

'Hush, wait a minute. This man is in pain.' The soft voice in his ear grew closer, and someone sat down next to him and gently lifted his injured arm. Keynes moaned again.

Keynes looked up into the dark eyes of the slender blonde girl. She smiled and ran her fingers around the burning pain and her fingers were cool and soothing. He felt the heat flow from his wrist into her hands. There was a tiny 'click' and no more pain.

'Ah,' she whispered. 'That's better, isn't it?'

Amazed, he nodded. She shook her hands as though shivering droplets of water from her fingertips, rubbed both hands together, then lifted one and laid it carefully over his forehead.

The cool sensation tingled through his scalp and his head seemed to float upwards, light and freed from all tension and sickness. The girl stood up.

'Thank you ...' he whispered, startled by his clarity of vision. He felt completely sober, and tingling with disbelief. The girl smiled.

Then someone behind her growled, laid large hands on her thin shoulders, and tugged her away into the darkness. Keynes rose to his feet, suddenly angry that this kind, strange girl should be mistreated. 'Hey!' he yelled.

A black figure lurched towards him, and a dark, hairy face glowered into his. The man spoke with a low rumble that chilled Keynes's spine.

'Leave her be, you cretin. Someone has obviously thumped you once already tonight, but I'd be happy to do the same. Any time. Understand?' A fist became a pointing finger and jabbed at his chest.

Keynes sat down suddenly, recognising Isaac Talboys, and decided that silence was the best policy. Isaac swung away into the darkness and he heard the couple's footsteps scurry away.

Then Celia appeared beside him again. 'Here we are; have you bandaged up like a mummy in a moment.' He moaned again, this time for the impossibility of explaining what had just happened.

'Am I hurting you?' she asked carelessly.

'Oh, no, it's just that, well ... I feel better now. You needn't do that. My wrist is okay.'

Celia stopped winding the sling around his shoulder and stared at him.

'Yes, really. Look.' Keynes shook his hand and flexed his wrist. 'Not broken, mended.'

'Is this some kind of sick joke, Dr Keynes?'

Keynes sighed heavily. 'I wish it was. I'm sorry to have bothered you, but I do appreciate your concern, it's just that ... it's better now.'

'You have a broken wrist, could be a compound fracture, don't be such a ... a man.' Her voice was scornful.

'No, honestly.' Keynes tugged the sling away. 'Feel ... see, it's fine.'

Doubtfully, Celia twisted and pulled at his wrist, gently at first then surprisingly hard. 'What is this?' she asked eventually.

'Dislocate your own wrist to get attention, then click it back into place? Some kind of weirdo chat-up line, trying to get sympathy?' She stood up, yanking her jacket from his shoulders and putting it on. 'Well, not from me. If you have a genuine problem, I have open surgery tomorrow morning, nine until twelve. Otherwise, forget it.'

As she turned to go, Keynes jumped up and ran after her. 'You won't believe this, but it was broken, and while you were on the 'phone that singing blonde girl came by and touched my wrist, and well … mended it.'

Celia stared at him. 'Balls.' She walked away, heels clicking firmly on the surface of the road.

'I know it sounds ridiculous,' called Keynes. 'Ask her! It's true!'

There was no reply except a tittering and whispering from the gathering crowd by the tables behind him. Unable to face anyone else, Keynes set off back to his hotel, keeping a steady distance behind Celia until she turned away into the car park. Further up the road, she passed him swiftly, without dimming her headlamps or turning her dark head in his dazzled direction.

Keynes's journey was a slow and mournful one. He also had to avoid the shadowy couple walking ahead of him. When he reached the hotel gateway, he turned into it thankfully and went straight to bed.

In the dark, beneath the crisp sheets, the images of the gentle blonde and the scornful Celia danced together inside his head. Dark eyes and long legs and slender waists and the soft curves of breasts competed for his attention. Keynes discovered that he was grateful that his right wrist was not broken, after all.

*   *   *

'Well, Gareth, I certainly learned some interesting stuff tonight,' commented Sue Hopkins-Jones as she climbed into her side of the bed.

'Oh, yeah?' yawned Gareth. 'Come here.'

'No, listen to me. No! Hands off! I need to tell you about this.' Gareth switched his light off.

'That stiff type in the suit, well, he's up to something very serious indeed. He wants to buy the Glyn off Dad.'

'Oh, I thought as much.'

'What? You know about this? What do you know?'

'Um … Isaac told me that your dad offered him forty thousand for the Glyn.'

'My dad? Forty thousand? When? The sneaky old bastard. Tell me when!'

Gareth considered. 'Tuesday, I think.'

'When did Isaac tell you this?'

'Wednesday, I think. God, that's only yesterday.'

'Yesterday! Why didn't you tell me?'

'You've been too busy, Sue. It's not all that important.'

'It bloody well is!'

'Okay, so it is. We'll discuss it tomorrow.'

'Tomorrow! With the Folk Festival to run! Don't be a complete nerd! What exactly has Isaac told you? Tell me now!'

'I don't want to tell you now. I want to make love to you and then I want to go to sleep.'

'Well, you can sodding well forget about that, for a start. Sit up. Sit up, you bastard!'

'Is this how you treat your kids at school? We only had detention when we were at school. Not slanging matches with the teachers. But then, if you want to talk dirty … come here!'

'Gareth Hopkins, you complete asshole, answer my bloody questions.'

'Ooh, I love it when you talk dirty … do you need to spank me?'

'I need to twist your bloody balls off. Good. Now you're listening. Tell me what you know about this business with the Glyn.'

Gareth sat up and kept his hands firmly in his lap. He took a deep breath. 'Isaac says your Dad came to see him, offered him forty thousand quid for the Glyn. Said he's going to offer the ballroom to us. I said no way, I don't want to live in that rotting mausoleum, don't sell the Glyn to him. Isaac said he might, because no one else would be idiot enough to want to live in the Glyn. He says the choice is up to Ainee; if she wants to move on, he'll sell up and follow her. Isaac's in love, he's getting his end away, he's willing to move. I'm in love – with you, in case you hadn't noticed – I'm not getting my end away, I don't want to move, and I certainly don't want to move into anything your father lives in, especially since he might think that he can move in with us. I'm knackered, I'm fed up with arguing, Berian'll probably wake up soon and it'll be me that has to go and feed him, and I want to go to sleep. That's it. Goodnight.' He lay down again.

'Oh, my God, that's worse than I thought. Gareth, listen carefully. The reason this bloke wants to buy the Glyn is so that they can dump nuclear waste in it.'

'What?' Now Gareth did sit up.

'Celia says this stiff bloke was telling her ... well, she wangled it out of him, you know Celia ...'

'I can imagine.'

'Don't interrupt me when I'm talking. Where was I ... Oh, yeah, he told Celia that the geology is perfect for drilling for dumping nuclear waste. It's a secret. They think that there won't be any fuss because the Glyn is uninhabited. Well, except for Isaac. He's only just found out about him. If Isaac sells up and moves out, they'll poison our village! Think of our babies. Leukaemia. Cancer. Destruction of our water table, our fields, our trees. Sellafield. Three Mile Island. Chernobyl. Our home!'

'Oh, shit.'

'Yes, oh shit. We've got to do something about it.'

'What?'

'What? There's loads of stuff we can do! Glasmaen Environmental Action Group. The Coven. The Women's Group. The entire Folk Festival!'

'Same people. They might be good at footpaths, but this is a lot more serious. What about your dad? Which side is he on?'

'God knows. My Dad's. Bryn Jones's. I wonder how much they've offered him.'

'Not forty thousand, you can bet that for a start. But, Sue, he always gives out this eco-awareness spiel, so maybe he doesn't realise ...'

'Oh, he'll know what they're up to. It doesn't go very deep with my dad, concern for other people's well-being. I should know. My poor mum knew.'

111

'Oh, Sue. Poor Sue.'

'Don't you 'poor Sue' me. She didn't fight back. I can. I will. I shall. If my father is threatening the lives of my babies by his selfish greed, then I'll murder the bastard.'

'Oh, Sue ...'

Sue burst into tears and sobbed and bawled and howled. Gareth clutched her to him until Berian woke up and had to be fed. When he came back to bed, Sue was fast asleep, lying across the middle of the bed. So as not to disturb her, Gareth spent another night on the sofa.

*　　*　　*

Ainee Sealfin walked straight down the shallow steps and into the stream which ran alongside Isaac's cottage. She knelt and washed her aching feet, rinsing off the dust and dirt caught on the delicate webs between her toes.

'Come on,' said Isaac, 'I want to take you to bed.'

Ainee stood in the stream and gazed up at the stars. The black traceries of branches latticed across the blue-black summer sky. The stars spangled the branches like tiny glowing lanterns. The glittering, many-coloured constellations outlined unicorns and queens, dancing across the Milky Way. The Pleiades revolved in their rhythmic circle. Cassiopeia tapped the branches with her foot, and Orion strode deathless and sworded across the horizon.

'Look!' cried Ainee, and pointed, as a shimmering cascade of golden-petalled silent flowers slid in slow arcs across the jewelled sky.

'Meteorites,' explained Isaac. 'Shooting stars. Falling lumps of burning rock.'

'Souls,' whispered Ainee. 'The souls of faerie falling, lost for eternity.'

'Which one's yours, then?'

Ainee swung round and stared up at him. She gave a sudden laugh. 'You expect me to tell you!' She turned to the sky again. 'I dance with my eleven sisters, of course. But not in this sky. No, far, far to the south and west. Dancing in a circle. Our last, glittering dance whilst you mortals destroy our palaces and forts and glades. Before long, we will be just another community of

112

sisters burnt up and finished. And now that you have chased
the faerie from the Earth, you are travelling out into the very
stars to destroy us there.'

'Not me,' said Isaac. 'I'm going to bed. Come on.' Reluctantly,
Ainee climbed out of the stream and followed him into the
house. Isaac was already lying in bed, and pulled her towards
him as her wet-hemmed dress slithered to the floor. Her hair
and skin gleamed in the candle-light.

'And I can tell you, Ainee Sealfin, that if – if – I am to take
you to the Folk Festival this weekend, you can forget about
singing and dancing and storytelling and making eyes at all the
other blokes, like you were doing today.'

'Why?'

'Why? Why! Because you're mine, Ainee, and mine only.'
Isaac ran his hands along the smooth curves of her shoulders
and neck. 'Aah …' he breathed, 'I do love you, Ainee. I love you
so much that I want to fold you up and tuck you safely away
inside my heart!'

Ainee's soulless dark brown gaze froze over with an ice-hard
glitter. 'Just as you have folded up and tucked away my sealskin
cap, denying me any choice of freedom?'

Isaac, resting on his elbow, looked at her for a long moment.
Then he caught her slender wrists in his large hands and rolled
over on top of her. 'Yes,' he hissed, his black brows furrowed.
'Yes, or I wouldn't have you here, now. And I will keep you.
That is my choice, my decision. Ainee, you're the only person,
the only thing in my life that's ever been precious to me.' Ainee
winced against the pain in her wrists. 'You're mine, Ainee Sealfin.
I love you. You're all that matters to me. I'll never let you go!'

His gaze dropped onto her whitened wrists; surprised, he released her. She rubbed the reddening marks silently. Isaac might
have begun to apologise, but any words fell as rough kisses
onto her cheeks and throat and breasts.

He did not see her eyes, glazed with black frost, as she glared
at the fiddle which hung like a sleeping bat on the wall at the
end of the darkening bedroom.

16

The morning of the first day of the Folk Festival dawned with a mist which had dissolved into another glowing summer's day by the time Keynes had finished breakfast. He spent several hours wandering in the cool shade of the Glyn woodland, but ventured no closer to the cottage than the green lawn. Sitting there, in the pool of dappled sunlight, he resolved to try to make his peace with Celia Llewelyn. He gathered a bouquet of the many tender wild flowers which embroidered the lawn, and set out for the village.

The surgery was held in a converted cottage with crisp white-painted doors and windows and a tidy recent thatch. In the waiting room, half a dozen villagers had been sitting chatting, breaking off to stare at Keynes in interested silence as he walked in. He felt extremely self-conscious and fumbled with the flowers.

The receptionist was an middle-aged woman with bright eyes and a professional frown. 'Can I help you, sir?'

Keynes hesitated. 'I have to see Dr Llewelyn.'

'When would you like an appointment?'

'I wouldn't. I'm not a patient. But I need to see her this morning.'

The receptionist waved her hand to indicate the number of other patients. 'Open surgery this morning, sir. You'll have to wait – oh, about an hour.'

Keynes frowned. He hadn't planned for this. He remembered his resolution to take action. 'My card. Dr Edward Keynes. Please ring through to Dr Llewelyn. I need to see her quickly, on a professional matter. It shouldn't take long.'

The receptionist glared at him. He glared back. The patients stared. Eventually, she reluctantly took the card. 'This is very irregular, Dr Keynes. But if it is a professional matter ...'

'It is.'

She dialled through and spoke in hushed tones over the phone.

Then she replaced the receiver. 'Dr Llewelyn will see you in a few moments, sir, if you'd like to take a seat.'

Keynes found a place on the end of a bench as two elderly men unwillingly edged up for him. 'Doctor,' one of them nodded as he indicated the seat. 'Nice bunch o' flowers.'

Keynes bowed his head in acknowledgement and checked his watch. Two minutes later, he checked it again. The waiting room was very hot with the windows closed, and he felt himself beginning to sweat. A few of the patients whispered amongst themselves. He wished that he had brought his briefcase, so as to look more businesslike. He checked his watch again. It was almost eleven.

Eventually the inner door opened and a very elderly lady shuffled out, bent over a walking frame. Celia held the door open for her and supported her to the front door. 'There you are, Mrs Evans. I'm very glad you've decided to take a stroll today, on this lovely morning. But you are sure that the minibus will meet you to take you back to Glasmaen House?'

'Oh, yes, dear,' croaked the old woman. 'They're picking me up outside the Golden Oak at one. Take me so long to get there it'll be opening time, and I'm looking forward to a drop of sherry!' She cackled with glee. 'They're bringing us down to see the procession tonight, n'all. Fireworks, they told us. That'll be nice. I likes fireworks.'

'Good for you, Mrs Evans. Enjoy yourself!' Celia smoothed the friendly smile from her face, and turned to Keynes. 'I can spare you five minutes, Dr Keynes.' As he stood up to follow her, he caught her glancing back to the waiting patients and spreading her hands in a gesture of helpless impatience. He thought it best not to comment.

Her consulting room was cool and fresh, with French windows opening on to a tiny, sunny patio bright with geraniums in pots. Framed prints of Monet's waterlilies hung on the mint-green walls. Her chair was arranged to one side of her desk, next to, rather than opposite, her patient's identical chair. The large Victorian desk was tidy, and garnished with several healthy-looking ferns in pots. Celia sat down and indicated the other chair to Keynes. She wore a spotless white silk blouse and a short silver-grey skirt. Keynes tried not to look at her legs as she crossed them.

115

'Yes?' she enquired, stiffly.

Keynes took a deep breath, and held out the bouquet to her. 'I've come to apologise. These are for you.'

She looked at him for several moments. 'So your wrist is better, Dr Keynes.'

He nodded. 'Edward, please. I feel the need to explain, but I'm not certain of the words.'

Celia took the flowers. 'Very nice. So, try to explain. I'm waiting.'

Keynes took another deep breath. 'It would take more than five minutes. Would you have dinner with me tonight?'

'So it was a chat-up line.'

Startled, Keynes sighed. 'I'm not sure, to be quite frank with you, but I do feel that I owe you an explanation.'

Celia was studying the bouquet with interest. She pointed to a frail, translucent flower. 'What's this one? I thought that I knew my wild flowers.'

Keynes peered at the flower. 'Oh, that one. I haven't found it in any of the books I've got. There are quite a few of these, growing on the edge of that green lawn in the Glyn where the stream curves round. I'd like to know what it is, too.'

Celia looked up at him again. 'I'll ask around. If I do have dinner with you, I'll want to know exactly what work you're doing around here.'

Keynes looked at her, then shrugged. 'Why not? I need to discuss the project with someone with good local knowledge. The Golden Oak at seven?'

Celia laughed scornfully. 'Amongst the Festival five thousand? I don't think so. St Briavel's Hotel, six-thirty. I don't want to miss the opening procession at nine.'

Keynes stood up. 'I shall look forward to it. Thank you for accepting.'

Celia nodded. She looked at her small gold watch. 'That's your five minutes up. Goodbye. Send in Mr Pettifer as you go out, please.' She turned back to shuffle the bundles of notes arranged on her desk.

* * *

116

Don Craven loped slowly down the track to Isaac's house at noon. He carried several old plastic bags stuffed full of the dresses which Ellen Sutherland had given to Ainee, and walked carefully past the verdant bushes because of the guitar slung over his shoulder.

Isaac and Ainee were sitting in a patch of dappled sunlight on the terrace. Ainee was curled up like a kitten, apparently asleep, whilst Isaac drew her. Her pale pink dress fell around her like the petals of a drooping rose. Isaac put down his charcoal stick and pad of paper when Don strolled across the slab-bridge, and watched him put down the bags and guitar and seat himself comfortably on the warm stone flags. Ainee eventually uncurled and stretched.

'Tired are you, Ainee?' Don asked.

Ainee yawned and stood up. 'He keeps waking me up,' she stated, coolly. 'Thank you for bringing my dresses.' She picked up the bags, and turned to walk into the house.

'You may as well put the kettle on whilst you're in there,' commanded Isaac. She made no response and disappeared inside.

'You ought to let the poor girl get some sleep,' grinned Don.

'Would you?' Isaac returned. Don passed him his tobacco tin, and they rolled up cigarettes. 'Finished the framing?' Isaac asked eventually.

Don nodded. 'Got any money? Thought I saw that Italian fancy boy give you an advance.'

Isaac fumbled in his trouser pocket and pulled out the roll of notes. He gave most of them to Don.

'Great! Now I can buy a few rounds this Festival! Here you are. Gareth gave me these two tickets for you and Ainee. He and Sue were having another set-to this morning. She's been cussing and swearing like a trooper. She reckons that her Dad is trying to buy the Glyn off you for sinister reasons. That true?'

Isaac exhaled smoke. 'I don't know about sinister. The old dog came down here the other day and offered me forty thousand quid for the Glyn. Selfish and cheapskate and daft, but not sinister.'

'So he didn't tell you what he plans to do with it, then?'

'Live here, I suppose. I might let him have it; I might not. Depends on whether Ainee wants to stay here or not, really.'

Don's eyebrows rose. 'You are serious about her, then!'

'Why not? She's special.'

'She is that. You know, I thought she was simple, until last night when she suddenly started to tell stories like a poet, and sing like an angel.'

'Simple, she is not.'

'She's a real mystery lady. Come on, where d'you find her? If she's really got eleven sisters, I want to meet them! That's the stuff of fantasy, man!'

Isaac shrugged. 'Tell me about this 'sinister' business that Sue's been on about.'

Don stood up, stretched, and pulled over a kitchen chair. He sat down and tipped the chair onto its back feet, stretching out his long denim-clad legs. 'Her dad wants to buy the Glyn back off you and then sell it to the Government.'

'Why?'

'To dump nuclear waste in.'

Isaac dropped his cigarette and sat up with a jolt. 'In the Glyn? I don't believe you.'

'Ask Sue. Ask Gareth. Ask Bryn Jones. Ask Celia Llewelyn. Ask that tall straight bloke with the flash car who's been hanging about all week. Ask the two guys who've been doing surveys for him all week – road access, Gareth reckons.'

'I nearly thumped that bloke last night. I would've if I'd known about this. Can't be true.'

'That bloke told Celia Llewelyn that the geology was just right, and that they'd be drilling in the Glyn. Dropping nuclear waste down shafts. They thought the place was uninhabited, so nobody'd make a fuss about them doing it.'

'No. That's all wrong. They can't. Anyway, I live here.'

'Not if you sell it to Bryn Jones.'

'I won't. But I can bet they've offered him a damn sight more than forty thousand for it.'

'I expect they have. He might not care about having nuclear waste in his back garden. He's the sort that'd rather have the money. But you can't sell it to them, Isaac.'

'Why not?' The voice was Ainee's. She handed round mugs of tea.

Don stared up at her. 'Because it's poison, Ainee. It'll poison the Glyn, Glasmaen, the valley, for thousands of years to come.'

'Poison how?'

'Don't you know anything? Poison! It'll get into the earth and the water and the air, and kill people, kill children. Painful, slow deaths: cancer, leukaemia. Kill fish, kill birds, kill animals. Farmers won't be able to sell their milk or meat or vegetables.'

'What is it, this poison?'

'Nuclear waste? Where have you been for the last fifty years? It's what's left over from making electricity in nuclear power stations. Impossible to get rid of.'

'But electricity seems to be a useful thing. Light, warmth, cooking, music, television, cinema.'

'Don't need it,' growled Isaac.

'You don't, but other people seem to find it useful,' observed Ainee.

'Well, it is useful. But there's other ways of making electricity, ways that don't poison the earth for ever more. Wind, wave power, hydro-electric, all sorts of ways. But the Government prefers to pay a fortune to build nuclear power stations, and then doesn't know what to do with the waste afterwards.'

'Then why do they want to put it here?'

Don shrugged. 'Quiet place, not many people to make a fuss about it. Cheap land. Right sort of rock for them to drill into.'

'Isaac?' Ainee looked at him. He had buried his face in his hands. 'Will you let them do this thing?'

Isaac slowly lowered his hands, and reached out for another cigarette. He rolled it slowly, and lit it, exhaling to watch the smoke twirl upwards amongst the trees. Eventually he lowered his eyes, and rested them on Ainee. 'What do you think about it, Ainee?' he asked quietly.

'I would need to know more about it. But I do know that you humans have been doing your best to poison the world for the last hundred years, in as many ways as you possibly can. I don't understand why you do it. You are all destroyers. You have almost destroyed my race, and almost destroyed the whales, and almost destroyed the seals and the dolphins, and now you want to destroy the world.'

Don whistled. 'Are you for real? I don't believe what you just said.'

Isaac ignored him. 'I haven't destroyed anything, Ainee. But

119

it's up to you if we stay here together, in the Glyn. If you want to go somewhere else, I'll take you. But this is my home, and I want it to be yours, too. You know that.'

'Go where? You won't let me go anywhere. You are holding me prisoner.'

'How is he holding you a prisoner, Ainee?'

'Shut up, Don. Piss off. This is between me and Ainee.'

'He keeps me prisoner. He has stolen me from my sisters. He has stolen my sealskin cap. He has hidden it inside his violin, and forbidden me to touch it. He has taken my body and my freedom and my future.'

'What is this? What are you talking about, Ainee? Who are you, anyway? Who is she, Isaac?'

'Shut up, Ainee. This is nothing to do with you, Don.' Isaac stood up, knocking over the mug of tea at his feet. The mug skidded across and smashed into the stream, leaving a trail of steaming yellow tea on the flagstones. 'It doesn't matter who she is.'

Ainee folded her arms sullenly. 'It matters very much who I am. Very much indeed.'

'Of course it does, Ainee. So who are you?'

'Shut up, Ainee. Don't tell him anything. Don't tell anyone anything. Get lost, Don.'

Don tipped his chair forward, tossed his cigarette butt into the stream, and stood up. 'What's going on? Come on, Isaac. We've been friends for years.'

Isaac's hands clenched into fists. 'No, we haven't.'

'Come on! We live in the same village, play in the same band. We've slept with the same women, for chrissake. You can tell me. I only came here to tell you some interesting gossip, and practice some duets with Ainee. She'll be a star turn at the Festival, you know.'

'No she won't. She's not going.'

'I am.'

'She will. Why shouldn't she?'

'Because it's too dangerous. She's too dangerous.'

Don grinned at Ainee. 'Ah, I get it. You don't want her to go, because she's so beautiful and talented that every man will want to steal her away from you. I know that I do. Come to the

Festival with me, Ainee. I'll show you how to have a good time.'

Isaac roared, and threw a punch at Don's jaw. Don yelped and flew backwards, tripped over and landed full length in the stream. He lay there moaning and coughing for several minutes before dragging himself to his feet and unsteadily wading towards the small stone steps rising to the terrace.

Isaac tore at his own hair and beard, then ran into the cottage, covering his face with his hands.

Ainee watched Don clamber onto the terrace, nursing his jaw. 'The bastard,' he muttered. He walked over to Ainee and stood before her, dripping. 'Come with me, Ainee.'

'Why?' As she waited for his answer, she reached up and, pushing his hand aside, laid her own hand gently on Don's jaw. She held it there for a moment, then dropped her hand to her side, continuing to gaze into his eyes.

'Hey! That feels better! You have a healing touch, Ainee Sealfin.'

Ainee nodded, and continued to wait.

'Come with me. Because I want you. Because you want me. Because it's the best way I can think of to make Isaac mad.'

'Those,' said Ainee solemnly, 'are not good reasons. Whether I go or stay, I will do so by myself, and in my own time. I shall not be the prisoner of another man. I will choose.'

'Fair enough. But what's this about being a prisoner?'

Ainee looked at him and her eyes were dark and soulless. 'That is an issue which rests between me and Isaac.'

'You have to be careful, Ainee. I'm supposed to be his oldest friend, and if he can thump me he can certainly thump you.'

Ainee shook her head. 'He will not do that. But soon, he may be driven to smash his own violin and so release me. Then we can discover the strength of our union, or its weakness. He is bound to me, just as I am bound to him.'

Don reached his arms out for Ainee, but she stepped back. 'Come on, girl, you were stroking my hair in the van the other night. I want you, and you want me.'

'Perhaps. But not just now. You should go now. I should offer Isaac some comfort, and some grief.'

'You'll drive him mad. You'll drive me mad. You are mad.'

Ainee shrugged, and turned away towards the cottage door.

Don watched her disappear inside and close the door behind her. Then he picked up his guitar and walked away, back up the track, careful to keep the instrument away from his wet clothes and the grasping foliage.

'She's mad. She's beautiful,' he muttered as he walked. 'Isaac's a fool. He doesn't deserve her. I do.' He glanced back down at the cottage, already half hidden by trees. 'There's one thing that's for sure. This will be a damned interesting Festival.'

17

Outside the surgery, Keynes, feeling pleased with himself for a change, wondered what to do next. He checked his watch. The pub might not be open for a while. Perhaps, he thought cautiously, it might be a good idea not to go to the Golden Oak yet; Richard Beavis should be given a chance to cool down after last night's fracas. Keynes felt a sudden wave of anger at the young man's impertinence. The situation had got entirely out of control; but perhaps the threat of a transfer to Saudi or Kuwait might bring the lad to his senses once he had spent time considering the drawbacks.

Keynes also suspected that at Head Office his own recommendation for transferring an employee might not be treated with the weight it deserved. His position with the Department had been uncertain ever since his return from Riyadh in the Spring. He remembered, with a slight surprise, how angry he had been at the posting to rural Wales only a week ago. What a week it had been!

Perhaps he should go and see Isaac Talboys and find out the true situation with the Glyn? Keynes dismissed this thought rapidly. The artist had threatened him with violence, for no particular reason, only twelve hours ago. Keynes felt rather afraid of Isaac Talboys, the man who possessed such a desirable residence and such a remarkable young woman. Whatever had she done to his wrist? He winced in memory of the pain which she had so suddenly smoothed away. He had been certain that his wrist was broken, and Celia had seemed to confirm that opinion. Keynes shook his head in puzzlement.

He looked about. He had become aware of a great deal of traffic on the usually quiet road. Several camper vans and a number of cars laden high with camping gear had passed him, heading for the village. All these people must be going to the Folk Festival. Keynes was uncertain about what this festival might involve. He vaguely recollected seeing television news coverage of dreadful open-air rock festivals in the sixties and seventies; young people sprawling drunken and half-naked over one another, taking drugs and rioting. Hell's Angels dressed in filthy leather motorcycle gear stabbing each other and fighting. Neglected children wading in acres of mud. He shuddered. Was a folk festival any different?

But the music last Saturday had been pleasant enough, and last night's folk club had been enjoyable, despite the personal problems which he had encountered. The audience had appeared to be a reasonable enough crowd of intelligent and friendly people. There had obviously been an understood rota system for performers, and everyone had seemed to know everyone else. Bryn Jones, whilst personally unappetising, had seemed to be quietly in control of proceedings. Perhaps he should go and see Bryn Jones, and try to sort out the misunderstanding about the ownership of the Glyn?

No, perhaps not. Bryn Jones had specifically named Tuesday for an appointment. He was obviously deeply involved in organising this folk festival, so he would be too busy during the weekend. Anyway, Beavis and Ferris would be around, helping out. If Beavis had the grace to help out, that was.

Keynes looked up at Bryngaran Hill, and decided to walk up and see the famous stones. The view would be interesting, anyway. He set off, back towards St. Briavel's Hotel, and eventually turned up a lane signposted to 'Arthur's Circle'. The lane was steep and narrow and overgrown with summer foliage, which shaded it from the heat of the sun.

A sunbleached heathland spread out across the summit, with patches of tall bracken already turning brown along the edges of the fronds. A few trees were stunted and twisted by the wind. Even on such a hot, still day there was a faint breeze across the heath and the air was cool and fresh.

Arthur's Circle rose from the very crown of Bryngaran Hill like a ring of jagged teeth. The nine stones were all upright, although several leaned at drunken angles. A simple wooden fence enclosed the site. Keynes clambered over the stile.

Approaching the stones, Keynes shivered slightly. He realised that he had never visited any megaliths before, not even Stonehenge. He had always avoided the sites associated with cranky, unscientific mysticism. But whoever built this, for whatever mysterious reason, had certainly picked an impressive location. He stood outside the ring of stones, and looked around at the breath-taking view.

To the East, the lush plains and pasture of England spread out like a counterpane, patchworked with hedgerows and fields speckled with grazing cattle. To the West rose the Black Mountains, steep and massy with dark green conifers.

The valley ran between these two worlds like a miniature version of both. The river gleamed and twisted its way alongside the silvery willows and rowan trees of Wales. Towards England, gentle slopes rose towards Bryngaran Hill, sprinkled with cottages and farmhouses, roofed with silver-grey slate or the golden hues of thatch. Gazing around, Keynes could identify one, two, three, no, many castles; he could see the towers and spires of dozens of churches, right over to the cathedral in Hereford. A sense of living history slid over his shoulders like a heavy cloak. This land was alive, and ancient, and inexpressibly beautiful.

'Oh,' Keynes spoke aloud. 'This is home. I want to come and live here.'

As he spoke, he stepped forward into the ring of stones and his hand brushed against the largest. An electric tingle shot down his arm as though he had knocked the humerus. Astonished, he cautiously touched the grey mass again, and felt a trembling sensation emanating from the rock. A week ago Keynes would have refused to believe the evidence of his senses, but now he felt a glow of well-being filter through his body, and smiled. He walked deeper into the circle and stretched out his arms as though to embrace the friendly warmth which surrounded him. Then he glanced down, and saw that in the very heart of the stone ring lay a circle of scorched earth. The bonfire which he had noticed a week ago! On Midsummer's Eve; wasn't that the solstice night? Keynes realised that the mysterious white-robed dancers around the bonfire must have been sensing an eerie pleasure, like the one which he felt now. He had hardly wished to believe his eyes then, but now he could acknowledge some primeval 'rightness' in dancing with friends on such an occasion, in such an extraordinary place.

Keynes turned slowly around, looking up at the nine stones.

On top of each one was balanced a small lump. Peering, he identified bread rolls. He laughed aloud. One of the rolls had fallen off. He walked over and picked it up. It was rock-hard and partially pecked by birds. He solemnly lifted it and replaced it on top of its stone.

'A gift,' he whispered to himself. 'A tribute to the ageless beauty of this place.'

Keynes strolled easily around the circle, smiling at himself. How could he have changed so much in a week? This valley had laid an enchantment on him. And more; the Glyn itself had enthralled him. He giggled aloud to find himself using such poetical images.

'But I don't want to spoil it,' he realised suddenly. 'I'm not going to let them drill in the Glyn, and I'm not going to let them dump nuclear waste there. I have devoted most of my tedious, dull, lonely life to drilling holes and to concealing radioactive poison in one place or another around the world. I don't want to do that any more. I have savings. I'll sell my flat in Cambridge. I'll buy that cottage in the Glyn, and I'll live in it, and study wild flowers and be happy. Maybe I'll even get married one day. Perhaps to Celia, or ... Maybe I'll start a family! Maybe I'll be happy ...'

Keynes was suddenly aware that he had spoken aloud. The nine stones stood silently around him, and he realised that he had just made a vow to them. He was standing beside the largest stone, and he laid his hand on it again, enjoying the tingling through his palm. 'I will,' he whispered. 'I will do it. I'll change my life.'

*　*　*

As soon as Bryn Jones saw Sue Hopkins-Jones marching towards him over the grass, shoving Berian's push chair before her like a battering-ram, he knew that he was in for trouble. He glanced about, seeking an escape route, but Sue was too quick for him. In her sergeant-major voice, she yelled 'Bryn Jones, I want to talk to you!' and he was unable to slink away.

'Sue, my darling, how lovely to see you! And dear little Berian as well! What a pleasure! How is everything going at the ticket office?'

Sue folded her arms and frowned grimly. 'And just what, I'd like to know, is this plan of yours to buy back the Glyn and sell it again ?'

Bryn Jones shuffled his feet. 'Oh, you've heard about that, have you? My, my, isn't this village one for gossiping about things which don't concern it?'

'Most rumours in this village have started with you, as you know perfectly well. But this particular gossip concerns the village, and myself, very much indeed.'

'Oh, yes? And how might it do that then, Sue?'

'Don't you start acting the mystified innocent with me. I know you far too well, much to my grief. Tell me what you're up to.'

'Oh, just a little financial transaction which will be greatly to the benefit of all concerned, particularly you, my dear.'

'Why me?'

'As my heiress and the mother of my beloved grandchildren, of course. I'm just gathering up a comfortable little inheritance to pass on to those I love most in the world.'

'Don't talk rubbish. We don't want your dirty money, and we never will.'

'Oh, Sue! How can you be so unkind to me! What would your dear mother have said?'

'Don't you, of all people, ever tell me what my mother would have said. You never listened to her when she was alive, and now you have no right to talk about her in that way.'

Bryn Jones stepped back, visibly shocked, and allowed small tears to well in his eyes. 'Sue, Sue. How can you say this to me? Me, of all people? I've worked so hard all my long life to make things comfortable for you.'

Sue laughed scornfully. 'Worked hard, indeed! Written a few filthy books and sold off everything you could at extortionate rates, just to please your miserly self.'

'Now, then, Sue, I'm beginning to get a little bit angry. Think of all the things I've done for this village – organising the folk club and this wonderful festival, repairing the church tower, building you that marvellous new school hall – and I did that at your suggestion, my dear, if you care to recall …'

'Bullshit. You did all that for your own self-glorification, and certainly not for any worthwhile reasons.'

'Susan! Your language!' Bryn Jones sighed and rolled his eyes. 'Oh, if only you'd been born a boy. You'd have made such a splendid, forthright man. As it is, you seem barely capable of doing the little tasks which fall to a woman's lot. It's a good thing, I suppose, that you married that wet little wimp of a husband of yours, so that he can do all your childcare and housekeeping while you strut about shouting at your school-children like a martinet, and pretending to run your ineffectual little women's group. Look at yourself! You look a complete mess. Pink hair? Is that your sole contribution to femininity? You're an embarrassment and a disgrace to the good name of Jones.'

Sue gaped, turned white, and burst into tears.

'And now you're getting hysterical. Why don't you go and do some womanly little job, like feeding and changing your neglected baby?' Bryn Jones grimaced at Berian, who also burst into tears. 'There, he needs your attention. Run along now, while I get along with doing the important things at this festival. I can't waste my precious time chatting to you about nothing in particular.'

Jones sauntered away, leaving Sue none the wiser and a great deal angrier. She pivoted the pushchair about and pounded away to disrupt the ticket-office duty which Gareth had been managing quite efficiently.

* * *

Isaac Talboys lay curled up in a huddle on the far corner of the bed, his head hidden under his arms. His body occasionally shuddered. Ainee stood watching him silently until she spoke in a low soothing voice. 'Isaac, I am willing to forgive you. I had not intended to cause you such pain.' She slid off her pink dress and climbed onto the bed, kneeling beside her lover. She began to softly stroke his thick black hair where it straggled over his shoulder.

Eventually, Isaac seemed to relax, and then he suddenly rolled over and buried his head in her smooth lap, nuzzling her belly. Her skin smelt vaguely of warm honey and lemon juice, with a tang of salt. He stretched out his arms and wrapped them tightly around her waist.

After a while, she gently prised his face away and bent down to kiss his tear-stained cheeks. She ran her tongue along his clenched eyelids, tasting the salt and flicking the crushed eyelashes straight again. She kissed his mouth, and he raised his lips to hers thirstily, as though to drink in the warmth of her affection. She noticed that he held his right hand painfully, and she paused to unfurl his fist and stretch out his long fingers between her palms. She drew out the bruised soreness from his knuckles and then kissed his fingertips, one by one. He opened his eyes warily, surprised at the disappearance of the pain, and flexed his fingers. His eyes were streaked with reddened veins like marbling, but his pupils began to glitter again as he looked up into the brown depths of her eyes.

'I love you, Ainee Sealfin,' he whispered unsteadily. She nodded and kissed his brow. He held her closer and pulled her down to lie next to him. 'I love you.'

'Isaac,' murmured Ainee, 'why did you never marry?' Isaac shrugged and wrapped his arms around her. 'I suppose I could have done, but I've enjoyed living alone – until you.'

Ainee shook her head, and repeated her question.

Isaac twisted slightly until a veil of her hair lay across his face. It smelt faintly of the sea, of ozone and salt and seaweed and the wind from the ocean.

'What woman would live here with me?' he asked in a whisper. 'Women these days want material things, carpets and washing machines and fancy cookers. All I can offer them is what their grandmothers rejected.'

'And passion ...' added Ainee.

Isaac stared up at her through the glistening fronds of her hair. 'Will you stay with me, Ainee Sealfin?' he paused and swallowed. 'Will you marry me? Will you live with me for ever? Will you give me kisses, and children, and ... and happiness?'

Ainee smiled. 'Will I, or shall I, or should I, or can I? That is a difficult question, Isaac. That is many questions.'

He continued to stare at her. 'Okay,' he said eventually. 'Ainee Sealfin, do you love me?'

She smiled again. 'Often!' she replied. She kissed him on the mouth again, her hair rough between their lips and the tips of their tongues.

He lay in silence for a while. 'Ainee Sealfin, will you stay with me?'

She smiled and shook her head, her hair sweeping clear from his face. 'In that, I have no choice.' She laid her silky cheek against his bearded jaw.

'Should I give you that choice?' he mused. 'If I give you back your sealskin cap, won't you just slide away into the stream, then the river, then the ocean, and be gone forever?'

'I may.' She turned her head and licked his ear lobe, nibbling it between her small sharp teeth. She paused and whispered into his ear: 'But then, I may not. How can I tell, until I have the choice?'

Isaac sighed, a long, deep, slow sigh. 'I've done yet another stupid thing. I can't get your sealskin cap out of my fiddle without breaking the damn thing.' His eyes glittered as she continued to breathe into his wet ear. 'You, Ainee Sealfin, are nothing but trouble and anguish, and violence too. I've been a peaceful man for many years, if a lonely one. Yet last night I almost thumped a stranger because of you, and today I thumped one of my best friends because of you, and now I'm contemplating smashing my most precious possession into matchsticks, because of you. You bring out the worst in me. You make me feel greedy, and selfish, and guilty.'

He stretched his right hand in the air above Ainee's shoulder. 'Although I did think I'd broken some of my knuckles on Don's chin, and wouldn't be able to play or to paint again, but you seem to have cured that. So perhaps my hands are more precious.' He ran his hand along Ainee's curving spine, then clutched her close to him. 'No, you are, my mystical, magical maiden-no-more. You are more precious to me than my home, or my music, or my art, or perhaps my heart and my sanity. Oh, you are so lovely ...'

Ainee tilted her pale oval face towards him, and opened her eyes wide; they were liquid and sparkling, like deep pools of clear moonlit water. 'Isaac ...' she said softly. 'Give me the choice.'

Isaac gazed into the depths of her eyes; he could not see his own reflection there. He felt his stomach contract with some emotion between fear and dizziness. Her eyes were like dark tunnels, down which he was falling ... floating ... flying ...

'After the festival,' he promised. 'I need the fiddle to play music for you to dance and sing, Ainee Sealfin, because you're a star, a real star, a jewel sparkling in an elusive heaven. I will keep you as mine through the festival; but I'll try to be gentler, kinder to you. And after the festival, I'll break open the fiddle and give you back your choice.' He sighed deeply. 'But until then, Ainee, you're mine, mine to have and to hold for three days more.'

And Isaac rolled Ainee beneath him as he pulled off his clothes and kissed and licked her arching body with all the passion and tenderness he could offer.

18

Don Craven stepped inside the open caravan door where Gareth was selling tickets for the Folk Festival. Gareth handed over a set of camping vouchers to three wise-cracking hikers from Birmingham and wished them enjoyment of the Festival, before turning round to greet Don.

'Hiya, Don! Can of beer?'

Don sniffed inside the large coolbag before opening one for himself and handing one to Gareth. 'Thought you might like company, stuck out here by yourself. But it's quite restful, really. Where's Sue?'

Gareth shrugged. 'Oh, she's gone home to give the kids their tea and an early bedtime. I'm enjoying the peace and quiet. She's had a row with her dad.'

Don grinned. 'Well overdue, isn't it?'

Gareth shook his head. 'It's me that she takes it out on. I love Sue – even if I have trouble remembering the fact now and then, and she's been giving me a damn hard time recently. You ought to get serious, Don; married life is hard work, but it has its rewards.'

'I'm glad to hear it, coming from you. As for me, I'll get serious when I get the right girl. I'm fed up of a bachelor life. Anyway, how's ticket sales going?'

'Oh, with luck the festival ought to break even and maybe make a profit for a change, if the weather stays as good as it is now.'

Don sipped from his can whilst Gareth sold more tickets to a pair of excited middle-aged parents shepherding five gawky teenage girls like sheepdogs with their flock.

'Gareth,' he announced once the family had departed for the camp site, 'speaking of rows, I just broke the latest news to Isaac.'

'Oh, yeah? I want to hear about that. Hang on a minute.' Gareth broke off to answer questions from potential customers. 'What did he say about this plan to dump nuclear waste in his private valley?'

Don scowled. 'Hard to tell with that miserable bastard. He reckons that he knew nothing beyond your charming father-in-law trying to buy the Glyn back off him for peanuts. But Isaac seems to be incapable of making any decisions without the say-so of the delicious Ainee Sealfin. You won't believe this, but he thumped me and knocked me right into the stream, just because I was chatting her up a bit! She's really got under his skin. What a stunner, although she's weird, all right. I can't tell whether she's for real, or lying, or scheming, or just plain insane. I never met anyone like her before.'

Gareth grinned. 'No, I don't think any of us have. Oh, hang on. Five tickets, name of Carter? Here you are. Thank you very much!'

Don drained his can, throwing it onto the floor. 'You're too busy, Gareth. I'm off. I'm on stewarding duty at six, so I'll go and have an hour's kip. See you later!'

'Okay, Don. Keep away from Sue if you see her; she needs a chance to cool down. Ah, the Scrattingby Mummers! We've been looking forward to your arrival! I didn't recognise you without your blacking. Here's your seven, no, eight performers' tickets.'

Don swung himself out of the caravan door and sauntered away towards his cottage, avoiding the queue which was beginning to form outside the caravan window from which Gareth leaned and smiled and collected money.

*   *   *

Dr Edward Keynes was sitting in the dappled shade of the unkempt rose arbour outside St. Briavel's Hotel, feeling rather smug. By the deft application of ten-pound notes to the greasy palms of the manager, the chef, and the young lad with fuzzy cropped hair who was acting as waiter that evening, he had managed to persuade the staff to carry out a dining table and two chairs into the garden.

The table was attractively laid with a thick white linen cloth and heavy silver cutlery which had been discovered in a cupboard somewhere. There was thin white-and-gold bone china from the surly manager's flat. The array of crystal glasses sparkled since the chef had brought out a polishing cloth and a bowl of hot water to steam them with. Keynes had personally selected several sprays of tiny pearl-pink roses; these cascaded from a silver-plated vase. Thick stiff napkins stood furled on the side plates, and a bottle of overpriced champagne was chilling in an ice bucket on a stand by Keynes's chair. The table had been prevented from wobbling by the insertion of broken beer mats beneath its feet, but you couldn't expect perfection, Keynes generously decided.

Keynes was dressed in his dinner jacket and white silk shirt, to which he had rather daringly added a dark red paisley silk bow-tie, handkerchief and cummerbund which had caught his eye in one of Abergavenny's gentlemen's outfitters. He had tucked a small spray of the tiny roses into his buttonhole. He had shaved carefully, and had added a few drops of expensive aftershave to his chin. He felt cool, relaxed, and comfortable as he sipped his dry sherry and admired the gardens, the table, and himself.

He had, of course, never done such an outrageously romantic thing before in his life. But after all his new resolutions during the last few days, he felt willing to be bold and daring for the first time ever, and, he smiled to himself, the fascinating Celia Llewelyn was well worth the risk.

Celia arrived, only ten minutes late, after being redirected from the hotel bar. Keynes, suddenly anxious, stood up and bowed before drawing out her chair for her. 'You look charming, Dr Llewelyn,' he observed sincerely as she sat down, spreading her full skirts around the chair.

Celia was rather taken aback at all this splendour, and unsure of her own response. She did discover that she was pleased that she had dressed with more care than she had originally intended. She wore a white lace and silk blouse and a circular skirt of dark crimson taffeta, nipped in with a wide black belt at her waist. Her bob of black hair gleamed, and she wore a trace of translucent deep pink lipstick.

'This is all very unexpected, Dr Keynes,' she remarked as he opened the champagne with a low 'pop'. 'But rather pleasant, I must admit.' She lifted her glass of pale gold champagne as its froth settled. 'A toast?' she enquired.

Before he could reply, a pair of swifts shot past his head, shrieking, and the shock made him cry out and drop his glass. Celia caught it deftly just before it rolled off the edge of the table, and shook out her napkin to mop Edward's sleeve dry. He mumbled in confusion as she reached out and refilled his glass.

'Devil birds,' she announced.

Keynes stared. 'I'm not certain whether that would be a suitable toast,' he said slowly. 'Although there does seem to be a lot of that sort of thing going on around here ...'

Celia paused, then laughed. Her laugh was rare, crisp and bright. 'No,' she replied eventually, 'that's the country name for swifts, because of that dreadful screaming noise they make. See, here they come again. Protecting their territory, you see.'

Keynes sighed. 'There seems to be a lot of that around here, too. This is really the most peculiar place I've spent any time in, you know, and Jeddah and Kuwait are pretty strange.'

Celia gave him an assessing look. 'You back recently?'

Keynes nodded. 'For good, I'm afraid. They've closed down my branch of operations over there, and I suspect that they're not sure what to do with me over here. Forty's too young for early retirement, and my field has always been very specialised, so they want to hang on to me. I hope.'

'What exactly are you doing in Glasmaen, then?'

'Ah,' Keynes topped up the glasses and hurriedly took a deep swig. 'Buying land, officially. But they should have sent a diplomat, not a physicist. It's all become very complicated.'

'Yes, the Glyn. Isaac Talboy's valley. Suitable geology, and out-of-the-way.'

Keynes stared. 'Did I tell you all that?' His recollection of the previous evening had become rather blurred.

'Oh yes, and how you were unsure of whether he or Bryn Jones actually owns the place. I can see the problem.'

Whilst Keynes fumbled with his memory, the scruffy young waiter deposited dishes of prawn cocktail on the table and sauntered away again.

'I'm sorry about the food,' muttered Keynes. He had forgotten about planning a menu. 'I just asked them for the best they had. I've not had prawns for fifteen years or so, living in Muslim states. I hope it's all right.'

'Not for a vegetarian,' said Celia firmly, setting her dish aside. 'Never mind. So why exactly are you drilling in the Glyn?' Her eyes glittered, and she smiled winningly. 'Dumping nuclear waste, isn't it?'

Keynes paled. 'Did I tell you that?'

Celia reached over and stroked the back of his right hand soothingly as he clutched the champagne glass tightly.

'Well, it's obvious, isn't it? When do you plan to start operations?'

Keynes's hand shook and he unwillingly withdrew it. 'Oh, not for years. Decades. Possibly never. We have a policy of purchasing suitable sites – we've got lots. This is just another one, a small one at that. But we do try to keep our actions quiet.'

'Oh, I can understand that. 'Not in my back yard' and all that. Anyway, I have some news for you. Did you pick my bouquet locally?'

'Yes … I'm sorry about that, but the nearest decent florist is in Abergavenny. Anyway,' Keynes added, 'I like wild flowers. I don't know much about them, but there seems to be a wonderful variety around here.'

'Oh, yes,' Celia agreed, 'and one of the ones you brought me is extremely rare. A protected species, in fact.'

Keynes frowned. 'Does that mean illegal to pick?'

Celia nodded. 'Don't worry, I won't tell. But I showed it to an amateur botanist friend of mine and she was astonished. It was the little pale flower with the translucent stem. A ghost orchid. Last seen in the Border Counties in 1910. What do you think of that?'

'But that's extraordinary!' gasped Keynes. 'Is it important?'

'Scientifically? Oh, yes. It means that wherever you found it will have to be declared an 'SSSI', a site of special scientific interest. Heavily protected, of course. Certainly protected from drilling …'

Keynes sat back, aghast. 'But this is terrible!'

'No, it's not,' Celia said sweetly. 'It's a wonderful discovery, and all the botanists will be ever so excited.'

As Keynes tried to absorb this unwelcome information the waiter cleared away their untouched plates and replaced them with gammon and vegetables. He only noticed the food after the waiter had gone. 'Oh, no!' he cried, 'you can't eat this, either. I'll call him back.'

Celia hushed him. 'I'll eat the pineapple and the vegetables.'

Keynes forked the limp pink mass on his plate. 'I don't think I can eat this, either. Pork. Something else I haven't missed for fifteen years.'

They nibbled at the vegetables in silence for a while.

'How many people know about this flower?' he asked suddenly.

Celia reached the bottle out of the cooler and poured out the last glassfuls. 'Oh, you, me, my botanist friend ... but she may have told her friends by now.'

'I bet she has,' replied Keynes sourly. 'I don't suppose we can keep it quiet, then.'

'No, I don't suppose so. I mean, people will want to know about this. It's not as though we were covering up dumping nuclear waste in an unspoilt corner of rural Wales, after all, is it? This deserves some real publicity, doesn't it? The front page of the *Guardian*, the letters page of the *Times*, that sort of thing?'

Keynes stared at her over the rim of his glass. There was a long silence. 'You don't approve of the nuclear industry, then, I take it?' he asked coldly.

Celia smiled. 'And you do?'

'Well, of course I do ... I've worked in it for most of my life. People need electricity, and if you think the alternatives are better, then perhaps you should have seen what a burning oilfield after the Gulf conflict was like. Do you realise how much pollution is given off by burning fossil fuels? That would show you just how much. You can't breathe for fifty miles in any direction. Or maybe you should go down a coal mine in South Africa, where the cheapest coal is mined, and see how cost-cutting endangers lives by reducing safety standards. I was terrified down there, you know. The heat, the dust ...the stink of sweat and coal and gas ... the cracking noises from the vast weight of the earth over your head. And the black workers do twelve to eighteen-hour shifts down there. Constant reports of cave-ins and explosions, men killed, that I don't suppose you would read in the local papers in Glasmaen. But you all still want the electricity.' He emptied his glass.

'Isaac Talboys doesn't,' put in Celia, softly.

Keynes shuddered. 'I expect he prefers wild flowers to power for the people. Ugh, that sounds like a song from the sixties.'

'There's a lot of people left over from the sixties around here. Or hadn't you noticed?' enquired Celia sweetly.

The waiter had rematerialised. He gazed at the gammon steaks hungrily as he cleared the plates, replacing them with enormous slices of chocolate gâteau.

'Wait! Another bottle of champagne ... or would you prefer coffee?' Keynes added lamely. Celia preferred coffee, so he ordered a potful. They poked at their gateaux in silence. The coffee arrived and was clumsily poured out. The waiter sloped away, grinning, probably to eat the leftover prawns and gammon.

'I'm sorry this dinner turned out to be so unpleasant,' said Keynes slowly. 'I meant it to make amends after that business last night.'

'I know you did,' said Celia kindly. 'But perhaps you could let me order my own own food another time.' Keynes sat bolt upright. 'Another time! You mean ...'

'I mean that I appreciate the effort that you've gone to, Edward. It's not every day that I'm invited to dine and drink champagne with a charming, intelligent man in a rose garden. The food may not have been perfect, but the evening has been very interesting so far.'

'Oh,' said Keynes. He was unsure of what to say next.

'Shall you be going to the Folk Festival?'

Keynes shrugged. 'I expect so. I don't really know what it's all going to be about.'

Celia consulted her small gold watch. 'The procession starts soon. Can I give you a lift down there?'

'Oh, yes! That's very kind ... but I shall have to change.' Keynes glanced down at his dinner suit. 'This is probably not the most suitable outfit ...'

'Oh, I don't know!' Her eyes twinkled wickedly. 'I think you look wonderful!'

Keynes suddenly felt deeply suspicious of her. Was she trying to make a fool of him, planning to hold him up to public ridicule? He felt a sharp wave of anger.

'I'll change. It should take a few minutes. If you want to drive down now, I'll walk down once I've dressed. I'll see you down there.' Stiffly, he accompanied her to her car, and held the door as she sat down and scooped her full skirts in around her.

'Thank you for a lovely dinner, Edward,' she smiled up at him. 'You've been very kind.'

'Thank you for accepting my invitation, Dr Llewelyn.'

'Celia,' she insisted.

'Celia. I don't suppose you could keep quiet about … our talk … at least until I have contacted Head Office?'

She smiled again, and pulled the door to. He stared at her through the open car window. Her dark eyes sparkled with merriment. 'We'll see!' she whispered, and turned the key in the ignition. She reversed gracefully around the crackling gravel drive and vanished through the gateway, one hand waving briefly over her shoulder.

Keynes glowered and hunched his shoulders.

'Ghost orchid, indeed,' he muttered as he turned toward the hotel. A sour taste rose in his throat. He glanced about, seeing no one as he spat surreptitiously into a bush. 'Women,' he muttered. 'They're all out to trick you.'

He sighed deeply, and walked quickly up to his room to change his clothes.

19

The dusk was darkening as the sun slid behind the Welsh mountains. The sky spread a glow of amber and saffron, fading to a
clear, dark star-sprinkled blue. Drifting over the hubbub of the
people lining the road, a faint strain of music could be heard in
the distance. The crowd hushed, and lifted their faces towards it
as though it were a delicious fragrance.

'They're coming!' hissed Gwen Orgee, nudging Keynes. She
wore a shapeless cardigan over a loose print dress. A little girl
clung to her left arm, yawning, and a sullen small boy dangled
by her side. 'The procession. Now you'll see summat, Totterikins!
The Nine Grey Men of Glasmaen!'

A flicker of torchlight appeared over the heads of the watchers.
The flaming wood-and-tar torches were carried by tall figures
dressed in flowing white robes. Streamers made from torn strips
of white cloth fell around their heads and over their sombre faces
from crowns of green leaves. They chanted unintelligible words
in a passionless timbre as they advanced with a slow, sliding
step.

'They're white, not grey, and some of them are women,' corrected Keynes.

Gwen shushed him. 'Not them, they'm the Thirteen Torch
Bearers, hen. Look!'

Surrounded by the ring of white figures, a line of strange
silent creatures emerged from the smoky darkness. They were
dressed in thick grey smocks over grey trousers. Heavy boots
revealed the old leather where the grey paint had cracked and
scuffed away. Steel toe caps struck white sparks from the road
as they tramped. Each wore a grey felt hat pulled low over his
face. Each face was so heavily daubed with thick grey mud that
the eyes, nostrils and open mouths had become dark holes.
Their hats bore great wreaths of mingled fresh, dried and plastic
flowers.

Their leader was enormous, a great bear-like hulk who swag-
gered from side to side across the road, threatening the watchers

with vast mud-streaked fists. He wore an ancient wooden mask, the brows and cheeks formed from flat carved leaves, painted in chipped grey-green. Wooden vines coiled out from his mouth, from which also lolled a large red tongue. His wreath was a thick tangle of glossy mistletoe.

The Nine Grey Men walked with a stylised lumbering march in time to the flat chant, placing each booted foot down with a leaden clump. They swung broad stooped shoulders and clenched fists, and each expressionless grey face was set towards the heels of the preceding dancer. They seemed burdened with the weight of centuries. They were more like a funeral cortège than a troupe of dancers.

'That's my old man Davy near the front,' hissed Gwen, pride in her voice.

'What, that huge man in a mask?'

'Naah, that's Spike Price. Allus has to be the biggest man in the village. And that's my lad Wayne at the back, I reckon.' She peered at the column of figures. 'You can't really tell o'course, what with them muddy faces. That's part of it, I expect.'

Keynes smiled stiffly down at Gwen's youngest son under his elbow. 'Will you be in the Grey Men when you're old enough?' he enquired.

The small boy frowned and scuffled his feet.

Gwen looked down sadly at her son. 'No, my Darren was born in the Cottage Hospital. Yes, and you, Jenny. They has to be born in Glasmaen to get in the Grey Men. My fault, really. But I feels sorriest for Grace, mind; she's not got no sons to carry on the name of Mortimer. I knows she frets. Mebbe them Morris Men can do summat for her!'

Keynes was embarrassed. 'Have these Grey Men been around for a long time?' He watched the next team of dancers go by, a jolly bouncing Morris side of bearded men with bells strapped to their calves. They skipped and cavorted to a brisk little tune played on a pipe held in one hand by a man beating a small drum with the other.

'Oh, bless you, for ever. Well, not since the Great War, mind. All of the Nine Grey men was shot in the trenches. Bryn Jones it was got 'em started up again, twenty year or so ago.'

Keynes was shocked. 'Nine? From a village as small as this? That's terrible.'

'Nine and more. You ask Vin Goldhanger to show you the War Memorial next time you're in the Golden Oak. Ooh, look at them lovely 'broidered tabards. Grace'd like them. She'm a dab hand at fancy work like that.'

'A war memorial in a pub?'

'Oh, yes. You jus' look.'

Keynes considered for a few minutes, as he watched a team of six pretty ladies jiggle by, swirling their lacy petticoats. They held beribboned hoops high over their heads, framing their faces with a ring of flowers and satin bows. 'Do the Nine Grey Men have anything to do with the nine stones in Arthur's Circle?'

Gwen grinned. 'You got it. Nine stones, Nine Grey Men. And the big 'un's King Arthur hisself.'

'Did they just march all the way from the Circle down the hill to the Castle?'

'Oh, yes. Sweaty work an' all. Ooh, look at them Ruskies! Them girls is as pretty as a picture. D'you reckon that their hair is real? And more 'broidery for Grace to see!'

A coiling line of Russian dancers was advancing, led by a graceful row of tall, smiling blonde girls hand-in-hand. They wore long red and gold dresses, thick with lavish embroidery, over which broad flat plaits of yellow hair fell to the hems of their aprons. On their heads they wore towering crowns of white and silver. They were exquisitely beautiful, as alike as matched gems in a necklace. The girls at either end held torches aloft, and the light from the dancing flames sparkled over their costumes.

'Ooh, you wait until my Davy spots them! They look like a cross between page three of the *Sun* and a weddin' cake! Mind you, them lads is a bit of alright, as well! Look at 'em springing about! Hey, what's that Rusky word they have in the papers these days?'

'*Glasnost*,' replied Keynes.

To the hectic strumming of balalaikas, the Russian youths leapt and twirled, whooping and shrieking. The audience clapped and shouted. As a young man with yellow curls bounded past, Gwen dropped her daughter's hand and leaned forward. She caught the youth by the arm, and shouted 'glasnoss!' in his ear. He grinned, and gave her a smacking kiss on the cheek before spinning away.

'Ooh, wait till I tell my Davy that a Rusky kissed me!' Gwen glowed with pleasure. Her torchlit face was almost pretty, thought Keynes.

As the last dance troupe and band passed them, the audience joined the end of the procession. Gwen gathered in her children and Keynes, and they strolled up the long ramp towards the castle gate.

'I went up to Arthur's Circle the other day,' Keynes remarked cautiously. 'There were the scorch marks of a large bonfire right in the middle of the circle. And someone had balanced a bread roll on top of each of the stones! Obviously, some had fallen off, and they were soggy, and had been pecked by birds, but it seemed to be a very peculiar thing to do to a historical monument.'

'Loaves, not bread rolls,' corrected Gwen absently. 'The Stones needs feeding, jus' like you or me. Now you hold my hand, Jenny, I don't want you wanderin' off. You better ask one o' them Thirteen about that sort of thing. I don't know nuffink. C'mere, Darren, before I gets 'ee. Now where's them tickets?'

Keynes trailed behind her into the castle grounds, where she showed her tickets to the stewards with electric torches at the gate. They directed Keynes to a small caravan parked on one side of the road, where he hurriedly bought a ticket from a young woman with pink hair who glared fiercely at him for no reason which he could fathom. He followed the crowd through the dark stone archway and long, dank, firelit corridor into the fairylit castle. He felt deeply puzzled by these mysterious ancient traditions which the villagers took for granted.

As he entered the vast ruined courtyard, roaring music and the exploding flashes of fireworks ricocheted around the high stone walls and took his breath away. With every explosion, the crowd shrieked, and with every cascade of flame, like chrysanthemums and willow boughs, the crowd sighed yearningly. Sheets of red and green shimmered, as fragile as the Northern Lights, and enormous bejewelled daisies bloomed above the black hulk of the castle keep.

When the last glorious fountain of silver and gold hung fleetingly across the dark summer sky, the crowd fell silent and watched it twinkle into emptiness, their eyes dazzled and unfocused. Even Keynes felt a wash of sadness filter through his chest, as though something indefinable and precious had just been irredeemably lost.

'Oooh, weren't that lovely!' exclaimed Gwen beside his shoulder. She sniffed noisily and dabbed at her cheeks. 'Allus makes me cry, fireworks – every year. Well, this'n bonfire night. Ooh, but in't it a shame when they've all gone.'

'I likes them big bangs best,' declared Darren.

'Naah, ye 'erbert, it's them pretty pink ones as is best,' hissed his sister. They began to punch each other. Gwen pushed them apart with sharp slaps.

'Now behave, or I'll send yer home,' threatened Gwen. 'Then yer won't see yer Dad dancin'.' The children sulked and pulled faces behind her back. 'Dancin's over there, on the stage, Doc, if yer wants to see it. I can see a bit, then nip back to help in the Golden Oak. Them Ruskies are on next, after the Grey Men. Yer comin'?'

Keynes hesitated, then followed her as she jostled her way into the thick of the crowd.

* * *

'I saw him, he came to buy tickets just before the fireworks, tall bloke, not bad-looking but a bit stiff. So how did your quiet little dinner together work out, then?'

Celia Llewelyn sat down on the caravan bench opposite Sue Hopkins-Jones, trying not to disturb the neat piles of tickets, papers and envelopes spread all over the small table. She flicked back her bob, and peered cautiously out of the open window. 'Oh, he's not around, thank goodness. Brilliant fireworks, Sue. Made my evening.'

'Oh, not the greatest night of romance you've ever had then?' jeered Sue.

'Romance!' Celia laughed sharply. 'You won't believe this, but he was all dressed up in a DJ and bow-tie, sash and everything! And sitting at a table in the middle of the rose garden, drinking champagne! I never saw anything like it, but then I've never read a Mills and Boon.' Both women giggled.

'He did look rather nice, I must admit. But somehow it was

144

like an interview for an important job rather than a date. He was incredibly nervous. Knocked over his glass at one point. And the food was appalling.'

'Well, that's St Briavel's for you.'

'He might at least have asked whether I was a vegetarian before ordering prawns and ham for me. Not the most caring man in the world, I suspect.'

'Huh. Caring men, they get up your nose. You can have Gareth any time you want caring ... drowns you in soggy sentimentality when he isn't running after you like a puppy-dog, all big eyes and wounded soul.'

'You're too hard on him, Sue. Father of your children and all that ... he's a real sweetie, your Gareth. I wouldn't mind a wife like him!'

'And a husband like your sexy nuclear physicist as well?'

'Get you, the perfect advocate of happy marriage. Oh, I don't know. I felt a bit sorry for him, trying so hard, but then, his morals! I was right about the nuclear waste dump, you know. And he's spent the last fifteen years in all the fascist regimes of the world: South Africa, Saudi, Kuwait. But he does seem to really believe in nuclear power ... I was quite taken aback at his sincerity about that.'

'I see. You aren't quite as scathing about him as I was expecting ... you like him!' Sue peered closely at Celia, who blushed.

'Well, at least he does have opinions, unlike most of the men I've met ... Most men will agree with anything a woman says. But I was pretty hard on him, you know.'

'Oh, yeah? Hang on a minute,' Sue leaned out of the window to sell a sheaf of tickets, then turned back to Celia. 'Here, stick that in the cash box while I fill in the ticket sheet.'

Celia clipped the notes into place inside the battered tin box. 'I tried to blackmail him, Sue.'

Sue stared, then laughed. 'You did what?'

'I threatened him with the *Guardian* and the *Times*.'

'You have one hell of a way of chatting up a bloke ...'

'Get serious, Sue. He's the key man in a plan to dump nuclear waste in our village. I can't forget the importance of that, even if you can.'

Sue prickled. 'I'm the one with babies to protect, remember.

I'm the one who has to teach classfuls of children about the terrible things going on in the world. Of course I'm serious about that.'

'And I'm just the friendly local GP who has to deal with a potential leukaemia cluster, with a massive drop in male fertility rates, with the increased likelihood of cancer in every member of the population. C'mon, Sue, we're on the same side, remember.'

There was a silence, during which Sue ungraciously sold more tickets.

'So what did you say to blackmail him, exactly?'

Celia sighed. 'He brought me a bouquet of wild flowers yesterday ...'

' ...Oh, so he does care about the environment, then ...'

'Don't interrupt. One of them was very unusual. I showed it to Katy Cobb ...'

'Oh, my beloved headmistress ... sorry. Go on – oh, hang on, tickets ...'

' ...and it turned out to be the most incredibly rare orchid, a ghost orchid, last seen in this area in 1910.'

Sue stared. 'Wow, that's interesting. They'd have to declare its habitat a Site of Special ...'

' ... Scientific Interest. Absolutely; and I'm pretty sure that he picked it in the Glyn, judging by his reaction.'

Sue threw her head back and roared with laughter. 'Yes! So we've got him pinned down! If he thinks there's no chance of drilling because of this protected flower, then they can't buy the site, and they can't buy the site because their special investigator has discovered this flower ... Yes! And we all know about it, the local environmental and anti-nuclear group ... We've won already!'

Celia stared out of the window. 'We've won, yes ... and he's lost ... lost his job, career, income, future. I feel as though we may be playing with fire, Sue. He's not the complete monster we imagined at first, you know.'

Sue looked at her friend sadly, then turned to sell more tickets. 'Go on,' she said softly when she turned back again. 'I can manage here. You go and enjoy the festival, Celia. See if you can find him; either squeeze out some more info, or teach him to dance, why don't you. Good luck.'

Celia nodded, smiled, gathered up her skirts, and stepped gracefully down from the caravan. 'I might just do that. See you later, Sue.' She turned and disappeared into the darkness spangled with fairy lights.

20

'Wow, doesn't Ainee Sealfin look good enough to eat,' declared Gareth. The band were resting between playing dances at the ceilidh in one of the two huge marquees within the castle grounds.

'Doesn't she just … I've been watching her dance all evening … delicious … you're a lucky man, Isaac,' agreed Don, re-stringing his guitar.

'Don't even think about it,' said Isaac slowly. He was trying to catch Ainee's eye, but she was gazing into space as a group of young men tried avidly to engage her in conversation.

'She can't half dance … she might not know the steps but she learns fast,' added Gareth.

'And it's not as though she lacks for willing partners …' Don remarked, staring at her.

'I said …' Isaac began.

'We heard you. And me a happily married man, too. Well, married, anyway … Where's my beer?'

'Sue got the kids tonight, then?' Don asked.

'She's got Berian asleep in the ticket caravan. Babysitter's looking after Emrys.' Gareth sighed. 'At least that way there's a chance of her feeding Berian tonight for a change, instead of me doing it.'

'Didn't think you'd got the gear, Gareth!' bellowed Davy Orgee, on whom the last traces of the Grey Men mud clung around his low hairline, wispy beard and hairy ears. He took a deep drink from his beer glass, slurping and licking his thin red lips. A battered clarinet hung from a noose of orange baler-twine around his muddy neck. 'Summat you've not been telling us then? Amazin' what them pills can do these days, innit?' He guffawed again.

'You just concentrate on the tune, Davy. You were way off in the middle of the last set,' growled Isaac.

Davy pulled a long face. 'Bloody artists. Ah, but we'm all bloody artists tonight, that's for sure! Bloody piss artists, yeah!'

He waved his empty glass in the air. 'Where's yon bloody jug, anyway?'

Isaac looked grim and grabbed the empty beer jug. He jumped heavily down from the stage and crossed the brightly-lit dance floor towards the bar, grabbing Ainee's wrist as he did so and yanking her along with him.

'Just cut the flirting, will you, Ainee ... and can't you dance a little – less? You look like an electric eel,' he hissed into her ear.

Ainee stared up at him, relying on him to dodge the crowd around the bar as he pulled her towards the counter. Men stared down hungrily at her pale radiance, some grinning. Isaac reached across waiting customers' heads to pass the empty jug over to one of the bar staff, who promptly refilled it without a word. Clutching the now-heavy, frothing jug, Isaac drew Ainee back towards the stage.

'Just don't step out of my sight, Ainee Sealfin,' he whispered more gently into her small pink ear. 'I like to see you.'

'To see me, or to watch me, or to – what do you say – to keep an eye on me?' she responded. 'And what exactly would you do if I were to vanish into the night, oh Isaac, such an Important Player In The Band.'

Their eyes fell simultaneously on the violin casually resting on a small stool on the stage.

'Just remember, my beloved ...' Isaac murmured, nuzzling the long, loose silver hair falling over her shoulders. 'You're mine, and only mine, and mine forever.'

'Or for as long as you keep my sealskin cap from me,' announced Ainee. She turned and looked up into his face, her eyes dark brown and endlessly deep.

Isaac stared into her eyes for a long moment, then caught her roughly in his arms and kissed her passionately in the middle of the dance floor. The beer slopped onto the yellow wooden floorboards, and onto the hem of her floating rainbow skirt, making it cling wetly to her slender legs. He released her unwillingly and climbed back onto the stage, passing the jug to Peter Mortimer, the thickset bass guitarist. The dance-caller, a sharp-eyed woman with a cloud of long black hair, nodded to Isaac.

'Think you can concentrate enough to give us a five-bar jig set, Isaac?' she asked crisply.

Isaac swung the fiddle up onto his shoulder and drew a long, deep, vital chord from his bow. The caller frowned, and turned to her microphone to call the next dance. Ainee had already dissolved into the crowd.

There she met Dr Edward Keynes, a puzzled member of the audience. Recognising him, she smiled up into his face. He bowed awkwardly.

'I healed your wrist last night,' she whispered. 'Now dance with me.'

Flustered, he tried to explain that he hadn't danced for years, and certainly not this kind of dancing, but she smiled softly and slid her small hand into his. As if in a trance, he followed her onto the dance floor, where a set of people appeared magically around them, and was led, confused and stumbling, into a walk-through of the dance.

As Ainee wove her way through the circle of dancers back to his side, she reached up and whispered into his ear: 'Walk the figures, don't try to dance them if you don't know how … I find that easier, because I too am learning these strange new dances.' As the music struck up, Keynes, already unsteady from very little food and a quantity of champagne, found the marquee and the dancers spinning all around him. Hands tugged or pushed him in all directions, and every so often the blonde girl's shining face laughed up at him. She was all he could manage to focus on, but she continually vanished. One moment she was slipping her hand into his, and the next she was sliding away from him, laughing over her shoulder as she faded away. Then suddenly she was in his arms, her hands stroking his shoulders and whirling him around and around. She dropped him and spun away, and other hands caught his and twisted or twirled him around. Other people's feet appeared under his, and he faced backs when he should see faces. The music throbbed as wildly as a migraine, deafening his ears. Shadows and lurid fairy lights flashed and whooshed in his dazzled eyes. Then he was spinning again in the arms of the blonde, and he clutched her shoulders to steady himself, desperately staring into her deep brown tranquil eyes as the room hurtled around them like a merry-go-round. She smiled up at him, and he gripped her tightly. Her shoulders were cool and lithe beneath his sweating hands. Her hair, fine and pale as cobweb-strands, floated around her head. Through the rhythm of her body he began at last to relax into the music. Keynes felt his feet seem to lift from the floor, and it was as though he and the lovely girl were flying, floating free in spangled space. His strained face broke into a sudden grin. He had never felt happier; this was magical, wonderful, marvellous!

Then the music stopped, and he crashed back down to tumble into a slump over the blonde's fragile shoulders, gasping for breath. The room unpredictably started to spin slowly in the opposite direction, and he felt her sag beneath his sudden weight. His stomach began to churn and thrum, and his throat and mouth became thick-tasting.

'Oh God, this is awful,' Keynes groaned aloud into a hushed room, instantly regretting speaking aloud.

The blonde disentangled her right hand and laid it coolly on his forehead. A cool, light sweetness cleared his brain, and he stood up straight, surprised and smiling in relief.

'How do you do that?' he gasped.

She laughed softly. 'Fresh air?' she asked.

He looked around; they were standing close to the doorway of the tent. She stepped down from the dance floor onto grass, and led him out through the hot crowd into the cool night.

'Tell me your name,' begged Keynes, inhaling the fragrant air in the shadow of the castle wall.

The blonde girl smiled up at him. 'Ainee Sealfin,' she replied. Her face seemed luminous in the darkness around them, her eyes dark hollows, and her voice was soft.

Keynes instinctively reached out to lock his arms around her smooth shoulders and pull her towards him. Mysteriously, she smelled of salt and sea and some elusive spice – cinnamon, perhaps. Her lips were inviting; he lowered his face to hers, and closed his eyes as he kissed her. She lifted her lips to meet his and he tasted her small sharp teeth and a flicker of her pointed tongue. Her breasts pressed against his chest. His head swam, and heat surged through his belly. Her flavour, the softness of her skin, the silkiness of her hair engulfed his sensations.

Then she drew back, her small hands stroking his throat, and regarded his shadowed face.

'You are so lovely, Ainee …' he whispered. 'You are the first

151

woman I have kissed for … years,' he completed vaguely, dizzied by her perfume. He bent his head to kiss her again, but she stiffened in his arms. Someone, a man, was loudly calling her name nearby. She ducked under and slid out of his arms before he could release her or clasp her, and moved softly towards the voice.

'Ainee! There you are!'

Keynes recognised the dark outline of Isaac Talboys, and quickly stepped sideways into deeper shadow, his stomach lurching. He watched Isaac catch Ainee's wrists in his large fists and glower down at her. She looked like a delicate silver wand in the hands of a lumbering bear, Keynes thought suddenly.

Neither spoke, but Isaac turned, trailing Ainee behind him, and towed her back into the glowing marquee. Keynes stood and stared, dull-eyed, at the tent, his throat constricted and an ache in his chest. Sad questions prickled his eyes. Why did he have nothing? No woman, no lovely home, no laughing friends? Not even a job, now, of which he could be proud? Why should that arrogant, uneducated boor have everything he desired?

Leaden answers bowed his head beneath their weight. He had nothing because he, Dr Edward Keynes, unemployed and unemployable outdated physicist, was an alien, an enemy in this companionable community. The reason for his very presence signified the destruction of this fragile and lovely place. His arrival would be the cause of the uprooting of rare and precious wild flowers and of gracious trees, scattering singing birds and small animals. Demolishing warm pubs and charming cottages. Raising stinking black oily drilling rigs, bringing noise and clamour, mud and dust. Befouling crystal streams and limpid rivers. Crushing strange traditions and heritages; damaging the past and poisoning the future.

'I never wanted this wretched job anyway,' Keynes whispered to the unresponsive stones of the castle wall. He sighed deeply and rubbed his sore eyes. He walked slowly out of the shadows and through the torchlit gateway.

The Golden Oak pub rang with music and glittered like something from a fairy tale. The terrace was thick with people joking, laughing, greeting friends with handclasps and hugs. Trays laden with full beer glasses passed from hand to hand. Some woman sang a delicate melodic verse, and a chorus of harmonies responded. Another person tinkled tiny hammers over a strange flat instrument which looked like part of a stripped piano.

As he edged his way into the squash of the lounge bar, smiling faces looked him over. The smiles faded and turned away as he was not recognised, not included in the company. He glanced over the many tousled heads, and saw pairs of dark eyes greeting him from every wall; portraits of Ainee Sealfin, smiling as though he were about to kiss her again.

Disconcerted, Keynes made his way to the bar counter and waited amongst the thirsty rabble waving notes. Eventually a hurried Vin Goldhanger passed him a full pint.

When he raised it to his lips, the beer tasted smooth and warm; bitter as compensation, he jested to himself sourly.

After a deep draught, he shuffled into the noisy gathering. Someone hidden in a corner unwound a thin tune from a tin whistle.

'There you are at last, doctor!' a bright voice declared. He glanced down at a winking corn-haired blonde, Lucy Goldhanger. A curving tower of interlocking empty glasses nestled in the crook of each of her arms. 'What do you think of our lovely festival, then?' she grinned.

'Noisy and overcrowded,' he replied, but she had already melted into the crush. He glimpsed Graham Ferris reaching over the counter to receive the glasses, and saw him exchange a sparkling glance with Lucy. Keynes felt sickened by other people's happiness. He backed into a corner to drink his beer and stare grimly at the roisterers. Even Bryn Jones, surrounded by a cluster of elderly Morris men, was laughing.

Keynes felt extraordinarily lonely. He was used to being alone, of course. But this was a sensation of such aching inadequacy, such a sharp pain of exclusion, that his entire body seemed wounded. He wanted to be part of this, he realised, and felt the unfairness of it all sprinkle over his skin like a shower of tiny needles. How could he justify his inclusion? Impossible. He sighed helplessly into his beer. He had been sent here to destroy, not to celebrate.

Suddenly a cool hand was laid across his, and he raised his head to meet Celia's bright eyes.

Before she could speak, he caught her arm. 'I've resigned my job!' he announced. Her eyes widened in surprise, then narrowed again.

'That didn't take long,' she remarked, coldly. 'One tiny threat to your livelihood, and you instantly back out of any possible confrontation.'

Keynes gaped. 'No, Celia, it wasn't like that. I'd already decided, I was going to tell you over dinner, but ... I didn't get the opportunity,' he finished, lamely.

'You could have made the opportunity,' she said firmly. 'If it was at all important or relevant ... or true.'

'Of course it's true,' snapped Keynes. 'You don't exactly make yourself easy to tell important things to, you know. You're so ... so ...'

'Professional?' asked Celia sharply. Her voice was hard and low. 'Not the sort of adoring, begging little girly-wirly you imagine a woman ought to be, eh? Just what do you think the work of a village GP is all about? I spend all day, and often chunks of the night, patiently listening to other people's problems. I thought that you, apparently possessed of some in-dependent intellectual capability, might actually be able to carry on an informative and entertaining dialogue. But I was wrong. You speak in fits and starts like an overwound clockwork train. Well, I've got better – and better-paid – ways of spending my time than in winkling confessions out of such an uptight, self-centred, chauvinistic, fascist – man!'

With this final insult, she twirled on her heel and flounced through the assembled customers, many of whom formed a bemused audience to their little drama.

Keynes drained his beer, his cheeks burning with vexation. 'Bloody women,' he muttered into his empty glass. 'I don't understand them at all.'

'Too bloody right, mate,' came a voice in his ear, 'but don't they make a fascinating lifelong study – from a safe distance!'

Keynes stared directly into the crinkled eyes of Bryn Jones.

'Cheers!' Jones leered, raising his empty glass. 'Mine's a pint of Owd Roger!'

Keynes took a deep breath and gradually unclenched his fists. He took Jones's glass from his grimy paw. Well, he thought, as

154

he dodged through the mass of people, at least Bryn Jones would be company of sorts, if only to get extremely drunk with. And they could always discuss the unnecessary nature of women. Jones, it was obvious from the filth and dust in his icy ballroom-house, had also had the sense to live alone for most of his life. This might turn out to be a faintly bearable evening, after all.

21

Lucy Goldhanger, her evening's work at the Golden Oak completed, was collecting broken plastic glasses into a black rubbish bag in the Festival beer marquee. The bar had been closed for over an hour, since Grace and Peter Mortimer had finished their duty and returned home to their children. Although most of the Festival-goers had gone back to collapse in their tents, a last group of drunken revellers was singing folk-songs in one corner. They reminded each other of the words as they forgot the next verses. The tent was lit only by a string of fairy lights across the trestle counter, and the bar was, at last, officially shut.

'Here, that looks heavy,' said Graham Ferris, grinning. 'Let me take it from you.'

Lucy paused and stared up at him. 'I can manage,' she replied stiffly.

Graham put down his own rubbish sack and leaned on one of the tables. 'Lucy, can I ask you what the matter is? You've been lovely and smiling and friendly to me, right up to an hour ago, and suddenly you've gone all cool. Why?'

Lucy continued to pick up pieces of litter for a while before she spoke. Eventually, she straightened up and looked directly at the lenses of Graham's glasses, rather than into his eyes. 'I heard something about you that I don't like,' she said in a cold voice.

Graham looked surprised. 'What, Lucy?'

Lucy sighed. 'Is it true,' she asked, 'that you three are here in Glasmaen because you're surveying the Glyn for a nuclear waste dump?'

Graham blushed. There was a long silence. 'Ah. Where did you hear that, Lucy?'

'Never you mind. Is it true?'

'Well, yes and no …'

Lucy waited for him to continue.

'Yes, we are here to survey a proposed site, but no, it wouldn't necessarily be used for ah … depositing intermediate nuclear waste … well, not for years, probably not in our lifetimes.'

'Is that what you do for your job? Find bits of Wales that no one will miss if you dump poison in them?'

'You make our job sound a lot grander than it really is. All Richard and I do is make maps, really. Other people do all the geological investigation and make all the decisions. People I hardly ever get to meet.'

'People like your friend Edward?'

'I'm not entirely sure just how much weight he carries with the Department, to be honest. He's been in the Middle East for most of his working life. He doesn't seem very comfortable with this job, that's for sure. I think that all he has to do is to buy the Glyn from whoever owns it, and then it's up to the Department chiefs to decide what to do with it.'

'Does your 'Department' buy up a lot of places like this, then?'

'Oh, dozens. Hundreds, probably.'

'So what will they do with it next?'

'Install drilling rigs. Down the old well by that little cottage, probably, and they'll go five hundred or even a thousand feet deep, to investigate whether the rocks are impermeable all the way down. There has to be no risk to the water table, no cavities in the rocks for instance. That's what Keynes is qualified to be in charge of. He did drilling rigs all over Saudi and Kuwait, he told me.'

Lucy stared. 'How on earth will they get a drilling rig into the Glyn?'

'They use our maps to make a road to bring them in. That's why we have to be so accurate – so that they can work out the cost.'

'This must cost an absolute fortune!'

Graham shrugged. 'Well, the pay is good. But we have to put the waste somewhere: the world's population is just enormous, and expanding all the time, and all those people want electricity. The high radioactive level waste is reprocessed at Sellafield; the low level stuff is chucked into the sea. They used to chuck the intermediate level stuff in the sea, as well, in yellow drums, like the ones that blonde girl described in her weird story last night. But we aren't allowed to do that any more, so we have to find other places to put it.'

157

'Like the prettiest valley in Wales, I suppose?'

'Well, it's got to go somewhere. All valleys are pretty to start with.'

'Until they're churned up to make roads and drilling sites and places to dump poison?'

'Well, Lucy, we've got to sacrifice something so that there's a better future …'

'We! We!' Lucy shrieked, hurling her bag onto the grass. 'This is all about 'you' and 'us', isn't it? 'You' march in here, chat up the local girls, make your maps, destroy the countryside, march out again, and go on to the next place, and do it all over again! Don't you ever stop and think, for a change?'

'Think about what?' asked Graham, turning pale.

'Think about the consequences of your actions, for a start! Think about the future, and your part in it all? Think about 'us'? Think about what exactly happens to your 'pretty little valleys' when you leave them, and go back to – where is it you live, any-way?'

'Reading,' answered Graham sadly.

'Reading,' repeated Lucy scornfully. 'Filthy great big place. I went there once on a catering course. All railways and blocks of flats. But no drilling rigs and nuclear dumps, I bet. No, not any-where where 'you' people like to live. No, you'll happily wreck the countryside for strangers you don't care a toss about, and then you'll sod off to your cosy little citified houses.'

Graham giggled faintly. 'My flat isn't cosy, it's a complete mess. I can't remember when it was last cleaned – last time my mother visited, I suppose. It's just a place to sleep before the next job. Your pub's a much nicer place to live.'

'For a week. How long are you staying here, anyway?'

'I dunno. Until the job's done. Could take months. Could be gone on Monday.'

'Monday?' Lucy was suddenly silent. The drunken singers, as though they had been listening, launched into a chorus of 'The Girl I Left Behind Me'. Lucy glared at them, and tossed back her long golden hair with both hands. 'That does it!' she announced, and marched over to the noisy group. 'Home!' she commanded. 'It's nearly two o'clock in the morning! Off you go, back to your tents or wherever you're staying, or you won't be fit for the Festival tomorrow.'

'You look fit!' roared one slumped figure, raising his pewter tankard in a salute to her. 'Take me home with you, darling!'

Lucy went behind the counter and brought out a large broom, with which she advanced menacingly upon the laughing singers. 'Out! Out! Out!' she cried, shaking the broom at their knees. They rose unsteadily to their feet and stumbled out into the black night, joking and giggling. Lucy quickly put the remaining litter into bags and dumped the broom and rubbish behind the bar. After a last glance around, she unplugged the fairy lights. The marquee fell silent and dark.

'Well done, Luce!' cried Graham. 'Um, where are you?' Silence answered him. He peered into the empty void. 'Lucy?'

She must have slipped out of the flap in the side of the tent, he decided. He followed the path of the revellers out into the night, and stood blinking in the dim light of the stars and of the half-moon peering over the ramparts. He could see no movement. Eventually he walked slowly through the shadowy castle gateway and down the rough ramp towards the pub.

Across the terrace, two large low black shapes ran toward him, growling. 'Demon! Dil!' he called out, and the dogs slowed their charge and came up to him for petting. The moonlit form of Lucy appeared in the pub door.

'Lucy! You left me all alone!' he cried softly.

'Well, now you know how it feels,' she replied icily.

Graham shooed the dogs in front of him as he walked towards her. 'I didn't want us to end like this,' he said, bravely. 'Especially since nothing has even really begun.'

'Oh, yes? And what did you expect to begin, then? Just another brief flirtation with just another landlord's daughter, in just another village?' Red and yellow light from the interior of the pub spilled out behind her, and her hair became flickering wisps of flame around her shoulders. Her arms were stiffly folded across her breasts. Graham noticed a tear glisten on her left cheek. He reached over and wiped it softly away.

'Sorry, Lucy. It's not like that at all, really.'

Lucy clicked her fingers and the dogs followed her into the empty pub. She poked the embers of the log fire in the hearth as the dogs settled down to sleep by its fading glow. Graham sat down in one of the cushioned wheel-back armchairs to watch her.

'Then what is it all about, Graham? What is your life all about?'

'To be honest, Lucy, I'm not very sure why you're so cross with me. I'm only here to do my job, such as it is. It's not as glamorous or important as you make it out to be. I'm not changing the world, I'm just living in it. And a pretty dull life it is at times, I can tell you. That's why Richard and I go windsurfing or climbing or hang-gliding; to get a bit of excitement. Spend some of the money. Try to have a bit of fun now and then.'

'And that's my job, I suppose, providing a bit of fun for a change? That's the job of the landlord's daughter, eh?'

Graham shifted awkwardly in the chair. 'You'll put that fire out if you keep hitting it with the poker like that.'

Lucy turned on him. 'Don't you want to ever stop in one place for long enough to have a life, to have kids, to see the future as worth protecting? Or are you just too scared of the future, of the fires that burn for years and years inside – inside people's hearts and souls – make them light up and glow and smoulder and burn and keep warm through the longest, darkest nuclear winters?'

Graham stared at her. 'What are you talking about, Lucy? You seem to be giving me two entirely different messages. Are you saying that you disapprove of my job, or of me, or what, exactly? I don't understand what you want me to say.'

She pointed up at the heavy beam over the fireplace. 'Look.' Graham could just distinguish the blackened shapes of a row of large coins, each one nailed solidly to the age-silvered oaken beam. 'That's the village war memorial,' Lucy said slowly. 'Every time one of the men from the village went away to the First World War, his wife or girlfriend nailed up a florin, a whole week's wages, so that when he came home again they could take it down and spend it. Spend it in the pub, I suppose, celebrating with all their friends and relations. Those are all the ones who never came home. That was the end of the Grey Men Morris team, an entire team killed in the muddy grey trenches in France. They say that they daubed themselves with mud and danced for the last time on the battlefield, eighty years ago tonight. Look, a tiny little village like Glasmaen, and there are twenty-four florins up there. And one farthing. Was that all that he was worth to her, or all that she could spare? Twenty-five men who went away and never came back. Who went away and changed the world, and left the women behind, alone in their own changed world.' Lucy burst into tears.

Graham jumped up and put his arms around her. 'Hush, there, there,' he murmured into her silky yellow hair. His arms tingled to hold her close at last. 'What is it, Luce? You can tell me.'

She sighed deeply, and pushed him away quite gently. She turned back to the fire and mopped her eyes with her sleeves. 'No, I can't,' she replied eventually. 'You're the last person I could tell.'

Puzzled, he sat down again. 'Why not?'

Lucy looked up at the shadowy portrait of herself over the fire. Then she reached up to the coins and gently touched them in turn, each one a talisman for a lost hope.

'I don't know,' she whispered. 'I've spent all my life here, in this pub, in this village, in this countryside. I love it. I love it so much that I never want to leave it. I want to keep it all just as it is now, green and clean and beautiful. But,' she sighed again, 'but if I am going to stay here for the rest of my life, then what am I to do with myself? There you are, rushing around the world, changing things, and thinking that it doesn't matter very much, because the future's not important. And here am I, standing still, wishing that everything would stay just the same. Well, more or less the same. We live in two completely different worlds. And you just come here for a week, and talk to me, and make me laugh, and help out with the pub and the Festival, and give me some … well, some real human company for once. And all the time, you're working hard to change the Glyn, change the village, change me. And then you've gone. And I can't see that life will be fun any more after you're gone. Dirt and poison and destruction you'll leave behind, hurting all the things I care about most. And me. All alone again.'

Graham sat in silence, uncertain of what to say next.

'Oh heck,' he said eventually.

Lucy turned slowly around and stared at him. Then she shrugged. 'Huh. I've done it now. I shouldn't have told you what I thought, but I did. Go on, piss off, run away. Go back to your flat in Reading and your dangerous sports and all your light, bright, brief girlfriends. Maybe you'll remember me sometimes, rotting away out here in Glasmaen, like the countryside you destroyed. Maybe you won't.'

'I couldn't ever forget you, Lucy.'

'Why not? Why not?' she demanded, her eyes glittering with tears. 'Is that just part of your chat-up line, or your farewell line? Why couldn't you forget me?'

'Oh, sod this for a game of soldiers,' Graham muttered under his breath. He jumped to his feet, and turned towards the door to his upstairs bedroom. At the door, he turned back to wish Lucy goodnight. She stood outlined by the fire, gazing at him longingly, her fists clenched. He stood and looked at her for a long while. The stone-flagged floor between them seemed a mile wide.

'Goodnight,' he said.

Lucy raised her arm, and something heavy hurtled across the room, crashing against the wall beside his head. He looked down to see what it was, shocked to discover a large brass candlestick lying at his feet. There was a dent in the plaster of the wall.

'Oh, no …' whispered Lucy. She stuck both thumbs in her mouth and bit them hard. She took them out again, and drooped slightly. 'I'm sorry, Graham. I didn't mean to do that.'

Graham solemnly removed his spectacles, folded them, and hung them from one of the belt-loops of his jeans. 'You should never,' he said calmly, 'hit people who wear glasses. Now you can try again, with the other candlestick.'

Lucy stood in silence for a moment, but deep within her a giggle was starting to grow. She tried to suppress it, but it rumbled up into her throat and exploded as a long, rich, rippling laugh. Through tear-filled eyes, she watched Graham as he folded up against the dented wall and began to laugh himself.

'You,' spluttered Graham, 'are the craziest, prettiest woman I have ever met in my life.'

Lucy continued to laugh. 'And you,' she eventually managed to get out, 'are the daftest, most attractive man I have ever met in my life.'

Still giggling, they found themselves falling towards each other. They met in the middle of the lounge in an embrace which dissolved into a kiss before either of them knew what was happening. Dizzy and breathless, they kissed and swayed together, each clutching the other ever tighter. At last, Graham pulled his face away from hers for long enough to ask politely: 'My room or yours?'

'Yours,' replied Lucy softly. 'We wouldn't want to wake my father, would we?' They kissed again, running their hands over one another's bodies, imagining them unclothed and shining in candlelit darkness. Then they drew apart and looked into each other's eyes for a long time. Graham smiled his long gap-toothed smile, and Lucy smiled up, radiant in response.

They paused only long enough to recover the fallen candle-stick and light its candle, before they tiptoed, hand-in-hand and giggling, up the flickering staircase to bed.

22

'This is it,' declared Bryn Jones. 'There'll be a party on here tonight, and it's on the way home for both of us. We'll get a coffee and a few drinks here.'

Keynes transferred his weight from Bryn Jones's solid shoulder to the doorpost of the Hopkins-Jones's cottage. From within, the sounds of singing and laughter crept out into the cool night air. Bryn Jones hammered on the door.

As Gareth Hopkins-Jones opened the door, his welcoming grin faded as he recognised his visitors. Silently he held the door open, and Jones and Keynes rolled inside.

'Kettle on, our Sue!' commanded Jones to his glowering daughter.

'You know where it is. But you do look as though you couldn't manage it yourself, so I suppose I'd better make you some coffee.' Sue bustled with the kettle. 'That way, you'll go home all the sooner,' she muttered.

Keynes looked around the cottage, small, brightly painted, and warm. The windows stood open to the garden and a slight night breeze stirred the gaily woven curtains. The room seemed full of people, most of whom were in the process of packing away musical instruments. He recognised Isaac Talboys with an involuntary shudder. The long-haired thatcher slouched beside the lovely Ainee Sealfin, who shot Keynes a swift, secret smile. In a basket in the opposite corner, a mongrel dog cowered. Surprisingly, Celia Llewelyn was sitting on the floor, nursing a sleeping baby.

Sue thrust a mug of coffee into his hand, and glared at him. Her hair, cheeks, lips and dungarees were all an unhealthy shade of pink. She jammed her hands into deep pockets.

'Is this him, then, Celia?'

'It certainly is,' came Celia's cool voice. 'Looking rather the worse for wear, too. Dr Edward Keynes, meet Sue Hopkins-Jones.'

Keynes transferred his coffee mug, spilling some on the carpet, and held out a wavering hand. Sue's hands remained firmly in her pockets. He looked at the brown puddle on the floor, and tried to rub it away with one toe. Sue frowned but remained silent.

'So, Edward,' announced Celia, 'introductions all round, I think. You know Sue's father because he was so tactful as to bring you here: Bryn Jones, the original owner of the Glyn, in which you intend to dump nuclear waste. Bryn sold the Glyn to Isaac Talboys, over here, who has worked like a steam-engine for the last five years, diverting the stream out of the ruined cottage, and then restoring the cottage to one of the prettiest in Wales. You will, of course, have to demolish Isaac's cottage to build your new roads and drilling rigs. You have offered Bryn an unspecified sum of money to buy the Glyn, so he's offered Isaac the rather paltry sum of forty thousand pounds so that he can sell it back to you for rather more than that, one assumes. This is Don Craven, the local thatcher, whose income will doubtless be reduced when the market value of all our houses drops because of the pollution from your nuclear waste dumping. I'm the local GP, who will have to treat the rise in cancers caused by radiation. This is Sue and Gareth Hopkins-Jones, who have to live and work here once you've destroyed the countryside in which they grew up. They'll be leading the local protest group against your plans. This is their youngest son Berian, who will be exposed to the radioactive pollution which you will cause. This is the mysterious Ainee Sealfin, who has been singing to us like an angel, but now the atmosphere has changed and I would be pleasantly surprised if anyone feels like making any more music now that you're here.'

There was a long silence. Keynes drained his mug of coffee and put it down on the dresser. He felt very sober and very unhappy. Everyone in the room, with the sole exception of the sleeping baby, was glaring at him.

'I'm sorry,' he mumbled. 'I didn't think that all this would be, well, so important. I was just doing my job.'

'Doing your job!' spat Sue. 'Wrecking our countryside, our incomes, our health, our futures, the future health of all our children, our Folk Festival, and my damn party, come to that. Get out of my house.'

Keynes stumbled backwards towards the door. 'I told you, Celia, I've resigned my job, I'll try and stop it all!'

Isaac and Don stood up and clenched their fists.

'You too, Father-of-mine, you weren't invited either. You can get out, too.' Sue's face was pinched and white with fury. 'You and your disgusting friend – all you people ever care about is the chance to make some more money for yourselves. Get out! Get out! Get out!'

The door slammed behind Keynes and Bryn Jones, and they heard the rattle of bolts shot into place.

'Well,' drawled Jones as they walked slowly down the uneven drive, 'at least we got a coffee.'

'You shouldn't have taken me there,' said Keynes stiffly.

Jones laughed grimly. 'I found it all very interesting! Even though I just lost fifty-three thousand quid.'

'That,' declared Keynes in funereal tones, 'was the most humiliating moment of my life. I'm greatly relieved that I won't have any dealings with you, Mr Jones, in a business capacity ever again. You've lied and deceived me. I, as an outsider to your merry little village, have been treated as a target for abuse by every one of you. I've done my best to be sociable, reasonable, and helpful, and I have been reviled and threatened with violence by you all. I've become your scapegoat, driven out into the cold.' Warming to his theme, he shivered.

'This is my lane,' observed Jones. 'You know, I don't think you ought to take life so seriously. Loosen up, have fun …'

'That's exactly what I have been trying to do, damn you!' Keynes exploded. 'In fact, there's only one thing I feel like doing right now, and this is it!' He punched Bryn Jones on the nose.

Jones reeled backwards and fell into the hedge, clutching his nose. 'Well,' he mumbled through a handful of blood, 'I'm thorry. I hobe you feel better now. I fink I deserved fat.'

Surprised at himself and at Jones's response, Keynes stood swaying slightly and flexing the aching knuckles of his fist. 'Um, are you all right?' he asked eventually. He offered his undamaged hand to Jones, and pulled him upright.

The scene was suddenly floodlit by the headlamps of a car, which drew up sharply beside them. The door opened and Celia Llewelyn climbed out.

Blinking in the light, both men looked awkward.

'Your nose!' she cried.

Jones covered it with both hands. 'I'm oday. It's nuffink.'

Celia had pulled out a torch and prised Jones's hands away from his face. 'Hmm.' Jones yelped. 'Seems to be unbroken, anyway. Pinch your nostrils hard, there on the bridge. Don't let go. Get in the car, the pair of you, and I'll run you both home.'

Embarrassed, they obeyed. At the unlit turreted doorway to the ballroom of the Knapp, Jones clambered out of the back seat whilst holding a mop of tissues to his nose. 'Do you want a drink or anyfink?' he offered, reluctantly.

'You've both had quite enough for one night,' replied Celia firmly through the open car window. 'Now get to bed, and if it's any worse tomorrow, you know where to find me.'

As Jones shuffled away, she turned the car around and drove back down the narrow lane, turning into the gateway to St. Briavel's Hotel. She drew up outside the door and switched off the engine and the lights. She and Keynes sat in silence for several minutes.

Celia sighed. 'Why did you punch him?' Keynes made no reply. 'Don't deny it: I've treated quite a few punched noses in my time. Usually after a football match and not a folk festival, admittedly, and not usually on the nose of one of our more respected and senior citizens.'

She looked hard at Keynes, who was staring at his feet, his arms folded across his chest. He glanced up as she started to giggle, and then briskly turned away to open the car door. She reached out and laid one hand softly on his shoulder to prevent him, smothering her laughter with her other hand.

'I'm not laughing at you, Edward,' she said softly. 'In fact, I'm absolutely delighted that you thumped Bryn Jones, that miserable, conniving old bugger. It was high time someone thumped him, and I'm very glad that it was you.'

'Unprofessional,' muttered Keynes.

'Oh, sod professional! Well done!'

Keynes turned and stared at Celia. Her dark eyes sparkled in the dimness. She was smiling! He shook his head, slowly.

'I simply cannot understand you, Celia Llewelyn. I've done my best to please and impress you today, and everything I did was met with – well, rudeness more painful than I could ever have imagined. And now I've committed an act of gross and unpardonable violence, you tell me that you admire me.'

'Oh,' said Celia. She bowed her head and covered her mouth with both hands. Then she looked back up at Keynes. 'Put like that, you do have a point, Edward.'

'Good night,' said Keynes, and climbed out of the car.

Celia remained sitting alone as he went into the hotel. She watched the string of windows lighten and then darken as he made his way upstairs, and saw his black outline draw the curtains of his own window. Only when his bedroom light was switched off did she start the engine and drive away. They were both wiping tears from their eyes.

*   *   *

The party at the Hopkins-Jones house broke up quickly once Celia left. Sue whisked around the room, collecting glasses and slamming them down in the sink. Gareth slunk away to put the baby to bed, and then to tumble under his own quilt and fall gratefully asleep. Don, Isaac and Ainee collected the guitar and fiddle, and slipped out into the night.

'You may as well sleep over at my place,' offered Don. Isaac stared at Ainee, but she was admiring the half-moon. 'You can have the double bed,' he added.

Isaac caught Ainee's wrist and led her down the silvered driveway and into Don's thatched cottage.

'If you want a coffee, you know where the stuff is,' Don said, pointing at the kettle.

'No,' said Isaac, and tugged Ainee up the rough uncarpeted stairs to the bedroom. Don shrugged, and settled down on the sofa with one of his glossy magazines. He kept thinking of Ainee naked in his bed, and had trouble getting to sleep.

Don's duvet smelled unwashed, like stale yoghurt and cold toast. The board floor was littered with dirty clothes and half-empty cups of decaying cold tea. Wardrobe doors and drawers hung open, and jumpers and unironed shirts trailed out of them. Isaac pulled the flimsy cotton curtains to, then watched Ainee slide off her dress. He tugged off his own clothes and stretched out the hard knotted muscles of his arms.

'My shoulders ache, Ainee; massage them, please.'

She yawned and sat cross-legged on the bed. 'Two more nights,' she said thoughtfully. 'Very well. Lie down here.'

Isaac collapsed onto the high, creaking bed and closed his eyes. Ainee reached out to the light switch, and turned off the naked bulb in the centre of the ceiling. She began to run her hands soothingly across his warm skin. His flesh cooled and tingled as she touched it, then warmed again into a faint sweat.

Eventually, she spoke again. 'Two more nights,' she whispered. 'Then I can do exactly as I wish.' She leaned down to drop a soft kiss on the nape of Isaac's neck, but he was already fast asleep.

23

Keynes woke unwillingly. Brilliant sunlight was creeping through the curtains, and he felt extremely thirsty. As he buried his head in the pillow, memories of the previous day crowded in on him. Each one made him cringe with a worse embarrassment. He had tried so hard to please so many people, and one after another each had rejected him. His head and heart ached. He wanted to disappear, to fall asleep again and never wake up.

The thirst grew stronger. If he got up and had a long drink of water from the tap in the bathroom, and then a cooling shower, perhaps life would be a little more bearable. He glanced at his portable alarm clock. Ten o'clock already! He forced himself to struggle out of bed and hurried to the bathroom. The tap water in his tooth-glass was sweet and cold and delicious, and he refilled and drained the glass several times. Then he stood under the shower for a long while. Much of the worst pain slid away down the plughole, and he began to feel more wholesome. Now he felt very hungry.

As he dressed, he glanced around the bedroom. The suitcases which he had angrily pulled out last night lay ready for packing. He was very tempted by the idea of driving away and never coming back. Cambridge seemed a very long way away.

Keynes shook his head solemnly. First he had to apologise. These villagers could not care less whether they saw him again or not, but he could not live with himself until he had admitted how sorry he was for all his appallingly rude, uncouth behaviour. Should he bother? He shrugged. His life had fallen apart. His letter of resignation would be irretrievably in the post on the way to Head Office. If he drove there first thing on Monday morning he could perhaps prevent the letter being delivered. But then he would have to explain why he had failed in his mission to purchase the Glyn, that wretched, beautiful, enchanting valley. They would only send someone else out to buy it from Isaac Talboys. Someone more efficient, more dynamic, more ruthless than himself. Anyone at all, really.

Then the valley would be ruined: by roads, drilling rigs, noise and dirt, by becoming a receptacle for intermediate nuclear waste. The lovely birds, the busy little animals, the rare and precious wild flowers would all be destroyed. The flowers! What was the name of that dainty little orchid which Celia had identified? The ghost orchid. That would be killed off.

But at least it wouldn't be his fault. The locals would blame the Department, not him. Other people would receive the same kind of victimisation which he had suffered. He thought back over the last few days. Through the bitter memories of sour words, other images kept slipping.

Smiling faces in the pub. Singing voices and tapping feet. Rippling music. The taste of good beer. The myriad clean, fresh colours of the flowers in the hedgerows. The greenness of healthy trees and springing grasses. The astonishing sense of welcome and well-being which he had experienced in the stone circle.

So not everything in the last week had been misery and humiliation. He had actually enjoyed himself at times. And how many years had it been since he had last experienced happiness? He couldn't remember. But happiness it had been, there was no doubt about that.

Keynes sighed deeply. He realised that he didn't want to sneak away as though nothing had happened to him here. He still felt that he ought to apologise to everyone concerned, but he also wanted to thank them for the pleasure which they had taught him. He would! He would make one last attempt – not to ruin these people's home for them, but to explain to them that they were very lucky to live such rich and wonderful lives, and that they should fight his own Department to preserve what they could so easily lose.

Resolved, Keynes strode downstairs and commanded a full breakfast. The resentful kitchen staff eventually produced the food seventeen minutes later, which Keynes generously decided was a miracle of efficiency for them.

After eating most of the greasy breakfast and consuming several cups of lukewarm coffee, Keynes felt physically refreshed, even though his mind was still churning over the difficult interviews ahead of him. However, he resisted the urge to scurry back upstairs and pack up his possessions, and went out to the car.

The BMW looked dusty and out-of-place in the glittering sunshine; as he inspected it, he realised that he didn't want to keep it. If he was going to change his life, he would sell it and buy a smaller, more economical car. Or a bicycle! Inside the car, the smell of fresh leather was overpowering and nauseating after so many days sitting unopened in the sun. He pressed the buttons and lowered all the electric windows to ventilate the car. He drove steadily up to the Knapp, and parked in the shade of a huge chestnut tree, still fragrant with the last pink candle-flowers of May-time.

Keynes hammered at the vast Gothic door at the top of the conservatory steps for a long time before Bryn Jones answered. He was dressed in a grey string vest, torn at the shoulder, over too-tight brown flared trousers. His nose was faintly coloured green and purple.

'May I come in?' asked Keynes stiffly.

Jones held the door open wider, and Keynes followed him into the kitchen. It smelled of rancid grease and decaying vegetables. Unwashed pots and pans stacked the sink drainer, and mug handles and the rims of plates poked out of the white film covering the cold washing-up water in the bowl. Overflowing bin bags, split in several places, piled up beside the door. Jones sat down at the table, sweeping aside stale crumbs and odd forks with his bare hairy arm. He indicated the other chair to Keynes.

Gritting his teeth, Keynes knocked several grey dish towels off the back and seat of the chair and sat down. He took a deep breath. 'I've come to apologise,' he said. Jones stared at him with glittering dark eyes, but made no reply. 'How is your nose?' Keynes asked. 'I do hope it's not too painful.'

Jones touched his nose briefly, and nodded slowly. 'I'll live,' he replied gruffly.

'I shouldn't have done that,' admitted Keynes. 'I've never done anything so … so unforgivable before in my life.'

Jones shrugged. 'Forget it. You're a stranger. But I've got my daughter so hopping mad that I doubt she'll ever speak to me again.' He sighed. 'And she's a good cook, too, so I've blown my chances of Sunday dinners at her place. With my grandsons,' he added.

'It's very decent of you to be so reasonable, Mr Jones.'

'Decent! Reasonable! Be sure to tell folks that! I haven't exactly been anyone's best friend and companion in my life. Not to anyone in the village, or anywhere else come to that. Folks have always been suspicious of me. Even my girl and her kids. Even my wife.' He stared out of the dusty window pane over the green-and-gold valley below.

'I didn't realise you were married,' observed Keynes politely.

Jones continued to stare out of the window. He touched his nose again, delicately, as though to remind himself of pain. 'I'm not,' he said slowly. 'She died. Hanged herself.'

'Oh,' said Keynes uncertainly. 'I'm sorry.'

'So am I. She was a good woman, and I made her life miserable. Without her, my life has been miserable. Well, look around you.' He waved his arm at the filthy kitchen. 'Horrible, isn't it?'

Keynes was silent for a moment. 'Yes,' he replied. 'It is horrible. No one should live like this.'

'What's the point of bothering, though? Why should I make an effort? No one would notice, and it'd only get mucky again. Sue refused to bring the boys up here ages ago. You're the first visitor I've had for ... well, a long time.'

'But you could keep it nice for yourself.'

Jones shrugged. 'Why should I? I'm not very nice. I'm a smelly, lonely, dirty old man. That's all there is. I've got plenty of money, mind, to pass on to the kids, but I might live for another thirty, forty years yet. There doesn't seem to be any point in anything. Not in living, really.' He sighed deeply and rubbed his furrowed brow. 'I enjoy a drink at the Folk Festival, a bit of tradition every so often, starting up the Grey Men again. Giving money to do up the church, or the school. But I've done all that now. Other people can run those events. No one needs me.'

Keynes felt very sad. He glimpsed his own future through Bryn Jones's hooded eyes. He, too, could so easily become a forgotten, unwanted, grimy old man. He didn't want that to happen, he realised bitterly. He would have to do something to prevent this happening to him.

'What could you do to change things, Mr Jones?' he asked uncomfortably.

Bryn Jones looked startled. 'Change things? Change what?

Change my life, I suppose? I don't know. I've worked hard at doing nothing, all my life. I don't know if I could change things. I don't know how to.'

Keynes thought about possibilities for his own life as well as for Jones. 'You could sell up and move somewhere else. Start again. New house, a little place you could keep clean. Hire a cleaner. Or maybe a nice big place which your daughter might want to share with you. Their house is very small for a growing family. Or if they wouldn't share, you could give them some money to get a bigger place. Then they might let you visit them.'

Jones gazed into the blue distance, rimmed by the Welsh mountains. 'You reckon? Sounds like a lot of trouble. But it would be pleasant to live somewhere warm. Hilltop village in Italy would be nice. Then the boys might want to visit. I like living on top of a hill.' He turned and looked hard at Keynes. 'You saying you want to buy the ballroom?'

Keynes laughed nervously. Then he considered the view. 'I could. But I wouldn't unless it was cleaned up and redecorated. I'm certain someone would want it if you did that. You might want it yourself, if you spent some money on it. It's in a wonderful place. The conservatory is splendid, and so is the fireplace in that room you showed me last time. You could do something really special with it. You could put in a decent heating system, and insulation. Paint, carpets, good furniture. Pictures.'

'Pictures?' Jones scanned the naked plaster walls. The only ornaments were out-of-date calendars and curling posters for old movies. His eyes glazed over as he imagined the possibilities. 'It could be nice, you know. I often think what I'd do with it if I could be bothered. But I could get Gareth to choose the colours and fabrics and stuff. He might even paint it, put up wallpaper if I paid him. He has his uses. Cost a lot, of course.'

'Be worth it if it made your life comfortable, and pleasant. And warm. People would want to visit you, then.'

'Would they?' Jones stared at Keynes until Keynes shifted uncomfortably on the hard seat. 'You're being very helpful for a bloke who punched me on the nose last night.'

Here it goes again, thought Keynes. 'I said I was sorry. I'd just had enough. So many people had been so rude and, well, unfair to me recently, I just felt like lashing out.'

'And because I was the rudest and most unfair, you lashed out at me, eh?'

They looked hard into each other's eyes.

'Yes.'

'I don't blame you. Well, maybe it brought me to my senses. Perhaps I ought to do what you just did to me, and go round and apologise to Sue and Gareth. Bloody brave thing to do, for both of us.'

'I'll come with you,' offered Keynes. 'We could go in my car.'

'That fancy black jobby down there? Bit posh for round here.'

'I'm going to sell it.'

'Oh, I see,' said Jones slowly. A smile creased his face and showed his chipped teeth. 'You want to change your life, too. Good for you.'

Keynes smiled back, glad to be able to share his decision with someone, even if it was just this odd old man. 'Yes. It's about time I started to get some pleasure out of life, for a change.'

'Pleasure, eh? What kind of pleasure is that, then?'

Keynes disliked the leer on Jones's face. 'All sorts,' he said firmly. He stood up, scraping the chair across the dusty floorboards. 'I'm going now,' he announced.

Jones glanced down at his vest. 'I'll put a shirt on and come with you.'

Clad in a pale blue nylon shirt, he followed Keynes to the car. Keynes felt a moment's reluctance to let this grimy person sit in his clean car, but overcame it by glancing at the bruise on Jones's nose. They drove companionably down to the Hopkins-Jones's cottage, and pulled up on the gravel drive. Jones grinned to see his youngest grandson playing on a blanket on the lawn, whilst the eldest ran towards his grandad, laughing and holding out his arms for a hug. Keynes felt a pang of envy. No small child had ever held its arms out to be picked up by him. He would like to experience that pleasure.

Sue appeared at the open door, wiping her hands on a towel. She stood very stiffly as she recognised her visitors. 'What do you two want? Can't you get the message? I don't want you here.'

'A quick word, Sue,' offered Bryn Jones, lowering the little boy to the ground. 'I've come to apologise to you.'

Sue's eyes opened wide in astonishment, then narrowed in suspicion.

'Me, too,' interjected Keynes. 'I'm sorry to have disturbed your party. I'm sorry to have upset you about the Glyn. I won't let it happen, the drilling or the waste-dumping. You ought to know that.'

'Ought I, eh? Well, miracles will never cease. Now sod off, I've got two children to feed and a folk festival to run.'

'Can I stay for lunch, Sue?' asked Jones humbly. 'Please? I want to talk to you. About my future plans.'

Sue glowered. 'Only if you help with the cooking and the boys. I've got a lot to do.'

'Fair enough. See you in the Golden Oak later, er ...'

'Edward,' Keynes offered graciously, nodding. He got back in the car and drove slowly through the village to the pub car park. As he drove, he admired the geraniums and lobelia, brilliant red, white, and purple in the sunshine in the window-boxes of almost every thatched cottage. Although the pub had only just opened, the terrace tables were thronged with laughing people, the girls all pretty in summer frocks. The sun-hot air bathed everyone, and someone lazily played the blues on a guitar. Bunting fluttered gaily across the terrace and bright sun-umbrellas twirled idly over the tables. This, thought Keynes to himself, is pleasure.

24

The kitchen at the Golden Oak gleamed with stainless steel and sparkling white tiles. After preparing the morning's breakfasts, Gwen Orgee had left the room spotless in readiness for the lunch-time rush. Lucy Goldhanger was refilling the coffee machine when Graham's lips brushed the nape of her neck. She shivered deliciously, and turned to greet him with a warm smile.

'Hello, gorgeous,' he whispered. 'Where have you been all my life?'

'Happy?'

He grinned, and enfolded her in his arms. 'Very. That was a wonderful night.'

'And dawn,' she added.

'And breakfast and morning,' he responded. 'Mmm, I wish everyone else would disappear, and we could go and do it all over again ...'

'And when would we ever get to sleep?' Lucy giggled.

'Who needs sleep, when you've got love?'

'Love?' Lucy regarded him with wide-open eyes.

Graham swallowed. 'Well, that was love-making ...'

' ... and not just a one night stand?'

Graham shook his head. 'You're a very special lady, Lucy.'

She sighed. 'Oh, I bet you say that to all the girls.'

He shook his head solemnly. 'There's never been one called Lucy before.' He kissed her tenderly. 'But ooh, that coffee smells good, Lucy. I could drink three cups of that.'

She glanced at the gurgling machine. 'It won't be ready for a few minutes.'

'But I am ...' They giggled and kissed again.

'Lucy! Are you there?' They looked up to see Richard Beavis standing in the kitchen door, staring at them.

'Morning, Richard!' beamed Graham. Lucy untangled herself unwillingly from his arms.

'Oh, there you are,' observed Richard coldly. 'I might have guessed.'

'Did you want something, Richard?' asked Graham, still grinning as he replaced his hand on Lucy's exposed shoulder.

'Not me. Four coffees for the gang of hippies at the far end of the terrace. I thought you'd like to know. They've paid.'

'I'll bring it out,' promised Lucy. She busied herself setting out a tray, whilst the two young men tried to outstare each other. She poured extra mugfuls for Richard and Graham. As she advanced with the laden tray, Beavis stepped aside sharply to let her pass, as though her touch might contaminate him.

'I know what you're thinking!' declared Graham. 'What a lucky beggar I am!'

Beavis frowned. 'You don't know what you're getting yourself into.'

'Oh, no?' sneered Graham. 'And what might that be, then?'

'She's not the usual sort of girl you can have fun with, then dump and leave behind you when you go on to the next posting.'

'Like I usually do, you mean?' There was a note of triumph in Graham's voice. 'No, Richard, she's different. She's a stunner, I can tell you.'

'I don't want to hear all your sordid details.'

'You usually listen, eh? About time you got a girl of your own, isn't it?'

'I wouldn't treat a dog the way you treat women.'

Graham giggled shrilly. 'I would hope not!'

Richard glowered. 'Don't be so crass. How dare you treat a lovely, gentle, kind girl like her in this way? You disgust me!'

'Do I? And what could possibly be disgusting about a girl like her, then?'

'That's not what I meant. If I'd known you'd be seducing Lucy, I'd have …'

'Tried harder? Used more imagination? Or just tried to warn her off, in a dark corridor somewhere, eh?'

'I'd have bloody well married her myself!'

A sudden silence fell between them.

'Married her, Richard?' asked Graham eventually. 'God, you have got it bad.'

'Well, I don't expect that thought has ever crossed your filthy little mind.'

'The thought of marrying Lucy Goldhanger? Of giving up my well-paid and varied job and settling down here in the Golden Oak Inn to play happy families, out in the wilds of Wales? No, that thought had never crossed my mind.'

'Exactly,' Richard growled.

Graham sipped his coffee. 'But now that you mention it, it doesn't sound all that bad an idea ...'

'Oh bullshit, Graham. You're incapable of doing a decent thing, and always have been. I've seen you! I've watched you for years, half-doing your job, creeping off to chat up the next girl, dropping her as soon as it's time to move on. You don't deserve anyone as good as Lucy. I hope you end up a sick, bitter, lonely old man.'

'And you won't, I suppose? Of course you bloody will. You're trying to be like that uptight Keynes, you are, and what has he got to show for twenty years in the Department, eh? Sod all, that's what. You'll be just the same.'

'So what do you plan for yourself?' asked Beavis slyly.

'Me? Oh, a job I enjoy, plenty of friends about, good food and booze, a lovely place in the country, a gorgeous wife, several kids, dogs and cats and horses ...'

'Sounds just like Lucy and the Golden Oak.'

Graham stared at him, then nodded slowly. 'Does, doesn't it? Perhaps I never thought about it before.'

Lucy returned with the empty tray. 'You ready for another coffee yet, Graham? I'd better take one in for my Dad.'

'Yeah, you do that ... sweetheart. And I'll come and change that barrel.'

As Graham followed Lucy out of the kitchen, Beavis leaned close and spoke in his ear. 'Just you treat this one right for a change, Graham Ferris. Just you bloody well treat her right.'

*   *   *

The 'gang of hippies on the far side of the terrace' turned out to be Don, Ainee, Isaac and Gareth. Don's coffee-making facilities appeared to be non-existent, and Gareth was temporarily escaping the trials of fatherhood and his father-in-law.

'Good morning!' sang out Lucy, as she delivered the tray of coffee to them. 'Another glorious day!'

'You seem very cheerful this morning, Lucy,' observed Don. He was idly tuning his guitar. 'What's got into you, then?'

'Ooh, wouldn't you like to know!' she giggled. She looked around at them all. 'You all look very sorry for yourself. Late night, was it?'

'Too right,' groaned Gareth, dropping his head into his hands. 'Running a folk festival, crying babies, foul-tempered wife, and the whisky didn't help, either.'

'I can't imagine why you put up with it,' grumbled Don.

'No, you couldn't, could you, Don,' Lucy said sharply. 'You weren't cut out for a happy home life, were you?'

They stared at each other for a moment. She turned her gaze on Isaac. 'Nor were you, come to that, Isaac. All charm and no sincerity, both of you. Pair of layabouts!' She smiled, but her smile was thin. She turned and walked away to the pub.

'That was a bit pointed,' commented Gareth. 'Was that a reference to the time when she went out with you both?'

Isaac and Don simultaneously reached for the tobacco tin.

'So it was, I see. But that was over a year ago, wasn't it? She hasn't taken up with anyone else in the meantime, as far as I know. Has she?'

Silence met him again, as they separately lit their cigarettes.

'Ah,' Gareth nodded sagely. 'She has. That young man with the glasses from the visiting survey team. I noticed them making eyes at each other last night. So she's in love, at last. Good for her.'

'So why did she find you both inadequate?' asked Ainee suddenly.

'Ask her,' muttered Don.

'She wants a bloke willing to take over running the pub whilst she plays at being a housewife, I reckon,' replied Isaac. 'That must be hard to find. She wants a man to give up his job and all his interests for her.'

'Oh, well then, maybe she should have chosen Dr. Edward Keynes,' suggested Ainee. 'He announced that he was giving up his job last night, whatever it is.'

'Don't believe a word of it. Guy like that, says anything to keep the dangerous public-spirited population in check. A politician and nothing else … speak of the devil.' Gareth pointed to Keynes as he advanced cautiously towards them.

'Good morning,' offered Keynes.

'Ah, the murderer always returns to the scene of his crime,' Don remarked. 'Come to break up another pleasant little session?'

Keynes shifted awkwardly from one foot to the other. 'May I get you each a drink? To apologise for last night?'

They all looked at each other. 'Mine's a pint,' said Don.

As they watched Keynes disappear into the pub, Ainee smiled sweetly at the men. 'I like him. He is an air man, all cold logic and discomfort.'

'Really?' Isaac stared at her. 'He's a meddling idiot.'

'Give the bloke a chance. He did offer to apologise, after all.'

'Heart of gold, Gareth, that's you. No wonder you let Sue walk all over you.'

'Thanks, Don. I do happen to love the woman, you know. She is the mother of my children …'

'… and the family breadwinner,' inserted Isaac.

'Well so she is,' replied Gareth coldly. 'And just why can't a woman get on in her career whilst her husband takes care of the kids, which just happens to be what he enjoys doing?'

'Cool down, Gareth! It must be great to lounge around at home all day, playing with kids, instead of slitting your hands to ribbons perched on top of a slippery thatched roof …'

'Or slashing them with the sharp edges of slates,' added Isaac.

'Don't be ridiculous!' exclaimed Gareth, offended. 'If you think bringing up two kids is easy, you ought to damn well try it. It's been left for women to do for a thousand years, and it's damn hard work. I'd never make enough out of my weaving to keep us if I worked eighteen hours a day, every day. And if I did, I'd never have time to see my little boys. I have a pretty good life, all in all, and it's a damn sight more comfortable and less lonely than you two merry bachelors.' Gareth suddenly looked very awkward.

'Is it a merry life you lead, then, Don and Isaac? You have never appeared to show much joy in life to me,' commented Ainee. 'Gareth and Sue may quarrel, but their home is clean and light and pretty, whilst yours are dirty, dark, and smell of decay and neglect.'

Keynes, sliding a tray of full glasses onto the table, provided a welcome pause in the conversation. The men raised their pints silently, whilst Ainee lifted a glass of white wine to sparkle in the sunlight.

'May I propose a toast?' asked Keynes tentatively. All eyes turned on him. 'To the protection and preservation of that enchanted valley, the Glyn.'

Surprised, they all sipped.

'So how do you suggest we go about achieving that, then, Doctor dig-it-up-and-bury-nuclear-waste-in-it?' asked Don.

'I did tell you last night that I have resigned my official appointment. I have come to realise that such an operation would be incorrect.'

'And how might it be 'incorrect'?' queried Gareth.

Keynes sighed. 'Because of the damage to the environment. And this village is an environment which you should fight to preserve at all costs.'

'And I suppose we haven't been doing that in the past?' asked Isaac brusquely.

Keynes looked at him carefully. 'You, Isaac Talboys, have done more to preserve the beauties of the Glyn than anyone else.'

'Well, I do just happen to own it, to have restored the cottage, and to have lived in it for the last five years. Is that what you mean?'

Keynes swallowed a sip of beer, attempting to disguise his awkwardness and failing. 'Well, yes and no. Yes, because what you have just said is true, although I was initially misdirected into believing otherwise. No, because you have created a work of art from that charming cottage, and so you have in fact improved the valley's loveliness by your efforts, rather than merely preserving it.'

'Is that a compliment?' asked Isaac gruffly of his companions. 'I find it rather hard to tell with this guy.'

'It is,' said Ainee unexpectedly. 'And it is a true one. You do live in a beautiful place, but you do not necessarily inhabit it in a beautiful way.'

'What the hell are you talking about?' growled Isaac.

'Er, may I ask you something very important, Mr Talboys?' Keynes interrupted.

'Go on.'

Keynes looked around. Everyone at the table was watching him with suspicious interest. People at several other tables were watching him, too. 'Could I speak alone with you for a while?'

'If you've got something to say, say it here, in front of my friends.'

'Friends!' scoffed Don, under his breath.

Keynes swallowed another large sip. 'It's rather a – well, delicate affair ...'

Isaac continued to stare from below his heavy dark brows.

Keynes swallowed again, slurping slightly and spilling some of the beer down his chin. He mopped it off with a clean white handkerchief. Then he took a deep breath.

'I'd like to buy the Glyn from you.'

His words hung in the air for several moments.

'I would, of course, offer you the full valued price, as the Department offered Bryn Jones when they thought he owned it. Ninety-three thousand pounds.'

'I'd give you my cottage for that, and it's thatched,' offered Don.

'You could have my place as well!' suggested Gareth.

Isaac remained silent.

Keynes suddenly realised his omission. 'I would be buying it to live in myself, of course. Not for the Department to drill in. I would take steps to prevent that ever occurring. I've plenty of savings and investment income, from a long career at a high salary, of which I have spent very little. I'd pay you cash.'

'Why?' asked Isaac.

Keynes hesitated. 'Well, I'm not sure exactly. I like it here. I don't have a job any more, so I could settle into caring for the valley, studying and recording the wildlife, that sort of thing. I'd be a sort of nature warden, I suppose. I just want to live there. Please,' he added, lamely.

Everyone drank. Keynes stood up. 'I'm sorry,' he muttered. 'I didn't mean to come out with it all quite like that. Please consider my offer. I can promise you that it's entirely genuine. I'll see you later ... I hope.' He walked away, heading in his confusion for the Festival site within the castle. The others sat in silence.

'Well, that was a surprise,' said Gareth eventually.

'Could be a trick to get hold of the valley for his filthy Departmental purposes. I wouldn't trust his word.'

'He spoke entirely honestly,' said Ainee calmly. 'You should consider his suggestion, Isaac.'

'Why?'

'Because you don't know what to do with your life, and here is a possibility for changing it.'

Isaac stared at her, then drained his glass. He stood up. 'Another drink?' he asked generally, then strode away into the pub.

Gareth smiled at Ainee. 'You don't say much, but when you do, you certainly know how to get your teeth into the heart of the problem, don't you?'

'I'm beginning to realise,' mumbled Don, 'that I'm glad you're his woman and not mine, after all.' He turned away, and began playing blues numbers.

Ainee smiled, stretched and yawned like a cat in the hot sunshine. 'Everything,' she said quietly, 'is obvious to me.'

25

Revealed by daylight, the Festival site fluttered with bunting and pennants on the marquees, as brilliantly decorated as any joust held in the castle over the last thousand years. The midday sun was so hot that the summits of the gatehouse tower and the Norman keep shimmered hazily.

Everywhere, people strolled, queued, and stood chatting in groups. A hundred children gripped the edges of a red and blue parachute, rushing to and fro, shrieking in joy. Jugglers sweating in particoloured hose and tunics tossed bats and spun plates. Stalls selling Breton pancakes and ice-cream floated their scents of molten butter and vanilla, and incense from craft stalls mingled with the savours of hot dogs and hamburgers. Queues of grim-faced women or jigging men led to the portakabin toilets.

Music from dozens of different sources competed for Keynes's attention. Customers at musical instrument stalls jangled dulcimers and mandolins experimentally whilst the stall holders winced. Recordings by the guest artists played from cassette and CD stalls, whilst the artists themselves practised jamming with each other at the tables outside the tea tent, which was still serving breakfasts to hungover late risers. The bar customers spilled out through the lowered flaps in the marquee onto the emerald green lawns, drinking, talking animatedly, and occasionally singing to one another. The musky smells of spilled stale beer from last night greeted Keynes as he edged his way to the bar. Grace Mortimer swiftly served Keynes with a warm pint in a wobbly plastic glass, smiling briefly. Keynes struggled with the pint whilst he put on his sunglasses, and wandered back out into the castle courtyard.

He fumbled to extract the Festival programme from his pocket, and waved it over his pint so as to unfurl and read it. Performers with peculiar names were about to appear in both the large marquees. Long queues shuffled slowly in through the entrances to both tents. Keynes, staring slowly around, saw faces he recognised scattered amongst the hundreds of Festival-goers. Gwen Orgee ushered her grizzling children into the mass games. Sue Hopkins-Jones pounded across the site, shoving her pushchair and tugging her toddler. Bryn Jones was holed up in a corner of the bar with his Morris men cronies.

After his chilly reception by Isaac Talboys and his associates on the pub terrace, Keynes felt unwilling to approach anyone else. He felt forlorn, an alien in an earthly pleasure-dome. Then someone tapped his arm. Turning, some of Keynes's plastic-encased pint splooshed onto his trouser leg.

He looked up to see Richard Beavis frowning at him.

'Sorry, sir,' Beavis mumbled, juggling with his own full pint.

Keynes nodded, and struggled with his handkerchief to mop his leg. His wrist twinged in memory of the break, causing him to drop his programme. Beavis recovered it for him.

'So, Beavis, you're out enjoying yourself now?' Keynes asked stiffly.

Beavis looked at his feet, shuffling them on the daisied lawn. 'Hmm. Other people seem to be, certainly,' he admitted reluctantly.

'Oh, yes? Who might that be?' Keynes enquired cautiously.

'Oh, Graham Ferris has no problem about having a good time. At other people's expense,' he added ungraciously. When Keynes made no comment, he continued. 'To tell no tales, he won the landlord's lovely daughter last night. I hope he treats her decently.'

'And you didn't?'

Beavis looked up suspiciously. 'I would always treat a lady decently, I hope, sir.'

Keynes recollected Celia Llewelyn's curt comments. 'I don't know why we bother doing so, er ... Richard,' he sighed. 'Perhaps the ladies prefer a bolder approach to the more, well, courteous one.'

Beavis also sighed. 'You may be right, sir. I feel very, well, out of step here. Old-fashioned. I thought this place was a real time-warp when I arrived here. But it seems to move faster than I do. I don't like it at all.'

'Really? I find it charming. Fascinating. Refreshing.'

'Yeah, well you haven't just had the girl of your dreams grabbed by your best friend – supposedly.'

Keynes thought of Celia and Ainee Sealfin. One was elusive and rude, and the other was elusive and protected by a boor. 'No, I suppose not.'

They both sipped in silence, watching the crowds.

'What are you going to do with your career, Richard?' asked Keynes.

'Finish this commission, do another, and so on. I was thinking about your comments on Saudi and Kuwait. I wouldn't actually mind going out there, you know. Although I'd miss the beer.'

'Those days are over. So's this commission, come to that.'

Beavis stared at Keynes. 'Sir?'

'Edward, please. I've resigned my post. You can pack up and go home tomorrow. Today, if you want. The Department will sort something new out for you, I'm sure. I'll write you both a good reference. For what my opinion is worth.'

'Why?'

'Well, you both worked very hard, despite the odd, well, 'personality clash' I think they call it these days ...'

'No, why have you resigned? I thought you had a key post.'

Keynes shook his head. 'I'm out of date and out of step, as you call it. They sent me here as a last resort. We British engineering specialists used to be vital to the developing nations. Now those nations have trained all their own nationals to do our jobs. I'd suggest that you learn a language and go into Europe. I can't be bothered any more.'

'But sir, with respect, surely you're not old enough to retire now ...'

'I'm forty tomorrow. You're, what? Twenty-eight? Don't get trapped in the bureaucracy. They'll stick you behind a desk and then they'll 'rationalise' your office, and out you go. They did that with my drilling rigs section. They sent me out here to fob me off with something, while they have dinner in their walnut-panelled boardrooms and decide on my severance pay. I just forestalled them by a few days. My job was on the line all along, ever since I left Kuwait.'

'But the nuclear industry is vital to the world's economy ...'

'Maybe. Maybe not. It certainly has an impact on the world's environment which we've managed to avoid noticing for thirty years.'

'But the greenhouse effect from burning fossil fuels …'

'Why burn them? What do we need all that power for? In India, I saw them install an electric light bulb in every hovel, in the city where we built a new reactor. The politicians ranted about progress. But the poor couldn't afford new bulbs or even to run the meter, and carried on burning cow dung to light their rooms and cook their rice. Even in the shade of the reactor itself. All those little children living in the dark. But they were only peasants, you see. So the rich felt that they ought to have worked harder and earned enough money to afford the power which the rich have. And the poor continued to die from starvation. The cost of that reactor would have paid for building and running fifteen hospitals for the poor, or for two luxurious ones for the rich. And we still have to dump the nuclear waste.'

'I never would have thought you were a communist, sir,' remarked Beavis stiffly.

'I'm not anything any more, Richard,' sighed Keynes, sipping his beer. 'I've seen a lot of marvellous new technology, and I've seen a lot of appalling poverty and desperate inequalities. And do you know what? I'm beginning to suspect that you can't have the one without the other.'

'Really,' muttered Beavis, unconvinced.

'I think I've reached the stage in my life when I want to do something completely different. I've been a technologist. Now I think I'll have a go at being a peasant.'

Beavis raised his face to the hot sun, wondering whether it had affected Keynes's brain. 'So you've resigned a well-paid, highly respected career, performing a vital service to the citizens of Britain. Have you thought about discussing this with a doctor, sir?'

Keynes spotted Celia Llewelyn, wearing a flowing sky-blue summer dress, appearing through the castle gateway. 'Good idea, Beavis! I shall do just that.' He began to walk towards Celia, discarding his unfinished pint in a wasp-infested litter-bin on the way.

Beavis stared, then turned to refill his pint. 'The man's gone loopy,' he muttered to himself. 'Listening to him is like reading the bloody *Guardian*.'

* * *

Back at the Golden Oak, the Sutherland entourage had descended upon the sullen group sitting at the table on the terrace. Jeremy Sutherland, a tall man, relaxed in an expensive grey silk suit, had at last arrived from London, delayed by official business. His wife Ellen fussed over him until she was sent inside to order a round of drinks and lunch for everyone. Dominic Batista, dressed in a startling paisley shirt and tight jeans, accompanied her, persuading Isaac away from Ainee's side to discuss the forthcoming exhibition in London. Despite the noisy multitude singing, chatting and drinking both in the sun and indoors, Ellen and Dominic's voices carried outside as they enthused about Isaac's paintings.

Lyndon Cotton slid his linen-clad tanned body beside Ainee, and began to whisper seductively into her ear in his smooth California drawl. Don, still playing his guitar, pointedly directed his softest love-songs toward Ainee.

Ambrose Fisher and Sonia Barnaby the anthropologists, wearing identical black clothes and sunglasses, listened calmly to the music and chatter around them.

Gareth, embarrassed by them all, tried to make polite conversation with Jeremy Sutherland, who had courteously invited them all to his wife's party after the last Folk Festival event that night. Gareth explained how delighted he and the other Festival organisers were to have secured Leon Grafton for his farewell concert, and Jeremy listened with a half-abstracted air.

'So do tell me, Gareth – isn't it? Yes. What is all the latest gossip in Glasmaen? We don't get down to stay in the Old Mill as often as we'd like.'

Gareth glanced around him. 'Quite a lot going on, really, Jeremy. Isaac has a new lady friend, Ainee Sealfin, as you can see. Although your American friend is doing his best to put a stop to that, at the moment,' he added, glaring at Lyndon. 'Lucy Goldhanger, the landlord's daughter, seems to have fallen in love with a bloke who's been surveying the Glyn. That's the big news, really. There's a bloke, a Dr Edward Keynes, has been going about causing an uproar.'

'Oh, yes, what's that all about, then?' asked Jeremy languorously, inspecting his polished fingernails.

'We've discovered,' confided Gareth, frowning, 'that the

blasted Department of Energy is trying to buy the Glyn from Isaac, to dump nuclear waste in.'

'Really?'

'So I understand. He's offered Isaac nearly a hundred thousand quid for the whole valley.'

'Lot of money.'

Gareth nodded. 'This Keynes seems completely clueless about the likely consequences.'

'Which are?'

'A nuclear waste dump! The whole village'll go mad. Sue, my wife, is already up in arms, and all the local environmental activists with her. You saw how wound up they got about you trying to close your footpath a couple of years ago. Just imagine what they'll be able to do about this. It's a great thing to have so many concerned people living in your village.'

'Yes, it was a shame about that footpath. I'm glad we were able to sort it out to everyone's satisfaction. So just what has this doctor–person been doing, then?'

'Oh, he's such a fool. Got drunk as soon as he arrived – couldn't take the Owd Roger. Offered the money to Sue's dad when he thought Bryn Jones owned the Glyn. Even punched old Bryn on the nose, Sue told me. Then he tried sneaking around and being friendly to everyone, and told all the wrong people about his aims.'

'Who are the 'wrong people'?'

'Oh, the right people for us, of course. He told Celia Llewelyn about his plans, and you know how committed she is to the protection of the environment.'

'Oh, yes …'

'And then, you'd never believe it, but he started chatting her up, and gave her a bunch of wild flowers that he'd picked in the Glyn.'

'One could hardly blame him for that. She's a charming young woman.'

'Ah, but you don't know the half of it! One of the flowers turned out to be really rare and special. Something called a ghost orchid, a protected species. She showed it to Miss Cobb, Sue's headmistress, who's dead hot on flower recognition. She nearly blew a fuse! With something as precious as that in the

Glyn, the bastards'll never be allowed in! The Nature Protection people'll turn it into an SSSI! Good, eh?'

'Fascinating. Ah, here's my dear wife with our drinks. Yours was another pint, I believe.' Jeremy graciously handed the drinks around. Isaac hung glowering over Lyndon Cotton until he moved away from Ainee.

'So, Ellen, I understand that we've been missing all the excitement here in Glasmaen,' observed Jeremy.

'Gossip?' gasped Ellen, her eyes sparkling. 'Do tell, Gareth! You must keep us informed all the time, you know!'

Gareth, primed with good beer, and shortly with roast beef sandwiches, told the visitors all about it.

*   *   *

Celia smiled radiantly up at Keynes. 'Good morning, well … afternoon, now. How are you today, Edward?'

Keynes looked down at her. She was astonishingly pretty. He frowned. 'Confused, Celia. I am confused.'

They were standing beside a small stall close to the castle wall. Celia studied the goods on display. She ran her slender hands over bedspreads striped with warm, earthy colours. 'These are lovely.' She smiled at the stallholder, a young hippy woman sitting cross-legged on one of her rugs spread on the grass. 'Oh, why does life have to be so full of difficult choices?'

Keynes looked even more confused. 'Well, if you're saying that I'm the one who's been causing all the difficulties round here recently, you may well be correct.'

'Life did seem calmer before you arrived,' Celia observed coolly.

Keynes squinted up at the sun. 'I seem to have arrived a lifetime ago, but it's only a week.'

Celia decided. 'I think I'll treat myself to this gorgeous bedspread. How much?'

The woman calculated airily. 'One hundred pounds.'

Celia tried to conceal a gasp.

Keynes brought out his wallet. 'Allow me. Some small compensation for my social inadequacies last night.'

Celia began to protest, but the woman stretched out a long

arm and pulled the two fifty-pound notes from Keynes's fingers. She folded them, and then stuffed them very deliberately down the front of her blouse. 'He can afford it,' she pronounced. She bundled up the fabric and dropped it into a used paper bag. 'Here.' She winked lasciviously at Keynes and stroked his arm as she gave him the bag.

'I think you may have got off very lightly there, Edward,' Celia commented as they walked away. 'She had something in mind for you other than extracting your money, I think.'

'I don't mind the money, but what a very disconcerting woman.'

'Ah, you've just met another of us wild Welsh witches, you see!'

Keynes stared down at Celia. 'A week ago, I wouldn't have believed such a thing possible. But already I can begin to see what you mean. There's a great deal of bewitchery in Glasmaen. That, I suspect, is the root cause of my confusion.'

Celia looked up into Keynes's face. Her eyes were wide and dark. 'You're a man of unexpected depths, Edward. I may have underestimated you. That young woman, however, did not. I would recommend that you stay well away from her today.'

'Why?'

Celia's eyes twinkled. 'Because I could get very jealous, of course!'

Keynes nearly dropped the bundle in surprise.

'Come on, let's go and listen to the concert. There are some excellent groups performing.' Celia laid her cool hand on Keynes's arm and steered him towards one of the marquees.

* * *

Lucy and Graham brought out large trays to clear the tables on the terrace at the Golden Oak.

'You don't have to be here helping me, Graham,' Lucy suggested. 'You ought to go and see the festival.'

'I want to see your own private festival, Lucy! That's plenty interesting enough for me. Here, are you sure you can manage that one?'

'Oh, I've got strong arms.'

'And don't I know it?' giggled Graham. He laid down his tray and nuzzled the nape of Lucy's neck, which was exposed by the parting between her long, thick golden plaits. She turned to him, and they fell into a long, deep kiss.

'Still at it?' asked a cold voice.

Disentangling, the couple turned to see Richard Beavis frowning at them.

'Did you want something, Richard?' asked Lucy sweetly.

He shook his head. 'I've got news for you two. The job's off. We can leave as soon as we please.'

Lucy gasped. 'Why?'

'Old Dr Keynes has resigned his post. Chucked it in. Got sunstroke, I reckon. Ranted on about ruining the environment, wanting to become a peasant, all kinds of weird stuff. Says he'll give us references. So that's it. We're off.'

Lucy picked up the loaded tray and walked rapidly back into the pub. Graham and Richard watched her go.

'So there you are, Graham Ferris. You've had your pleasure, and now you can dump her. Go home to Mumsy in Reading, and start chatting up the next girl in your life.'

Graham adjusted his glasses on his nose. 'Maybe I will. Maybe I won't. I like it here. I've got a fortnight's holiday owing. I was saving it for that diving trip to Ibiza. You can sod off as soon as you like. I'm staying, for a while at least.'

Richard Beavis stared at Graham. 'You're a lucky bastard. I hope you realise that.'

Graham gave his startling gap-toothed grin. 'I certainly do! See ya, kid!' And he followed Lucy into the pub.

26

As Celia and Keynes emerged into the sunset from the marquee, they marvelled at the shades of apricot and lilac spreading across the sky.

'This is such a beautiful place to live,' whispered Celia.

Keynes nodded. 'I can only agree. You know, Celia, I've decided that I'd like to live here, too.'

'Oh, yes? Where?'

Keynes sighed. 'The place I'd like best belongs to someone else. At the moment.'

'The Glyn? However did I guess. So you'd enjoy living in a nuclear waste dump, would you. Well, you are loyal to your cause, I'll say that for you.'

'Oh, for heaven's sake! Do you never listen to a word I say? I'm going to do my damnedest to stop all that! Your special orchid will help, too. We all have to work together on this, don't you see?'

Before Celia could reply, someone standing beside them cleared his throat, and she and Keynes turned angrily to look at the intruder.

'Good evening, Dr Llewelyn. How delightful to meet you again. Won't you introduce me to your companion?'

A little flustered, Celia obliged. 'This is Dr Edward Keynes, meet Jeremy Sutherland. Jeremy owns the Old Mill, it's their holiday home.'

The two men shook hands. 'My wife Ellen and I are holding a party at the Old Mill tonight. Please do join us, both of you, any time after ten o'clock.'

'Certainly,' agreed Keynes. 'But I can't speak on behalf of Dr Llewelyn. Celia?'

'Oh, I'll be there. Thank you, Jeremy.'

Jeremy looked closely at Keynes. 'I feel certain that we've met somewhere, Dr Keynes.'

'Have we?' Keynes felt this intrusion sharply. He had just spent several very pleasant hours sitting beside Celia in the concert tent. He did not remember any of the music as clearly as he remembered her citrus perfume. This stranger, with his suave public school accent and cold eyes, was breaking into the pleasure of his afternoon.

Celia glanced at her watch. 'Excuse me, gentlemen, but I must fly. I have to check the answerphone back at the surgery. I'll see you both later.' She walked rapidly away.

The men watched her cross the festival site and disappear amongst the crowds. Then Jeremy turned back to Keynes.

'May I invite you for a coffee or a drink at the Golden Oak, Dr Keynes? I'm certain that we can track down our connection.'

Keynes agreed. Without Celia, he felt that there was nothing better to do. The two men walked companionably to the gate-house, commenting occasionally on the multicoloured whirl of activity around them.

After ordering two coffees from Lucy Goldhanger, they sat at an empty table on the terrace outside the pub and admired the sunset. Tints of plum and mint infused the vaster shades of amber and pink.

'Ah, our coffees. Allow me to pay, Dr Keynes.'

'Edward, please. Thank you.'

After pouring and stirring his coffee, Jeremy took out his slim silver and leather wallet, and unfolded a piece of paper from it. 'This, Edward, I believe you will recognise.'

Keynes took the paper, and his heart stopped for a moment. He shivered. It was a faxed copy of his letter of resignation to the Department of Energy. He refolded the paper and handed it back. 'Well, that's a credit to the speed of the postal service, I suppose.'

Jeremy slipped the fax back inside his wallet. 'And also, of course, it does credit to the efficiency of our civil servants. It was placed on my desk shortly after nine this morning. There have been quite a few discussions about it, I can assure you.'

'I suppose that now you want another.' Keynes sipped his coffee, but it failed to warm the cold sensation creeping in from his toes and fingertips.

'Oh, I'm certain we can be amicable about it. After all, we're both professionals.'

'Who exactly are you, Mr Sutherland?'

'Oh, Jeremy, please. Let's not disrupt the charming informality of this occasion. No, I am merely an interested party. I have a post within the Department, certainly, but my sphere of influence does extend into other areas. This project of purchasing the Glyn was rather a pet of mine. Living locally, you might say. After all, who do you think recommended the valley for the Geological Survey in the first place?' He paused to sip coffee. 'I understand that you were selected for the investigatory work because you've spent so much of your working life abroad. Doing splendid work, too, I hear, Edward. You were always a very reliable employee. You didn't fraternise with the natives, you have considerable experience with these expensive new drilling rigs, you always got the job done quickly and efficiently. An excellent record.'

'Until now,' observed Keynes icily. He didn't dare risk another sip of coffee, since his hands were trembling alarmingly. He kept them folded in his lap. His memory suddenly reminded him of an interview just as alarming in the past, with a headmaster. Keynes couldn't remember what schoolboy offence had led to the interview, but the cold fear was exactly the same.

'Until now,' agreed Jeremy. 'Exactly. And now, of course, that simple plan seems to have gone astray. Rather wildly. I've been hearing some quite extraordinary stories about your behaviour during the last week. And then I found myself standing nearby when I – and many other people, no doubt – overheard your brief disagreement with the fragrant Dr Llewelyn. I really am a little puzzled, Edward, as to how this curious series of circumstances could have arisen in so short a space of time as one week.'

Keynes sighed deeply. Jeremy remained silent, expecting a reply. Keynes bit his tongue, and gazed at his cooling coffee.

'Well, let's be frank, Edward. Despite your professional abilities, unquestioned as they are, you've never really been part of the club, so to speak. That much was apparent from your handshake. Wrong school, I expect? You've always kept very much to yourself. Unmarried at forty – but nothing wrong with that, I daresay, no reports of any untoward activities in the trouser department! No particular friends or involvement in societies, as far as we can tell. And yet you, the ideal man for the job, a model of tact and discretion, have failed us. You've been mixing with some very – how shall I say? – undesirable characters this week. This pretty little village is rather a hotbed for them, I know. Let's see: you arrived and got drunk in a very public way,' Jeremy lowered his voice. 'Flirted with the daughter of our host at this very original pub. Our host, Vincent Goldhanger, being a good man to run a pub, but ejected ten years ago from our estimable police force for some very dubious social activities. Still up to his old tricks even now, I gather. Dancing around stone circles at every pagan festival. I also hear that one of the juniors for whom you were responsible has been sleeping with the daughter, which will have a detrimental effect on his career, I shouldn't wonder. We'll just have to keep an eye on that young man.' Jeremy raised the coffee cup to his lips again before continuing.

'Meanwhile, you very boldly attempt on several occasions to seduce the mysterious girlfriend of the owner of the Glyn, which might suggest a breakdown in tact. Especially since Isaac Talboys has been well known to us for many years for his lively role as a political agitator in a number of foreign countries. We thought he'd settled down quietly, but he might view any attempt to prise away his new lady friend by the man trying to buy his cottage with suspicion, to say the least.' Without offering Keynes a refill, he poured himself another cupful.

'And then you discover the lovely and capable Dr Llewelyn, and dine with her, telling her openly and honestly of all our plans for her village. Dr Llewelyn could have got on very well in her profession, if not for her predilection for joining political pressure groups. CND, Greenpeace, FOE, Doctors for Peace, you name it, she joined it. The Department of Health was quite glad to tuck her away in a small general practice in rural Wales, I can tell you. Very pretty, feisty young woman, too. I can quite understand your enthusiasm for her company, if not for her political philosophies. More coffee?'

Keynes shook his head.

'No? Very well. And then you got drunk with Mr Bryn Jones, who is a writer of quite extraordinarily debauched novels. Interesting, but debauched. His wife hanged herself in quite curious circumstances, did you know?'

Keynes shook his head again.

'Well, Jones seems to have inserted a finger into every sticky little pie around here. Covens, indeed. Nasty business. His daughter is very involved with such practices, too, which is giving some cause for concern to the Department of Education. I hope she has other strings to her dynamic little bow. She threw you out of her cottage, I gather? I might have been amused at that, if it weren't for her reasons. She's probably informed every political activist in the area by now about our plans. You seem to have been very publicly honest and forthright about them, after all.'

In the silence which followed, Keynes managed to raise his cup and finish off the cold coffee in it. Fortified, he asked: 'How do you know all this?'

'Ah, well. Do you see the young couple dressed in black, sitting at the table over there?' Jeremy raised one hand in greeting to them, and Ambrose Fisher and Sonja Barnaby nodded solemnly in reply. 'Well, they've been staying at the Old Mill and keeping an eye on you. As anthropologists, their trained observation can be very useful. Dressed in black, they're adequately camouflaged to sit quietly in pubs or to stroll discreetly in country lanes and woods, don't you think?'

Keynes put his empty cup down with a clatter. A cold anger had replaced the fear. 'Why exactly are you telling me all this? If you knew that Glasmaen was full of anarchists, why select it as a site for dumping nuclear waste?'

Jeremy inspected his fingernails. 'Land prices, my dear Edward. A hundred thousand pounds is very little to pay for a deserted valley of ideal geology in Britain today, and there is a recession. The Department has been feeling the pinch too, you know. If you hadn't informed the local populace of our intentions so efficiently, it could all have been done very discreetly. We thought that the cover of a site for a nature reserve would have been ideal. Even left us hope of a compulsory purchase order without attracting too much attention. The Department of the Environment is very image-conscious these days, you know.'

'But it has to become a nature reserve now,' Keynes pointed out coolly. 'It contains ghost orchids. Very rare. Of great public interest, nationally.'

'Ah, yes. From such tiny acorns do mighty oak trees grow. That could be the most serious hitch in our plans, after all.'

Keynes considered this. Deep within him a tiny flame of hope began to burn. 'You live in this village. Do you really want nuclear waste dumped in your own backyard?'

Jeremy shrugged. 'Frankly, it doesn't bother me at all. It has to go somewhere. I even proposed putting the stuff underneath Stonehenge – or Arthur's Circle – which raised rather a timely laugh at one dull meeting. It could rest undisturbed there for a very long time indeed.'

'But if you live in this village, surely the locals wouldn't be pleased to hear about your plans.'

Jeremy's eyes snapped open and looked at Keynes with a gimlet intensity. They were so pale as to be almost colourless, and the pupils were pinpricks of black. There was a long moment of silence between them, during which Keynes maintained his stare against the pressure of Jeremy's sinister regard.

'Dear Ellen, such a socialite, loves the Old Mill. It pleases her to play Lady Bountiful here. She gets a bit overwhelmed by the London set, poor dear. I can afford a holiday place anywhere, it doesn't bother me. So I'd forget about that tiny little hint, if I were you.' Jeremy sighed. 'We could come to an arrangement, Edward. Your letter of resignation could be filed away somewhere inaccessible, and a new posting, overseas, could be sorted out for you quite quickly. Where do you fancy? Middle East or Far East? Some lovely dark-eyed ladies in the Far East, too, if that's your preference.'

Keynes drew a deep breath. 'My letter of resignation stands. I will send copies out to every subdivision of the Department, if necessary. I don't want to work for you any more. I don't like what you do. After this conversation, I am only confirmed in my opinion.' He stood up. 'Goodbye, Mr Sutherland – or whatever your name is.'

Jeremy unfolded his silk-suited length and stood up too. 'We would both be wise to keep this conversation discreet as well as amicable. Please allow yourself a period of reflection. My invitation to our soirée stands. Please do attend. My wife is always enchanted to meet someone new.'

Keynes bowed his head briefly. Then he turned and walked rapidly away.

27

As the dusk fell slowly around him Keynes walked blindly for a while, then found himself at the bracken-gated entrance to the Glyn. So this, he thought, is where it has all led. He carefully picked his way down the rocky path into the valley. Bird-song chimed in the tall slender trees around him, and he noted the tiny wild flowers half-hidden by the undergrowth. The flower petals were closing now, as the sun slipped away. He intended to locate the ghost orchid. This was the only salvation for this precious place, he had realised.

With a new sense of purpose, he crossed the slab-bridge over the tinkling stream. Then he heard the muted chords of fiddle music. So Isaac Talboys was in residence, perhaps with his enchanting girl-friend. It was time to speak to the man. He knocked at the striped door, and the music stopped.

Isaac opened the door, fiddle in one hand.

'I have to talk with you,' said Keynes.

Isaac silently held the door open and Keynes stepped into the dark interior.

At the far side of the low-beamed room sat Ainee Sealfin in a pool of lamplight. She turned to gaze at Keynes, her face shadowed but her hair lustrous in the golden light. 'Welcome,' she said quietly. She pointed to a wooden chair beside the warm stove. A heavy dented kettle hissed on the stove. 'Tea?' she offered, and Keynes nodded. He lowered himself into the chair as she rose and prepared three mugs of scented tea. Isaac sat down in her empty wheel-back chair, and laid the fiddle in his lap. 'Well?' he asked. Although his face was shaded, his blue eyes glittered icily. Keynes bit his lip, unsure of how to begin. 'As you know, Mr Talboys, I arrived here a week ago, directed by the Department of Energy to purchase this valley. They planned to bring in drilling rigs, to test the geology here. If suitable, it would be used as a site for dumping intermediate level nuclear waste. This was supposed to be a secret project, but through my own failings, it's become public knowledge.'

Isaac's eyes glittered, but he said nothing. Ainee handed them their mugs of tea. Taking her own, she retired into a corner and curled up on a sofa piled with dark rugs.

'It's essential that you understand that I have changed my opinion on the advisability of this project,' Keynes continued. He felt awkward, embarrassed by the direct stare of Isaac and by the awareness of Ainee Sealfin watching him. 'The events of this last week have been of the greatest possible importance to me. Although I have been unhappy about the aims of the Department for several years, my work abroad has never affected me as much as Glasmaen has. This is a very special place.'

Isaac nodded, and drank from his mug.

Keynes looked around the room. 'I envy you, Isaac Talboys. You have an exceptionally beautiful home, in an exquisite place. You have a beautiful woman. You have many friends, and you have great talents as a musician and artist. Yours must be a very happy and fulfilled life. Unlike mine,' he added. 'But you need to know that all this is under a very serious threat. I have just had a long conversation with a man both powerful and dangerous, a man who lives in your village. Jeremy Sutherland. He tried to threaten my career, but I'd already resigned my post with the Department. He told me that – well, I can only call them spies, although I appreciate that this sounds like paranoia, – spies have been watching me, you, and several people in Glasmaen for a long time. Sutherland can do you all a great deal of harm. The nuclear waste-dump was his plan.'

Isaac sipped again, then spoke: 'Just because you're paranoid, doesn't mean that they aren't out to get you.'

Keynes looked up at him. 'You believe me?'

'Shouldn't I? We've been curious about Sutherland for a long time. He has some very odd connections.' Here, he glanced briefly across at Ainee. 'One of them has just offered to buy all my paintings, and has even given me an advance. I don't mind about that. It's high time that my work was appreciated.'

'Congratulations, Mr Talboys …'

'Call me Isaac.'

'Thank you. My name is Edward. Isaac, have you considered my offer for the Glyn? I meant it in all seriousness. I have the money, and I'd like nothing better than to come and live here. I know that I've managed to infuriate everyone in this village, but I'll make it my task to protect this place from the Sutherlands of this world.'

Isaac drained his mug, then ran his hands through his long black beard and hair. 'Ainee Sealfin, this is your choice. If I keep the Glyn will you stay here with me? Or shall I sell it and with the money from this man and the art dealer we can leave this place, together, go anywhere you like?'

Ainee stood up, and walked over to Isaac. She laid a pale arm over his shoulder, and pointed to the fiddle on his lap. Her voice was calm. 'Why do you offer me choice, when you deny me freedom?'

Isaac's eyes, captivated by her own, were desperate. 'I can't live without you, Ainee Sealfin.'

'You did so until a week ago.'

'But it's different now. Everything has changed. I love you, Ainee!'

'Only you can decide what to do, Isaac,' she said softly. 'As long as you hold me prisoner, I cannot help you in any way.'

Isaac groaned and tore his hair.

Keynes was mystified. 'Excuse me, but I don't understand what's going on.'

Ainee turned her soulless dark-brown gaze full on him. 'Oh, how curious human beings are! Strange, and fascinating. You have changed the world, and yet you cannot make sense of yourselves. I am astonished at your creations, and yet I despise you for your poor little confusions. You two are examples of the extremity of your strangeness. You, Isaac, are a creature of earth and dirt. Look at your feet.'

All eyes dropped to his naked feet. The toenails had not been cut for years. Thick, grey and curling, they dug into the flesh of his toes, long and horny like miniature goats' hooves.

'There is music in you, Isaac, a wonderful spirit of music, but there is no dancing. You are earth-bound; you walk in mud, and you stir up clotted swellings as you walk. You are filthy. The rot of generations stinks within you, the stink of greed and lust. You stole me from my sisters as we danced in moonlight. You tore me from the sea. You pressed sand and weed into my eyes and nose and mouth, and tried to press the very breath from my body. You tore my sealskin cap from my naked shoulders, and then you forced me to journey alone to your green valley, which you tried to make a prison around me. Even this evening, you have torn me away from my dancing, to bring me back here, afraid and jealous for me. And Isaac, you bit as you kissed, and you pinched as you caressed. You were so greedy for my body that you have tried to consume me within your body of clay.

'I am water and I am animal, and you have tried to cage me in your claws. Not I. I am not your prisoner or your slave. You are mine. You will paint and draw me for ever: you will yearn for my image, but in truth, my image is all that you really desire. You cannot form my body into the substance you seek. Your hands will be forever empty of my form, just as your eyes will be forever filled by my image.'

She turned to Keynes as Isaac hid his face in his hands and moaned. 'And you: you are a man of air. Your brain revolves in numbers. You strive for logic, but reality is your curse. You came here crippled by guilt and by embarrassment, and have been shown release. You each deserve something of the other. You, Isaac, deserve logic and clarity of purpose. You, Edward, deserve the passion of art and music. I give you both what you lack.'

Ainee Sealfin lifted her hands and pointed each slender webbed forefinger at the nearest hand of each man.

Surprised, they unfolded their own clenched fists, and reached out to her with their empty hands.

Ainee's forefingers went rigid. A thin blue spark shot out from each fingertip, vivid in the dimness, and catching hold of each man's hand, flickered around his outstretched palm. They both stared at the glow in astonishment, and everything else around them began to shift and blur. They both rose slowly from their seats as she began to draw them together. Isaac's long hair rose and crackled, and the violin tumbled unheeded from his lap onto the stone-flagged floor. Watching them, Ainee's pupils, dark as tunnels, swivelled almost imperceptibly until each pupil held the frightened gaze of each man. Both men grew pale. Ainee's eyes centred again, pulling each man toward the other.

They met at hands, arms and shoulders with a crack like a gunshot. The blue static leapt between them, and their bodies recoiled. They each fell back into their seats like lead weights dropping. They sat, dazed.

Ainee shook her freed hands, and blue fire dripped and sparkled from her fingertips. She clapped her hands sharply, then wrung them, until the last spark dissolved away. She softly kissed each man's brow as he slumped forward.

Then she bent down, and picked up something from the floor. The others looked down to see the fiddle lying broken, cracked apart like an egg. She unrolled her sealskin cap and held it delicately between her palms.

'Walk in peace,' she whispered, turned and walked out of the cottage. The door fell to behind her with a hush like a sigh. Silence descended.

'She's gone, she's gone back to the sea,' groaned Isaac, and a large tear rolled down his cheek, glistening in the lamplight.

Keynes sat in stunned silence. He felt empty, and yet it was as though he had been cleansed within. His shocked brain could only offer one explanation. 'Magic,' he whispered. 'That was magic ...'

Eventually Isaac wiped his eyes, and picked up the shattered fiddle. 'No more music for me. No more love. I have loved, and I have lost my love. All is emptiness.' Then he stood up and thrust the remains of the fiddle into the stove. Yellow flame caught the resined wood as he closed the iron door behind it. 'I need a drink. It must be late, now. The pub will be shut. The Sutherlands should have plenty of booze at the Old Mill. You coming too, Edward?'

Keynes nodded, still dazed, and stood up, following Isaac out of the cottage into the dark wood. As they crossed the slab-bridge, they both glanced down at the brook. A large silvery moonlit shape was almost visible in the water, dipping and swaying its way downstream.

'Was that a seal?' asked Keynes, surprised.

'It was,' said Isaac with conviction. They continued their journey.

28

Silver fairy lights glittered in the branches of the willow trees around the pool beside the Old Mill. Their reflections in the water tangled with the stars glimmering in the clear black sky above. The windows of the Mill sparkled with light, and the door stood wide open.

As Isaac and Keynes entered, Ellen Sutherland greeted them from the top of the wide pine staircase. 'Come in, come up, all welcome!' she cried, waving. They followed her upstairs, towards the sound of music, singing, and the chatter of guests.

The vast room on the first floor was thronged with people. Even the Russian dancers were there, drinking vodka in one corner, their embroidery and jewellery flashing like tinsel. The Scrattingby Mummers, faces blackened, sprawled in their brilliant tatters nearby, arguing amicably with the dapper Garpside long sword dancers. Miss Cobb, the village headmistress, sat in polite silence amongst them. The Ramsons trio of three burly bearded men supped ale from tankards and sang drinking songs with complex choruses, and several of the lace-clad ladies from Wendens Amber Ladies Ritual dance team sang the harmonies. Don Craven played the guitar to their tunes. Graham Ferris and Lucy Goldhanger held hands and gazed into each other's eyes, whilst Richard Beavis pointedly studied a selection of CDs. Gwen Orgee and Grace Mortimer gossiped in another corner, whilst their husbands drunkenly discussed sheep-rearing. Bryn Jones, his nose a muted rainbow of greens and purples, raised a tankard to Keynes and Isaac in greeting, as he listened patiently to his daughter and son-in-law argue about the baby-sitting arrangements. Celia Llewelyn put in occasional soothing observations. Dominic Batista, Lyndon Cotton, and the eternally black-clad Ambrose Fisher and Sonja Barnaby discussed everyone else.

'Oh, this is delightful; everyone seems to be here!' trilled Ellen. 'Help yourselves to drinks – dear kind Vin Goldhanger's doing the bar over there, and Jeremy's about somewhere. He was hoping you'd be here, Dr Keynes.'

'Was he?' asked Keynes coldly. He was given a large glass of ruby wine, whilst Isaac chose brandy. They raised their glasses to one another briefly, in a toast. 'To the Glyn and its safe future,' proposed Keynes. Isaac drank to that, and they crossed to the centre of the room.

'Oh, I do hope you've brought your violin, Isaac sweetheart!' gushed Ellen, following them. 'No? Well, never mind. Now, where's your beautiful girlfriend?'

'Gone,' said Isaac firmly.

Ellen looked flustered. She fiddled with the tiger's-eye necklace about her throat. 'Oh, well, I'm sorry. Lyndon was particularly hoping to show her the stills from his latest movie. He'll be so disappointed.'

'Really?' asked Isaac, looking away from Ellen and frowning at Lyndon Cotton, who had come closer and overheard the conversation.

'Yes, I am disappointed,' drawled Lyndon. 'She's a stunning girl. I could really do things with her – in the movie way, of course. You must give me her address and phone number.'

'No,' said Isaac. 'I don't know it.'

Lyndon grimaced, and drifted away.

'Ah, my good friend Edward,' said Jeremy Sutherland, offering his hand. 'I'm so pleased you've decided to return to the fold.'

Keynes did not offer his hand, but shook his head instead.

'No? Well, we must find time to talk again.'

Keynes shook his head again, and took a deep sip of wine.

'Come, come, we're all friends here, you know.'

Keynes spoke crisply. 'I very much doubt that's true. You're no friend of mine, nor of Glasmaen's.'

Jeremy's pale eyes iced over. Then he gave Keynes a sardonic grin. 'That sounds very much like a declaration of war, Edward!'

'I think so,' replied Keynes.

Jeremy smiled. 'I'm sure you're aware that I could make life very difficult for you, if it came to that.'

'I have some sound supporters,' Keynes declared. Isaac stood shoulder to shoulder beside him. The three men were much of a height. Jeremy's eyes flicked between Isaac's electric-blue eyes and Keynes's steely grey ones.

'This is frightfully brave of you, but I suspect that we shouldn't be discussing this in front of Mr Talboys,' Jeremy observed.

'Edward has told me all about your plans,' said Isaac. 'So I'm the ideal person to discuss them with.'

Jeremy became aware of a hush in the room. He sipped from his glass of champagne. Several people advanced on the group, and Jeremy glanced around to see Bryn Jones, Sue and Gareth, Don and Celia standing behind him. Miss Cobb joined them. Vin Goldhanger, wiping his hands on a tea-towel, completed the ring.

'Jeremy Sutherland, if you wish to continue with your plan to dump nuclear waste in the Glyn, then these people will form the opposition,' announced Keynes.

'And the Glasmaen Women's Group,' added Sue Hopkins-Jones.

'And the Glasmaen Environmental Action Party,' added Gareth.

'And all the wildlife protection groups,' cried Miss Cobb fervently.

'And the Coven,' put in Vin Goldhanger.

'Also Greenpeace and the Friends of the Earth,' Celia Llewelyn pointed out.

'And I think I could safely promise,' said Bryn Jones, 'that the folk scene would unite to prevent you.'

There was a chorus of agreement from the folkies in the room. They had all stood up, and were draining their glasses, apart from one or two who were using the opportunity to refill their tankards from the bar.

'Oh, oh,' gasped Ellen Sutherland, wringing her hands helplessly. 'Please, everyone, this is such a nice little party, let's all be merry again …'

'Be quiet, you silly woman,' snapped her husband.

'And you can forget about 'aving me to clean your great big fancy house if you're trying to do such a lot of harm to my village an' all the folks in it!' shrieked Gwen Orgee, enjoying the moment. 'You was niver exactly popular 'ere, you knows!'

Ellen Sutherland burst into tears. 'Oh, it's all too horrid, Jeremy. I can't stand it any more.' She rushed upstairs, wailing. Dominic Batista glanced behind him wistfully as he followed her to offer soothing kindnesses to his distressed hostess.

Jeremy Sutherland looked slowly around the room. 'I will remember this night, and all those participating in it,' he said loudly. 'Now, I think you should all leave.'

There was a noisy exodus from the Old Mill. The confused Russians were invited back to parties on the camp site.

Jeremy followed the last group to the door. He was white with anger and frustration, and slammed the door behind them all. Then he returned upstairs to watch them depart, through one of the open windows of the Old Mill. Lyndon Cotton stood beside him, and the pair of black-clad anthropologists hovered behind them darkly.

'It is such a wonderful house,' sighed Sue Hopkins-Jones, looking behind her at the glittering mill, and at its reflections in the mill-pool.

'Do you like it, Gareth?' asked Bryn Jones.

'Gorgeous. Why?'

'Oh, I imagine that it'll be on the market soon. I could afford to buy it, if you and Sue and the boys would consent to share it with me. I could make the top floor quite cosy for myself. I like a room with a view. You could have the run of the rest of it.'

'Dad! Are you serious? That would be fantastic!'

Gareth sighed. 'You do that, Bryn. I'm sure we could work out a few house rules between ourselves. It'd take a damned lot of cleaning, though.'

Bryn Jones laughed. 'Maybe Gwen would agree to coming in for two days a week.'

'Four,' said Gareth firmly.

Bryn Jones laid his heavy arms around his family's waists and they walked away in the darkness, arguing.

Isaac was staring into the mill-pool. Don, Celia and Keynes leaned on the rail beside him.

'What's that in the water?' asked Celia, pointing. A dark shape moved slowly towards them, leaving a faint v-shaped ripple in its wake. 'It looks like a seal, of all things!'

'Ainee!' yelled Isaac, 'you've come back!'

The shape glided to the brink below them, and a pale figure emerged from it, white in the moonlight and sparkling amongst the reflected starlight and fairy lights. Ainee's clear brown eyes gazed up at them.

'Ainee! I'm here! Come home!' cried Isaac, gripping the rail until his hands whitened.

Ainee shook her head, and brushed the long wet hair back from her face. She floated in the glistening water below them, naked as a nymph.

'I am leaving, Isaac. I wish you joy of your life. You gave me pleasure, and introduced me to this wonderful world. Now it is time for me to explore all the possibilities in it. I have a message, but it is not for you.' She looked around, and saw Lyndon Cotton leaning out of the open window, waving to her.

'Lyndon, wait for me,' she called to him. 'Wait on Monterey beach beside your Californian home. It will take me several cycles of the moon to cross the oceans, but I will be there, one night when the full moon lights a path across the sea. You have told me so much about the wonders of California, and of its clean seas and green forests and glittering cities of glass and steel. I will become your movie star, as I wish and you can make me. Wait for my full moon!'

'I'll be there, Ainee Sealfin!' called Lyndon. 'Me and the whole damned movie business! It'll all be yours, I promise you that!'

'California!' raged Isaac. 'I'll sell the bloody Glyn and follow you there!'

'No, you won't!' shouted Jeremy Sutherland. 'You'll never get a visa. I'll see to that! Now get off my land, the lot of you.' He pulled the window shut.

Ainee laughed, and dipped beneath the water. As her shape darkened and slid away, the watchers could just distinguish the shapes of eleven other seals in the darkness by the mouth of the mill-race. The dark shapes twirled in joy as she joined them, and accompanied her away into the night.

'So she's gone,' sighed Isaac.

'Bad luck,' said Don companionably.

Isaac turned and looked deep into Keynes's eyes. 'Yes, Edward. You can buy the Glyn from me. I don't want it without her.'

'Where will you go?' asked Keynes.

'Evidently not California. Probably I'll stay around Glasmaen. I've got a lot of painting to do. If Bryn Jones really does move out of that ballroom, maybe I'll buy it myself. Good north light.'

'It's a deal,' said Keynes, and they shook hands. The very faintest tingle of blue fire flickered as their palms met.

'Coming for a drink at my place?' invited Don.

'Yeah, I could do with getting extremely drunk tonight,' sighed Isaac.

'Not for me, thank you Don,' said Celia. She looked up at Keynes, and her dark eyes shone. 'But if you wanted to walk me home in the moonlight, Edward, I'd be delighted to accept. I live over the surgery, you know.'

'I know,' smiled Keynes. As they turned away from the mill-pool, Celia slid her hand into his and he gave it a soft squeeze.

They followed Isaac and Don in silence through the village. Faint strains of music, singing and laughter drifted through the warm night air from the folk festival camp site.

'Good night, you two,' said Celia when they reached the surgery. Don and Isaac murmured their farewell and continued on their way.

Celia looked up at Keynes. 'Coffee?' she asked, smiling. He nodded, and followed her through the door.

Upstairs, her flat was clean and neat, decorated in elegant floral fabrics and painted in cool greens and beiges. Framed landscapes in watercolours hung on the walls. Keynes inspected them whilst Celia prepared the coffee in the small cherry-wood kitchen.

Celia returned with a tray of bone china and a cafetière filled with fragrant Javanese coffee. She sat beside Keynes on the sofa to pour.

Then she looked into his eyes and smiled. 'You turned out to be quite a hero tonight, Edward. I was rather impressed.'

Keynes shrugged. 'Someone had to do it. I did have a lot of help.'

'Well, you did it very well.'

Tentatively, Keynes laid his arm along the sofa-cushions behind Celia's back. She looked extraordinarily pretty in her mint-green silk dress, and with her eyes and bob of black hair shining. She leaned back, and snuggled up against Keynes's side.

'I'm really looking forwards to you coming to live in Glasmaen,' she said.

'Are you? After all those harsh things you said to me?'

Celia shrugged. 'Well, I never seemed to put you off me, did I?' She sighed, and rubbed her cheek. 'Mind you, I thought you might be about to dive into the mill-pool and swim away with

Ainee Sealfin for a moment back there. What a very strange young woman. Just the sort an oddball artist like Isaac would collect. Did you think you saw seals in the water there? I did.'

'It looked oddly like seals. Impossible, of course.'

'As impossible as your broken wrist healing itself the other night, I would say.'

'Mmm. Yes, I'm still not sure what really happened there.'

'So you won't be swimming off to California?'

Keynes looked down into her smiling face. Her lips looked soft and warm. 'No,' he said. 'There's too much to keep me here. And anyway,' he picked up her wrist and glanced at her watch, 'it's my fortieth birthday today.'

'Ooh, happy birthday! What would you like best as a present?'

Keynes hesitated, and looked down at her coiled silk-wrapped body. 'You,' he said.

She smiled. 'Well here I am, birthday boy.'

He bent his head and kissed her. Their kiss grew deeper as she parted her lips, and he put his arms around her delicate shoulders and eventually lowered her back on to the sofa-cushions as their kiss made their entire world revolve around them.

Epilogue

The following year, on Midsummer's Day, Isaac Talboys went back up Bryngar Hill, just in case. The Methodists were already there and the harmonium worked as perfectly as it is possible for a harmonium to work. Its nasal tones fluted out across the entire hilltop. The Methodists sang their hymns lustily. Several families of tourists picnicked on the grass, much to the disgust of the congregation. Someone hidden in the bracken listened to the Test Match on the radio. The stones were silent.

Isaac sighed deeply and scratched his head. He was wearing costly new designer clothes, but they were already paint-stained and grimy around the cuffs and collar. He set up his expensive new easel to the east of the Circle and set out his new paints. Once these were arranged to his satisfaction he stood gazing out across the valley for some time. This year's field of rapeseed burned fluorescent yellow in the centre of the view.

Eventually Isaac bent down and rummaged in his sack. He drew out a precious tube. With great care, he unscrewed the lid and squirted the contents into the middle of his palette. It was fluorescent yellow. He began to paint.

Eventually the triumphant Methodists packed up their harmonium and went away. Some time later, several car-loads of excited witches arrived to build their Midsummer Eve bonfire in the centre of the stone circle. Isaac continued to paint, capturing the great sweep of sunlit clouds across the horizon.

At last, he put down his brushes and sat back to roll a cigarette and study his painting. He calculated the value of the picture on the London art market as the price of an interesting motorbike. Perhaps he would even bother to pass his driving test for the new bike. Then he could take a passenger around with him. It was about time he had a woman on the back of his bike. The ballroom could do with a feminine touch – the redecorations were going on apace.

It had been an interesting year, Isaac decided. The Glyn's new inhabitant, Edward, had become a close friend of his, and often asked his advice on the sensitively-done building work going on at the cottage, where a bathroom and kitchen were being added. He had turned out to be a fiercely protective warden of the new nature sanctuary in the valley. Botanists from all over England and Wales had been turning up in droves to inspect the ghost orchids. Edward and Celia Llewelyn seemed happy enough in their relationship, despite the occasional political argument. There was even a rumour about a forthcoming wedding.

Isaac hoped that the event would prove as entertaining as the rather hurried wedding between Lucy Goldhanger and Graham Ferris, who was now the proud father of a bouncing baby boy. Graham looked set to become a good landlord of the Golden Oak, and Vin was talking about retiring to Spain, but his new role as grandad seemed to occupy much of his time.

Don Craven had a new girl-friend, although secretly, as she was married to a neighbouring farmer. Don was hoping to cut a record featuring his songwriting and guitar-playing, supported by Isaac playing the fiddle, which the band had persuaded him to take up again. They had even clubbed together and bought him a splendid old violin.

The Hopkins-Jones household had moved into the Old Mill, once the Sutherlands had departed in disgrace, and seemed to be enjoying life there despite the rows, which were as frequent and passionate as ever. But they must enjoy the reconciliations, because Sue had recently told everyone that she was pregnant again. She had also managed to get the job of headmistress at the local school, Miss Cobb having retired to write a botanical history of the locality.

A baby boy had also been born to Grace Mortimer, but since Isaac suspected that Don was the father, the less said about that the better.

Bryn Jones and his family were planning an even bigger Folk Festival this year. There was going to be a major guest star appearing, although they had initially been cautious about telling Isaac who it was going to be. But the tabloid press had got hold of the star's name and Isaac took a lot of newspapers these days. He made the excuse to his friends that he felt the need to be in touch with what was happening in the rest of the world. They kindly refrained from pointing out that it was really to read the vast amount of publicity given to Ainee Sealfin's highly controversial and dramatic new movie. The papers even suggested that she was toppling Madonna from her throne as 'Sex Queen of Hollywood and the pop charts'.

In only a week, Ainee Sealfin was due to descend – by helicopter – on Glasmaen Folk Festival, to appear in a charity concert which was raising funds for the international protection of seals, whales and dolphins. Isaac knew why she had chosen such a charity, but he wasn't telling.

Isaac viewed Ainee's return with mixed feelings. He could never lose the aching desire he had felt for her since the moment he first saw her. But she had been such an inspiring muse that she had galvanised him into a dramatic new line of art forms. His first tentative sculptures promised to turn the art world on its head, and the soft rhythms running through his new creations had all been generated by Ainee.

Her image always danced before his eyes. She had awoken him into an electric new phase of creativity. But she haunted him, even in his deepest dreams. Perhaps it was about time for him to try expelling her image by falling in love with a different woman. Isaac sighed. She would have to be very different to compete in his affections with Ainee Sealfin.

He packed up his canvas and easel, and wandered over to Arthur's Circle. He felt a faint tingle stir the hairs at the nape of his neck, remembering the electric storm and lightning-strike here a year ago. But the stones today were calm and quiet, with none of the intense, ethereal passion which Isaac had experienced here before.

A figure sat in the golden evening light, her back to the largest stone. Isaac walked over to speak to her.

'Hullo, Grace Mortimer,' said Isaac.

Grace looked up at him and smiled serenely. Her baby was feeding from her naked breast, and she held it tenderly in her arms.

'You look good enough to paint as a madonna, Grace,' he observed.

'Can you sell a pagan madonna?' grinned Grace.

Isaac sat down beside her, and played with the baby's curling fingers.

'Earth mother,' he said.

'Thank you,' said Grace, pleased.

They sat in companionable silence as the baby fed and the sun slowly set over the Black Mountains.

'You out all night, Grace?' asked Isaac.

'Until dawn,' she replied. 'Solstice. Stones are very quiet this year. They were full of power last year. You could even say they were demanding a sacrifice.'

'Perhaps they got one,' Isaac answered thoughtfully.

Grace remained silent, adjusting the baby in her arms as her son fell serenely asleep.

Isaac smiled. 'You were always a graceful woman. Your name and motherhood both suit you.'

Grace smiled into his bright blue eyes. 'Are you staying here for the dancing tonight?'

'Got my fiddle with me,' he replied.

'Well then, we'll make a night of it, Isaac Talboys.'

'Let's do just that, Grace Mortimer. Let's do just that.'

The sun slipped behind the Black Mountains, and they sat together and watched the stars come slowly out.

Julia Hawkes-Moore was born near the ruins of Walsingham Abbey and grew up in the countryside around the Welsh Marches. Both places inspired in her a deep fascination with folk history and myth. After training as an architect in Liverpool she went on to run a London restaurant and to teach metalwork and woodwork in Suffolk, before settling down to write novels and run folk festivals. She now lives in Saffron Walden with her husband Bob and their finest production, baby Gabriel. *Dancing in Circles* is her first novel.